ABOUT THE AUTHOR

Jan-Philipp Sendker, born in Hamburg in 1960, was the American correspondent for *Stern* from 1990 to 1995, and its Asian correspondent from 1995 to 1999. In 2000 he published *Cracks in the Wall*, a non-fiction book about China. *The Art of Hearing Heartbeats*, his first novel, is an international bestseller. He lives in Potsdam with his family.

ABOUT THE TRANSLATOR

Christine Lo is an editor in book publishing in London. She has also worked as a translator in Frankfurt and translated books by Julia Franck and Senait Mehari from German into English. Her most recent translation is *Atlas of Remote Islands* by Judith Schalansky.

Jan-Philipp
SENDKER
The Far Side
of the Night

Translated from German to English by Christine Lo

This edition first published in Great Britain in 2019 by Polygon,
an imprint of Birlinn Ltd

Birlinn Ltd
West Newington House
10 Newington Road
Edinburgh EH9 1QS

www.polygonbooks.co.uk

Originally published in German as *Am Anderen Ende der Nacht*
by Karl Blessing Verlag, Munich

ISBN 978 1 84697 417 5

10 9 8 7 6 5 4 3 2 1

British Library Cataloguing-in-Publication Data
A catalogue record for this book is available on request
from the British Library.

Typeset by 3btype.com
Printed and bound by Clays Ltd, Elcograf S.p.A

For Anna, Florentine, Theresa
and Jonathan and Dorothea

PROLOGUE

Paul saw him first. A young man on a street corner. His hands buried in the pockets of a light jacket, waiting patiently on the spot as though he had turned up early for an appointment. Conspicuously inconspicuous.

He sized up every car that turned into Jia Jou Lu with watchful eyes.

It was the look of suspicion in his eyes that gave him away.

Christine kept her son hidden on her lap; he lay beneath a black blanket that stank of stale smoke. Her eyes were closed, as though she was asleep.

Paul knew she wasn't.

She had not believed that they would make it. Not when they had first fled, nor later on, as they had left Shi further behind them with each passing day. Not even this morning.

The traffic lights turned red and the taxi stopped. Christine opened her eyes briefly and he could see that she still did not believe it. One more street to go, he wanted to say. Look out of the window. Reassure yourself. Two hundred meters, maybe three hundred, no more than that. What was one more street after thousands of kilometers on the run?

The man on the street corner would not be able to stop them on his own.

Then he saw a second man.

And a third.

A black Audi with tinted windows, with its headlights off, drew up and parked not far from the security zone in front of the embassy. He noticed a group of young men lurking under one of the gingko trees, keeping watch.

"Don't stop. Drive on," he said to the taxi driver.

"The embassy is here."

"I know where the embassy is. Keep driving."

Christine. Alarmed. How strongly fear could show on a face, Paul thought. That was something it had in common with love.

"But you wanted to go to the embassy."

"Carry on driving. Go!"

"Where to?"

Sometimes there were no answers to simple questions. Especially not to those questions.

"Where to?" the driver said again.

———

Two thousand kilometers away, lunch was interrupted by a phone call.

The gentlemen were in a meeting and not to be disturbed except in an emergency.

Not an emergency, no, but a matter of great urgency.

Then please call back later.

An exchange of curses and threats followed, then the call was put through.

"They're here."

"Where?"

"In Beijing. In front of the American embassy."

A brief silence.

"What should we do?"

"Bring them here."

"All of them?"

"No. Only the child."

"And the other two?"

The City

Two weeks earlier

I

Paul had never liked dancing and he had not done it much. It was years since he had last danced. But he was one of those people who found it difficult to say no to a child, especially to his own, so he started moving.

He took a step forward to the beat of the music, a step to the side and a step backward. He swung his knees from side to side, and turned round in a circle with a flourish.

The weight of the world was on his shoulders. But it was so light that it was not difficult for him to carry.

David shrieked with delight.

Several hundred couples dancing the waltz surrounded them. Some of them took no notice of the two strangers in their midst. Others laughed at the sight of the tall man with the child on his shoulders, towering above them all by a head. They called encouraging words, waved and clapped whenever there was a break in the music.

David enjoyed the attention and Paul relished the lighthearted feeling of them dancing in the People's Square in Shi. Instead of being oppressed by the heat in Hong Kong, he and his son were enjoying the warm air of a mild autumn day in Sichuan. Above them was a clear blue sky. Heavy rain that morning had washed the grime from the air; the wind had blown any remaining dust out of the city in the last few hours.

After a few dances his son grew thirsty. Paul lifted him off his shoulders and they walked over to a row of stalls lining the side of the square. They were selling ice cream, pastries, and drinks, and were surrounded by crowds of people. Hong Kong Cantopop blared from loudspeakers and the smell of fresh coffee was in the air. Paul ordered a double espresso for himself and a scoop of ice cream and a soft drink for David. They perched on bar stools at the only free table. David wanted a straw. Paul got him one.

"No, not a yellow one. A red one."

"There aren't any red ones."

"There are. The woman at the next table has one."

"The color of the straw makes no difference to the taste of your soda."

"Yes it does."

"It definitely doesn't."

"It definitely does. Please, Daddy."

Paul fetched a red straw.

They sat in silence, looking at the square.

In the middle of it, a grayish-white stone statue of Mao Zedong towered into the sky, much, much larger than life. Mao's right arm was raised; whether he was waving at the people or showing them the way was not clear. The stone of his head and shoulders was noticeably lighter in color; the bird droppings had clearly recently been cleaned off him.

At Mao's feet, the city had laid large flowerbeds, filled with red autumn blooms. Behind him was a banner with 'Long live the Great Chairman' on it.

David did not pay attention to any of this. His glass was empty and he had finished his ice cream. He wanted to dance again.

"In a moment."

"When is that?"

———

At twilight, more and more people streamed into the People's Square: families enjoying the mild autumn evening, people laden with heavy bags of shopping, young couples pressing close to each other on the benches and chairs.

An old man came towards them and stared at them openly. When they met his gaze, he laughed. A strange toothless laugh. Not hostile, but not friendly either.

Drawn by curiosity, a couple of elderly women joined him, and immediately started talking in thick Sichuan dialect about the stranger and the unusual child. As far as Paul could make out, they were marveling at David's curly black hair and the dark blue color of his eyes, which, they agreed, did not suit his Asian eyes at all. He was certainly not Chinese, but not a real white person. What was he, then? Japanese, maybe? Paul suppressed a laugh and said nothing. They gave him a penetrating look and asked if he was the child's father or grandfather.

"Father," Paul said.

Skeptical looks. The odd laugh of disbelief.

He must be a rich man who had taken a young Chinese woman as a wife. Where was she? She had probably left him by now. From what Paul could understand, there were conflicting opinions on this point.

David grew restless. He wanted to dance.

Paul got up and put him on his shoulders again.

In the middle of the next waltz, the music stopped. The dancers paused. Questioning looks. A quiet murmur that grew louder, then quieter, until it subsided completely. A strange, tense silence spread over the square. David leaned down to speak to him. "What's going on, Daddy?"

"I don't know. They're probably changing the music."

A fight broke out in front of the loudspeakers. Several men and women were shouting at each other; the sound of their raised voices carried over to them. A different piece of music started up, then it stopped and the fight escalated. Then the new music continued. Paul recognized the tune immediately, but it took him a moment to put a name to it.

Rise up, the damned of this earth

When had he last heard 'The International'? A few couples had started dancing again but others hesitated, clearly waiting to see what the majority decided on. Gradually, everyone started moving again.

People, listen to the message!

David swayed enthusiastically to the music. Paul gripped his son's legs a little tighter.

"Why aren't you dancing?" David wanted to know.

Paul hated marching songs and fighting songs. But to please David, he moved a little, helplessly, against his will.

"Not like that," the disappointed voice said from above. "Dance properly. Like you did before."

Paul made an effort to do so.

Then came 'Long live the Great Chairman', a song in praise of Chairman Mao, which had been heard every day throughout the country when he had been alive. The old man next to them climbed happily onto a bar stool and started singing. His voice sounded like a crow cawing, but he knew the lyrics off by heart.

The young people sitting on the wall a few meters away laughed and grimaced.

Paul stopped moving.

"Keep on dancing," his son shouted.

"In a moment."

"No, now."

The next song was 'The East is Red'.

The East is red, the sun is rising
China has produced Mao Zedong
Chairman Mao loves the people
He leads us
To build a new China
Hurrah! Lead us forward!

More and more young couples starting joining in, dancing and singing. Most of the people in the two coffee shops were standing too, some of them on the chairs.

'The Song of the Red Star'.

The roar of a few thousand-strong choir singing echoed around the square.

The red star shines, it shines bright
The red star shimmers, it warms our hearts
The red star is the heart of the workers and farmers
The reputation of the Party shines for all time

The power of the people. Paul shuddered. He felt uncomfortable. He felt his pulse quickening and he was breathing heavily. Maybe he shouldn't have had that double espresso.

David had stopped swaying, as though he felt the unease. He held on tight to his father's head with both hands. Two men approached the food and drink stallholders and demanded in brusque tones that they stop playing Canto-pop music. When they refused, the men went to the speakers and yanked the cables out.

After that, they set to work on the young people. A few words were sufficient. The young men and women lowered their eyes, obediently got to their feet and joined in with the singing. Only one of them remained sitting in defiance. Despite the mild weather, he was wearing a leather jacket, ripped jeans, and fashionable motorcycle boots, and his hair was dyed a shimmering, almost white blond. Within seconds his nose had been broken by a punch in the face. Paul turned away, appalled.

David immediately asked to be let down from his father's shoulders and to be held in his arms instead.

The old man shouted something at them and some other men who were standing nearby joined in. Paul did not understand exactly what they were saying. It was clearly something about Japan, for some reason. He replied with a helpless smile, which made them even angrier. The women who had been curious about them a moment ago gave them hostile looks and the young people nodded. Paul looked around for Zhang, who was more than half an hour late. He wanted to get away from here.

David was shivering.

Paul clasped his son tighter in his arms. He saw Zhang approaching in the distance.

His monk's robes were flecked with spittle.

II

The Moshan monastery was only a few kilometers away from the People's Square, but the taxi still took over half an hour to get there. The six lanes of traffic on the road moved at a walking pace when they moved at all. The driver swore. He switched lanes constantly until Zhang asked him to stop doing so. They were not on the run from anything, even though it had seemed like that at first. They swung out of a side lane and were stuck in the jam again.

Paul found the confines of the cab and the stationary traffic difficult. He hated not being in control of how fast he was travelling, and he felt trapped. The singing of the crowd still sounded in his ears. The wordless silence in the cab made their song ring out even louder. He wished he could get out and continue the journey on foot.

Zhang sat next to him in silence, staring at a photo of Mao Zedong that was dangling from the rear-view mirror and, beneath it, a white plastic figurine of the Great Chairman fixed on the dashboard. Paul could see how worked up he was. The great gob of spit on his chest had still not dried up completely.

The cab turned into a side street near the monastery. They got out and Zhang bought a few groceries at a small market. Just like before, Paul thought, feeling glad at how familiar this felt. For a brief moment that nonetheless seemed too long, the sight of his friend in the gray monk's robes had unsettled him. He's changed his uniform, was the thought that crossed Paul's mind.

That of a policeman for that of a monk.

The thought subsided as quickly as it had appeared, but it still made Paul feel uncomfortable. He had known Zhang for almost thirty years now. They had met on one of Paul's first trips to China. Zhang had been a patrolman in Shenzhen, and had had to protect the foreign visitor from a horde of curious onlookers at a public toilet. They had become friends over the years. No one else in the world, apart from Christine, perhaps, was closer to him.

Three years ago, Zhang had suddenly left the police force, from one day to the next. He had gone to Shenzhen as a young man and had quickly risen from a mere patrolman to police inspector in the homicide division. In the nearly thirty years that followed, he had been overlooked for promotion with remarkable regularity. The official reason for this was his Buddhist beliefs and his refusal to rejoin the Communist Party after he had been expelled from it in the 1980s in a campaign against 'spiritual pollution'. The Party cadres might have forgiven him these misdemeanors given that he was one of the best and the most hardworking of the police inspectors, but what really ruled him out for higher office in the eyes of his superiors was his probity. Zhang was tenacious in his refusal to extract protection money from restaurants, bars, hotels, prostitutes, or illegal migrant workers from the countryside. He even turned down, politely but firmly, the red envelopes of cash, cigarettes, whiskey, and all the other gifts that were offered to him at Chinese New Year.

This honesty had often resulted in conflict in Zhang's family. A police inspector's salary and that of a secretary were not sufficient to take advantage of the promises of the new age. Not enough to buy a flat or a car. Not even enough for a regular shopping spree in one of the new malls filled with foreign branded goods. Zhang's wife's Prada bags and Chanel belts had been fakes of the cheapest sort.

Through the years of low-level but constant bickering and arguments – Zhang could not have said precisely when it had all started – the love between them had disappeared.

When he had been made head of the homicide division after a corruption scandal, but resigned from the position only a few months later because he knew that, being so honest, he could not but fail, it had been too much for his wife.

She left him soon after that, for a German businessman. Without saying a word to him, she had moved out with their son. When Zhang had come home from work one evening, half the contents of his household were missing. It looked as though she had even counted out the peppercorns and weighed out the sugar. Now she carried a genuine Prada bag and lived in a mansion in one of the suburbs of Shenzhen that rich foreigners and even richer Chinese people cloistered themselves in.

The split after twenty years of marriage had devastated Zhang. Paul had spent a lot of time with his friend in the weeks and months that followed. One evening, Zhang told him that he had left the police force and would be returning to his home province of Sichuan and entering a Buddhist monastery.

Paul had been disappointed and annoyed. Disappointed because Zhang was the only friend he had ever had, and he would miss him. Annoyed because this friend had not taken him into his confidence and asked for his advice or his opinion.

One week later, Paul took Zhang to the airport. He wanted to say goodbye and to help with his luggage. But Zhang was travelling with only a bright yellow imitation leather case that was so small he never needed any help with it. He had arrived in Shenzhen thirty years ago with nothing, and wanted to leave the city with nothing.

Since that farewell, they had not seen each other, only talked on the phone now and then and sent the odd email. Paul had been determined to visit Zhang, but something had always got in the way.

————

Now he watched Zhang and saw his friend the way he remembered him. The way he bent over the tomatoes with a skeptical eye and examined the pak choi carefully, picking up a dozen aubergines before finding the right one. The way he sniffed at garlic and Sichuan peppers or asked the market stallholder about the quality of the fresh tofu. Even as a monk, he had clearly not lost his passion for cooking.

Paul had missed Zhang very much in the last few years. But it had been easy to put thoughts of his friend aside in Hong Kong. He realized that it would be very difficult to say goodbye again in a few days.

The monastery was surrounded by a red wall, several meters high, and was hidden in a development of new housing, between tower blocks that were forty stories high. Zhang led them into the courtyard. Red lanterns hung from the roofs of the three temples in the middle, one behind the other. Plumes of incense smoke rose from the temples into the evening sky.

They walked past piles of building rubble, pallets of new roofing tiles and bricks, wooden beams and scaffolding. A rat scuttled across the courtyard.

David clung tightly to his father, burying his face between Paul's shoulder and neck. He raised his head only once and looked around.

"I'm hungry," he whispered.

The kitchen was basic, with a long table, a couple of stools, a work surface, stove, and sink. Pots, pans, and crockery were on a dresser. A fire was burning in the oven.

Zhang put the groceries down.

"How about some vegetarian ma po tofu, lotus roots in sweet and sour sauce, stir-fried vegetables, and then dan dan noodles to finish? I'll fry some spring onion pancakes for your son."

"Don't go to all that trouble. Rice and some vegetables will be enough."

Zhang gave him a disappointed look. "What's wrong with you? You want to celebrate our seeing each other again with just rice and vegetables?"

"No. I just don't want you to have all that bother."

"I'm not doing it on my own. We're cooking together."

Zhang fetched knives, chopping boards, and bowls from the dresser and put them on the table in front of them.

Paul was too surprised to say anything in response. He had never been allowed to help his friend cook before.

In the past, Zhang had barely spoken while cooking. If Paul had said anything he had not even heard him, so absorbed had he been in a world of aromas and spices, of herbs, oils, and pastes. Paul had long thought that cooking was just another form of meditation for Zhang, until he had told him the story of Old Hu. During the Cultural Revolution, Zhang had witnessed Red Guards beating the old man to death because he had dared to add some pepper to the soup from the commune's kitchen. That had been sufficient proof of his 'decadent, bourgeois' attitude.

The soup had to taste the same for everyone.

Ever since this experience, Zhang said, every meal cooked with care and effort was a celebration to him. A small, quiet triumph of life over death. Of love over hatred. And the better the food tasted, the more the taste buds were tickled, the nose stimulated, and the belly filled, the sweeter the victory. He could not prepare a single meal without thinking about Old Hu.

———

He put a bowl of water on the table and laid lotus roots, tomatoes, aubergines, courgettes, spring onions, red peppers, cucumbers and carrots down next to it.

"Hey, little one, you can wash the vegetables if you like," he said, turning to David.

To Paul's astonishment, his son knelt on his stool and set to work. He conscientiously dipped each vegetable in water, rubbed it, and showed each piece to Zhang, who nodded in approval.

Paul picked up the washed vegetables and cut them into thin slices. Zhang peeled garlic and onions, made the pancake batter and started busying himself at the stove.

The smell of garlic and spring onions frying and of sesame oil and ginger soon filled the kitchen.

Zhang fetched a can of Sichuan peppers from a drawer and sniffed it.

"Do you know what this used to be called?"

Paul shook his head.

"Barbarian pepper."

"Because it's so spicy?"

"No. Because it came from America to China."

Zhang smiled, and for a moment Paul thought he was joking.

"The world is filled with barbarians – apart from us Chinese, of course."

Half an hour later, dinner was on the table. Zhang had not forgotten how to cook even though he was now a monk. The lotus roots were neither too firm nor too soft. Paul knew from experience how difficult that was to achieve. The mapo tofu was delicious even without meat. Zhang had got the spiciness perfectly right – the Sichuan pepper spread its subtly numbing effect on the tongue and taste buds without the chili burning the throat.

Even David enjoyed it. He ate a second pancake, crept into his father's arms and, exhausted, fell asleep in minutes.

"Shall we put him in my bed?" Zhang asked.

Paul nodded.

———

Zhang's room was on the other side of the courtyard. It had space for a bed, a chair and small closet. A bare bulb dangled from the ceiling. Paul laid his son on the bed, covered him with a blanket and switched off the light. Zhang and Paul sat down on two stools by the door. An elderly monk shuffled across the courtyard. His back was so bent that it was an effort for him to look straight ahead. He did not notice them.

III

"What's wrong?" he heard his friend say.

"What do you mean?"

Zhang turned his head and looked at him thoughtfully.

"I've missed you," Paul said, a little embarrassed.

Zhang did not reply. He turned his gaze away and looked once more into the courtyard, which was lit only by a couple of lanterns.

After a long pause Paul said, "Everything's fine."

"I'm glad to hear that."

He heard David cough in his sleep inside the room.

"And how are things with you?"

"All fine too."

Perhaps he had underestimated the differences between the paths they had taken in the last three years, Paul thought.

The monk and the father (once more).

They were both searching.

But each of them in a different way.

There was so much to say but they didn't have much time. Where to begin? How to separate the essential from the inessential under such pressure?

The more oppressive he found the silence, the greater the tension within him. Until it unloaded itself in a torrent of speech. Until his longing to share his feelings with his friend was greater than his fear of talking about things that he would rather have kept silent about.

He tore through the last few years without stopping.

The birth of David and the hopes he had built around that.

Christine moving in. She had given up her flat in Hang Hau and had, along with Josh, her son from her first marriage, and her mother, moved in with him. That was a challenge; they both knew that. Although her mother had moved into a small flat in Yung Shue Wan after a few months, she was a permanent guest.

His efforts to share with them a house and life that had, until then, been occupied only by him and his dead son. His efforts to fit in, to meet the demands of living in a group of five people.

The way a family was meant to be only showed him what he did not have, or had only very little of: the ability to live in a community. To adapt. To tolerate closeness.

And how could he have learned that? He had not had any examples to follow. The day he left his parents' house, when he was eighteen, had been the best day of his childhood and youth.

Family life. Eating together. Looking at each other. Conversations in which hints were often sufficient to communicate with the other. Or to hurt them. Wordless understanding, or the lack of it.

Sometimes he sat there, listened, watched, and felt like an impostor. Like someone acting the role of a family member.

He was a stranger in his own home.

Christine did not understand it.

A stranger in his own life.

She would probably understand that even less.

How lonely a person could be under a shared roof. And it was his fault. His failure – he knew that. And it did not make things any easier.

What was even worse was how torn he felt with regard to Justin and David.

After David's birth he had done everything he had intended to do. Repainted Justin's room. Replaced the gentle pale blue with a rich yellow. Put away the stuffed toys in a box that was now under their bed. On his side. Taken most of the drawings and photos off the walls. Put away Justin's wellies and raincoat that had been in the hallway.

He had not been able to bring himself to paint over the doorframe with the markings for Justin's growing body.

28 February – 128 centimeters. The final entry.

But after he had thought about it some more, he had allowed Josh to paint the doorframe for him. David's growth must not be measured against that of his deceased half-brother.

And yet.

David's birth had not made his memories fade away. They had animated them instead. The first time he crawled. The first steps. The first words. How could he not think of Justin each time? And of course those memories were cast in a deep black shadow that mixed every feeling of joy with so much pain that he could no longer tell the two feelings apart.

Pain, joy, joy, pain.

He had sworn not to compare them. But he did it anyway.

What had Christine expected? That he would erase his dead son from his memories? (Of course not, she said.) Forgetting was like dying. (That's not what this is about, Paul!).

They fought often about that too.

Nevertheless, the love had not diminished. Not his, at least. Perhaps even the opposite had happened. But he was not so sure about Christine sometimes.

Zhang listened. Cast him sideways glances from time to time. The Zhang expression. An attentive, open face, with deep lines and more than a hint of melancholy in the eyes.

"Difficult," Zhang said quietly after a long pause. "Very difficult."

That was sufficient comfort.

The situation he was in was exactly that: difficult. Very difficult. No one could help him with it. He would have to find a path through it. Possibly a new one every day.

Paul heard his son cough violently so he got up and went to check on him. When he returned, Zhang was leaning against a pillar, looking at the night sky and smoking.

"I thought you'd given up?"

"I have," Zhang responded laconically. A thin smile.

Maybe, Paul thought, he would find life on Lamma easier if there were more evenings like this one. He swore to himself to visit his friend more often in future.

"What on earth was happening in the square this afternoon?"

"Shi has a new Party chairman, Chen Jian Guo. Have you not heard of him?"

Paul thought for a moment. The name seemed familiar. "Chen Jian Guo? That sounds like the name of one of the heroes who fought alongside Mao on the Long March."

"That's right," Zhang said. "Chen is his son. A rising star in the Communist Party. He must be a fervent fan of the Cultural Revolution."

"Didn't his father go to jail?" Paul asked.

"Yes. So did he. The whole family did. His mother committed suicide because of it. And yet he's reintroduced the singing of those revolutionary songs in public."

"Have all the placards and propaganda posters by the roadside got anything to do with that?"

"Yes. Every few weeks there is a new political campaign against some evil or other. And people love it. Hadn't you heard of him before?"

"Yes, now I remember. But I don't know much about him."

Zhang nodded. "Remember his name. He has lots of charisma and he is very ambitious. Many people think he will one day be the most powerful man in China. He has Shi completely in his grip, and is governing the city like a red emperor. There are often show trials and a couple of executions. He threatens the rich and criticizes corrupt Party cadres and fat cats even though he is one himself. But it's going down well with the people. He's very popular."

Suddenly they heard a voice in the darkness.

"Master Zhang?"

They turned around in surprise. A man was standing in front of them. He lowered his gaze and bowed.

"Xi, what are you doing here at this hour?"

"Please excuse me for disturbing you, but may I speak to you for a moment, Master Zhang? It's urgent."

Zhang winced every time one of his students addressed him as 'Master'. Even the sound of the word was unpleasant to him.

One year after his arrival, Zhang had, against the abbot's will, started inviting visitors to the monastery for evening discussions on the teachings of Buddha. A small but loyal group had grown out of this; they met every week, and regarded Zhang as their teacher. They admired his decision to reject the temptations of the world and enter a monastery. They regarded him as a wise man because he had acted on his beliefs. Some of them revered him as a guru because he had no interest in material things.

Zhang was flattered by their admiration, but he knew that they had the wrong man.

He was no master. By no means.

He was weak. He was small, frightened, and vulnerable to temptation.

He was searching.

Like they all were.

Xi must really need help to visit him so late at night. Zhang made his excuses to Paul, took Xi aside and walked a few steps across the courtyard with him.

"What can I do for you?"

"I got a call from a friend in the Party," Xi whispered. His voice trembled, betraying his anxiety. His brow was finely beaded with sweat. "I'm going to be arrested in the next few days."

Zhang took a deep breath and gazed steadily at him. Xi was one of his most eager students, hungry for knowledge. Recently, he had made generous donations to the monastery more frequently. The monks had drily called these donations 'soul salvation money'.

As far as Zhang knew, Xi had made his fortune with the construction of flats and retirement homes. He had a young wife, a son, and two mistresses and, in the last few months, mounting worries. He owed his riches to corrupt officials in the city administration who were now falling victim to Chen's anti-corruption purges one by one. The new cadres were no less greedy, but they belonged to another faction in the Party, and did their deals with their own people.

Zhang was not sure what Xi wanted from him. He must have known this could happen. "Are you surprised?"

"No."

"Do you think it's unfair?"

"Yes ... No ... Yes."

"Are there grounds to arrest you?"

"Yes."

"Aren't we all responsible for the consequences of our actions?"

"Yes."

"Why is this unfair, then?"

"Because ... because I only did what everyone else was doing."

Zhang sighed briefly. He did not want to engage in a longer discussion about Buddha's teachings now. "How can I help you?"

Xi hesitated before replying. He looked down at the ground and spoke in an even quieter voice. "I could escape to America tomorrow via Hong Kong. I have a visa."

"And?"

"I would have to leave everything. My son, and my wife too. I don't know what I should do."

"And you think I can tell you that?"

Xi nodded. "Yes."

Zhang shook his head gently. "You're wrong about that."

"Master Zhang, I trust you. You know what I should do."

"No." Zhang felt more and more uncomfortable. He did not like Xi's tone of voice and his body language; it was meant as an expression of respect, but he found it submissive and obsequious.

"Please, Master Zhang. Give me some advice at least."

"Who am I to give you advice? The answer is within you."

"No," Xi said vehemently. "No. Or I wouldn't be here."

"No one can take the decision for you."

"I know. But I'm so confused. I need your help, Master Zhang. You must tell me what I should do. Can I leave my family on their own?"

Zhang tried not to let his increasing annoyance show. "I can't tell you that. No one can, apart from you yourself."

He saw the disappointment in Xi's face. And the despair too.

But he felt no pity. "I can't help you with this," he said shortly. "Is there anything else?"

His student wanted to say something but then he thought better of it and stayed silent.

"Then you'll have to excuse me. I have a friend visiting from Hong Kong."

Xi swallowed, bit his lip, hesitated for a moment, then turned his back silently and slowly disappeared into the darkness. Zhang looked at him as he walked away and wondered for a moment if he should call him back, but that would have been dishonest. He had meant every word he said. There was nothing else to add.

———

Zhang went back to Paul and told him about the brief conversation with Xi.

"I never knew that you could be so . . ." Paul paused, searching for the right word. "So abrasive."

Zhang lit himself another cigarette, deep in thought. "Neither did I."

"I thought monks learned the art of serenity in a Buddhist monastery," Paul said teasingly.

Zhang closed his eyes for a moment and tried to breathe deeply, in and out. His breath was shallow. The exchange with Xi had disturbed him. What his friend was saying now had been on his mind for months.

Of course he had hoped for serenity. He had not left his old life in Shenzhen behind in order to go on an adventure. He had retreated to Shi only to realize that the city now merely shared its name with the place of his birth. He had not recognized anything: not a single building or street or park. His childhood and youth seemed to have been erased.

Zhang had traveled to a monastery in his home province of Sichuan in the hope of finding something. He had wanted to meditate and devote himself to the teachings of Buddha, but not as a goal in itself. The studying was to help him achieve more peace and serenity, to help him towards an inner equanimity. It was to drive away the melancholy that had followed him like a shadow ever since the Cultural Revolution. The older he grew, the more he longed for a peace of mind that, if he was honest with himself, he had never had in his life.

He had hoped to find answers but now he was no longer sure what the questions were.

He cleared his throat. Paul waited patiently.

"I don't know if I'm in the right place," he said. "Even after three years I'm finding it difficult to get used to life without Mei. I miss her laugh. I miss her smell next to me in the morning. I even miss her grumbling."

"And I miss my son, even though we were never as close to each other as I would have wished. Or maybe that's precisely why I do. Since I moved to the monastery we've had no further contact. My phone messages to his voicemail box remain unanswered, as do my emails. At some point I just gave up. I think that in his eyes I'm simply a loser. Someone who's too old or too stupid to adjust to the new times. He can't understand that I don't want any of it. Apparently he's working as an estate agent in Shenzhen.

"There are many ways a man can lose his children, Paul. I know who I'm talking to, so I don't say that lightly."

He had never formulated this thought so clearly, let alone spoken it aloud to anyone. It was only now that he heard these words himself that he understood how sad they sounded. How wounded he was.

Paul knew him well enough not to ask him any questions at this point.

"I imagined life in the monastery to be different. The first abbot was a Maoist in gray robes. He believed that the Enlightened One had preached his teachings directly into his ears and his alone. He was strict and severe in his interpretation of the words of Buddha. He knew of no doubts or contradictions and wouldn't hear of either. You were either a believer or a non-believer. This suited the other monks very well but I could barely tolerate it.

"When he left a year ago to lead a monastery in Yunnan, I was relieved. With the new abbot everything is different but no better. He wants to extend the monastery and turn it into a tourist attraction. We now have a souvenir shop that sells jade pieces blessed by us monks. It's clear that there is a big market for it in the city. Those were his words – can you imagine? Last week a marketing team from an advertising agency was here. The abbot wants to buy a second monastery in the countryside and offer retreats, yoga classes and weekend seminars there.

"I keep thinking about leaving the monastery.

"But what should I do instead? Who will employ a sixty-something former policeman, former monk and former husband? I could go and work as an advisor for a private security firm. I had an offer to do that once. That isn't affected by the ups and downs of the economy and it has a future.

"People are always fearful.

"I even find meditating more difficult here than I did in

Shenzhen. I don't know why. Questions pile up. Doubts. Yes, even fears. But look who I'm saying this to."

Zhang fell silent for a while and lit himself another cigarette.

"Living in a monastery requires passion and commitment," he said pensively. "It is full of privations, though I couldn't even say what I miss exactly, apart from Mei and my son. When I was in Shenzhen I didn't have any friends apart from you. I wasn't sociable. I was always a loner.

"Maybe it's the dedication that I can no longer summon up. The passion for an idea. The humility. Or is it the ignorance that a person needs to follow the dogma of another without question? Perhaps I lack the will or the ability to feel at home in a community. Or maybe I'm making it much too complicated and it really is very simple: perhaps I have simply had enough of believing in my life."

V

Paul woke before his son did. David had been restless in the night, as he had so often been in the last few months, talking in his sleep, and kicking Paul and waking him up several times. Now they lay quietly next to each other. Nose to nose. Paul looked at his sleeping child. The dry air of the air-conditioning had chapped the boy's lips. He must remember to put some cream on them later.

He listened to the rapid, regular breathing. He looked at the high forehead and the small nose. David had inherited the southern Chinese skin color from his mother; he looked completely different from Justin, who had had pale, almost transparent skin.

Justin. A small child. Even at birth.

Paul shuddered. He did not want to remember. Why did his thoughts have to turn to the past again right now? He was here. In Shi. In a hotel, in bed. Next to David. He wanted to experience nothing else in this moment. There was no yesterday. And no tomorrow. He repeated the words and concentrated on the breathing next to him.

For a short, precious moment he felt only the warm air that came from David's nose. It streamed gently over his skin. It still had the slightly sweet smell of childhood that would soon disappear forever.

Then the fear in him rose again, and he was unable to defend himself against it. It was the fear that the beating of this little heart could suddenly stop.

Just like that.

Why should it? Christine had asked him when he had told her about his worries once. She understood his fears, but David was a healthy boy who was growing perfectly well. That's what the doctors said at every examination. Children's hearts don't stop beating just like that, Paul. Not without a reason.

He had nodded sadly. How could he have expected her to understand what he meant?

Paul got up and opened the curtains a little. He sat at the desk, picked up his phone and looked up the Hong Kong stock exchange on the Internet. He had earned a lot of money on shares in the last few years. He always bet on a falling market, which, as Christine remarked, was in line with his pessimistic nature.

———

"Were you four once?"

Paul turned his phone off and looked round in surprise. "Good morning, sweetheart."

"Were you four once?" David repeated his question.

"Of course."

"And where was I then?"

"I don't know," Paul replied. The wrong answer. Admitting to not knowing anything always unsettled his son and led to more questions that Paul had no answers to.

David shot him a troubled look. "Why not? You always know where I am."

Paul pulled the curtains back, sat next to him on the bed and thought for a moment. "I was talking nonsense. You were in Mummy's tummy, of course."

His son nodded contentedly.

Paul didn't know what to say next. He found the silence uncomfortable. "Are you hungry?"

David did not respond. He was not a good eater.

"Shall we have breakfast in bed?"

"What are we having?"

"Whatever you want. An egg. Cornflakes. Bread rolls. Someone will even bring it to our room."

"Really?" David seemed to like the idea. He sat up and thought about it. "I want to eat in the bath."

"We can't eat in the bath. Everything will get wet there."

"In a cave, then!"

"What kind of cave?"

"Like the one you built yesterday."

Half an hour later, Paul was crouching with his head lowered under the blanket that he had stretched like a tent between the desk and the armchair, held down by an iron, an alarm clock, and a kettle. David lay in front of him under the desk and they ate toast with raspberry jam and drank orange juice, hot chocolate and green tea. They were escaping from a green dragon spewing fire, so they could only speak very quietly.

"What are we going to do today?" Paul whispered.

"See the pandas," David said immediately.

"But we saw them yesterday."

"That doesn't matter. Didn't you like them?"

"Yes, I did. Very much."

"Then we can go and see them again."

Since Paul did not have a better suggestion, he could not counter this logic.

He had actually liked the panda zoo very much. He had not seen a place like this in China before. The lawn was freshly mown and the trees were well tended. Elderly women emptied the rubbish bins. There were no plastic bags or empty bottles lying around. The toilets in the souvenir shop were clean and they worked. At every other bend in the path there were signs telling visitors what they were not allowed to do: spit, curse, push, step on the grass, be rude, wear dirty clothing. To Paul's amazement, people obeyed the rules.

They walked through a dense bamboo grove, whose tall canes leaned over them like a roof. It looked like they were walking through a long green tunnel. A gust of wind made the bamboo sway and the loud cracking sound startled David. He stopped. "Are there dragons in China?"

"No."

"How do you know that?"

"I read it somewhere. They died out many years ago."

Satisfied with this reply, David carried on walking. Soon he could no longer wait to see the pandas, and ran ahead, drawing curious glances. Paul was used to that: wherever he went with his son, the boy attracted attention, even in Hong Kong.

David waited for him at the first enclosure. He had climbed up on a bench and was watching five pandas, who, separated from the visitors by a trench, were sitting less than ten meters away from him and chewing bamboo branches undistracted by the many spectators. Behind them, a panda lay sleeping in the fork of a tree.

"Why is he sleeping in a tree?"

"Because he finds it comfortable. Do you want to try sleeping in a tree in the garden at home?"

David gave him a stern look. Before he could reply, disquiet rose among the spectators. Men with walkie-talkies came down the path and brusquely ordered everyone to make way. They pushed the visitors in front of the enclosure roughly to one side and everyone made way without complaining. Two children stumbled and started crying but their parents hushed them. David climbed into his father's arms.

Paul saw a dozen young people walking through the bamboo grove towards them. Their laughter and their loud voices could be heard from a distance. They were in their early or mid-twenties and were conspicuously well dressed. The women were carrying expensive handbags and wearing high-heeled leather boots, a lot of jewelry, and big sunglasses.

The other visitors shrank back as they approached. One young man was quite clearly the focal point of the group. Paul could see that from his body language and from the way the others looked at him, vied for his attention and made way for him. He was wearing a tight white T-shirt and his sunglasses were propped on his forehead. The prettiest of the women walked by his side. They stopped in front of the panda enclosure.

Suddenly the young woman shrieked several times.

"Oh, how sweet, how sweet!" she exclaimed rapturously.

Everyone around her looked at what she was staring at. The woman was not interested in the pandas – her eyes were fixed on David.

"How sweet!" she cried again. Her companions were also looking at David curiously now. A few of them laughed. Others pointed their mobile phones at father and son and took photos of them. Paul found the attention unpleasant. He turned away and made to leave.

"Hey!"

Paul flinched.

"Come here."

He turned back slowly. The young man waved him over. His voice did not sound unfriendly, just strangely authoritative for a person of his age. Every sentence sounded like a command.

The visitors stepped to one side. The gap in front of the young man seemed like an urgent demand to obey a summons. Paul did not wish to be impolite, so he took a few steps towards the group of people. The young man was a head shorter than he was. He had full lips, a large nose, unusually large eyes, and was very muscular. He sized Paul up.

The woman whispered something in his ear. He nodded and they both laughed.

"Boy or girl?"

"Boy," Paul said, doing his best to be friendly.

"How old?"

"Four."

"I'll be five soon," David chimed in.

Laughter.

"What's your name?" the woman asked.

"Bao."

"'Precious treasure.' What a beautiful name."

She stretched her arms out as though she expected David to come to her. "A photo." Paul involuntarily tightened his grip on his son. She stood next to him and her friends and many of the onlookers took photos, as though she was a Hollywood starlet. Then a friend wanted to join in the photo. And another one. And yet another.

She stretched her arms out again. David held on tight to his father. She took a black and white lollipop shaped like a panda head out of her bag and offered it to David, who cast a questioning glance at his father. Paul nodded.

"Only if you let me hold you," she said, smiling, withdrawing the lollipop.

David hesitated, and then he slid from Paul's arms into the young woman's. Her friends cheered and laughed and took more photographs. The woman herself was so happy that she was quiet. She gave David the lollipop, sniffed his hair and stroked his neck gently.

Paul was finding the situation more and more uncomfortable. "We must go," he said, taking his son back. He could feel that she did not want to let go from the way she clung to David and resisted, only reluctantly letting him go after some delay.

"One more photo with my friend," she demanded.

It was the tone of voice that annoyed Paul. "No, that's enough," he said curtly, turning away.

"You'll stay here until my girlfriend and I get one more photo with your son."

Paul wondered if he should respond to this outrageous behavior or ignore it. He did not want to get into a fight, but before he could take another step, two bodyguards were standing in his way. He moved to the left, then to the right, and the two men followed him each time. They meant business. He would not get past them. Paul turned around.

"Tell your men to let me pass."

The young man crossed his arms. There was a challenging look of mocking laughter on his face.

Paul walked right up to him, straightened himself to his full height and said, loudly enough for everyone to hear, "Asshole".

Without waiting for a reaction, he pushed him roughly to one side and walked with firm steps towards the bamboo grove that led to the exit. Half a dozen men with walkie-talkies caught up with him but were unsure about what to do. They were clearly waiting for orders. Paul heard the walkie-talkies crackling and a voice repeating words that Paul did not understand. After twenty meters they fell back and let Paul continue.

David had watched the whole scene attentively without reacting. Now he gave his father a stern look. "You're not allowed to say 'asshole'."

VI

Paul needed the toilet so urgently that his stomach hurt. He had wanted to go by the zoo exit but the line had been too long and David had become impatient. The streets had been jammed with traffic and the taxi ride to the hotel had taken almost one and a half hours. Paul could hardly hold out any longer.

He rushed across the foyer in long striding steps and parked the pushchair next to one of the pillars in front of the gentlemen's toilets. "Wait here for me. I'll be right back."

When he came back two minutes later, the pushchair was empty.

Paul looked around the foyer. More annoyed than worried. How often had he told his son that he mustn't just run off somewhere? On Lamma he had once nearly fallen from the jetty into the sea doing that. He owed his life to an alert passer-by.

"Bao!" When Paul was being stern with his son he often switched to Chinese.

He looked behind the pillars. Behind two luxuriant potted plants. A bench. A display cabinet.

David liked hiding under tables. Paul kneeled in front of a sofa suite and crawled around it on all fours.

Nothing.

"David?"

He got up again and realized that the chatter in the foyer had died down. People were frozen in their places and not moving. As though someone had paused a film. All eyes were on him.

"Has anyone seen my son?" Paul shouted in the quiet foyer.

Silence.

They averted their gazes. The receptionists, the concierge, the three businessmen next to him. The two hotel porters.

"Has anyone seen my son?" Paul called out again. Louder and more urgently. No reaction.

Paul walked toward the exit and everyone fell back into doing what they had been doing as if by command.

Several black Audi sedans and two Mercedes SUVs were parked in the driveway. The doorman stared at Paul.

"Have you seen my son?"

An empty, dismissive look in reply.

A deep bass beat was growling from one of the SUVs. The windows were tinted so Paul could not see if anyone was sitting in it. He knocked against the driver's window. The window was lowered a little. At the wheel was a man with a crew cut and a mole on the forehead of his pockmarked face. He gave Paul a questioning look.

"Have you just seen a child come out of the hotel on his own?"

The music boomed in the vehicle. Paul was not sure if the man had even understood what he had said. He repeated his question, more loudly this time. The man shook his head and the window was raised again.

Paul ran back into the foyer.

"David!?"

Paul was gradually beginning to feel panic rising in him. Please, David, please come out of your hiding place.

The lifts. David was fascinated by lifts. Why hadn't he thought of that in the first instance? He had probably taken the lift alone up to the room on the twenty-eighth floor.

But he wouldn't have been able to press the top-most button without help. Had someone lifted him up?

Paul ran down the long hallway. They had the second last room. He burst into it. David? Oh my David, where are you?

Nothing.

He felt ill.

Had David got out on another floor? He could be on any floor of the hotel.

In any room.

On the way back to the lift he heard a child's voice in another room. He knocked on the door but no one answered. He knocked more loudly, hammered on the door with both fists, and then he heard the child's voice again, coming from the room next door. A young woman opened that door, carrying a small, frightened-looking little girl, whose big eyes looked at him in alarm. Paul excused himself for disturbing them.

He tried to remain calm, to gather his thoughts. He must not let fear overwhelm him.

He noticed cameras beneath the ceiling of the hallway. The hotel had CCTV. He usually detested it, but it was now a blessing. With its help he would find his son in a few minutes.

The woman at the reception desk did not answer his question. Not in Chinese. Not in English. Paul started shouting.

An older man took her place and introduced himself as the 'Duty Manager'.

No, he had not seen the child, but it was no problem to look at the CCTV footage from the last fifteen minutes. No, Paul could not see it himself, only the trained security personnel could. Everything would be cleared up. He mustn't worry himself. He just had to be patient.

Paul kept looking. He took the lift down to the swimming pool. Ran through the fitness studio, the bar and the café next to it, more and more quickly and more and more upset. He wrenched doors open and screamed his son's name into empty rooms and dark basements.

When he returned to the foyer he was a different man.

I'm sorry to have to tell you . . .

There were two new faces at the reception desk. The duty manager was nowhere to be seen. Where was he and when would he return? They looked at him as though they did not know who he was talking about. Instead, a younger man came up to him. He was responsible for the security in the hotel. They had looked at the footage thoroughly and found nothing suspicious. The cameras covered about eighty percent of the hallways and the pushchair had been in a blind corner.

Paul did not believe a word he said.

VII

Paul sat collapsed into himself on a chair in the police station. Zhang, who was sitting next to him, thought he had aged years. He was muttering to himself, constantly blaming himself. How could he have left his son alone? Every so often he looked quest-ioningly at his friend as if Zhang could tell him where David was.

The two policemen were exceptionally polite and helpful to him. They acknowledged the presence of a monk with him casually. They offered Paul cigarettes and tea, placed a dish of roasted melon seeds on the table and tried to calm him down. David had most probably slipped out of the hotel without being noticed and got lost. The city center of Shi was almost one hundred percent covered with CCTV cameras. They would find him. No question about it. This sort of thing happened more often than you thought. Only the day before yesterday they had brought a five-year-old girl back to her parents after searching for hours when she had got lost while they were shopping.

All the things policemen say in situations like this, Zhang thought. He knew better. Time was not on their side. With every hour, no, every minute that passed, the chance of finding David grew slimmer and slimmer.

People smuggling. Zhang had no doubt that this was what they were dealing with. This was a business that made a lot of money in China. Tens of thousands of young women disappeared every year. Kidnapped, lured into traps with false promises or bundled into lorries in broad daylight and sold as wives in remote provinces. Thousands of children also disappeared every year. Especially boys around David's age, who were valued goods. They were snatched and sold to childless couples, to farmers without sons or sold abroad. Only very few of them ever saw their parents again.

Zhang had interrogated a few people smugglers in his time as a police inspector. Most of them lived miserable lives themselves: migrant workers from the countryside who had failed to make a living in the cities, who had no jobs but had families in the villages waiting for their monthly remittances, often depending on them for survival. That did not excuse anything, as he had always said to his skeptical wife and his son when he told them about these criminals. But it explained things a little.

None of those men would have dared to choose a victim from a luxury hotel. It was only in the last few years of his time as a police inspector that people smuggling had become professionalized. The criminals were younger, smarter, better organized, and educated, though he did not like to use that word in this context. They channeled their victims through the provinces quickly and efficiently. They took orders for size, age, appearance, and gender and gave delivery dates. People had become products.

Like everything else in this country.

Many of these criminals organized themselves into larger cartels, entirely in the spirit of the free market economy that now dominated, in order to increase their productivity and market share.

If David had fallen victim to one of these well-organized people smuggling operations, he would no longer be in the city, Zhang thought. Even if there was CCTV footage showing him disappearing into a car, the number plate would be covered up and the windows would be tinted. The color and the model of the car would be so common that it could not be identified. David had probably disappeared without trace this afternoon, forever.

He thought he could see from the looks that the two policemen exchanged that they thought the same thing. Paul described once more what had happened that afternoon and the minutes before David disappeared. No, he had not felt as if someone was following him. He had not noticed anything suspicious. No strangers had spoken to him. Neither the day before yesterday, after they had arrived, nor yesterday. And not this morning either.

He described his increasingly desperate search for his son.

The policemen thought there might be clues in the hotel's CCTV footage. Their officers were already on the way to the hotel to see the footage. They would soon know more.

It was the two gray SUVs in front of the hotel that made them suspicious.

Paul only remembered the man at the wheel vaguely. His face had been scarred. He had not noticed anyone else in the vehicle; he hadn't been able to see into it.

Any suspicious sounds? Paul thought about this. No. And even if there had been, the thumping music had drowned everything out.

The older of the two policemen rang the officers who were viewing the CCTV footage. They were to seek out the footage from the cameras by the driveway and entrance urgently, view it and look out for two gray Mercedes SUVs. He would stay on the line with them.

They waited in silence. The two policemen lit cigarettes.

The policeman on the phone did not like what he was told next at all. And it grew worse and worse. Zhang could tell from the flashing of his eyes, the thinning of his lips, and the way he ground his teeth.

"Nothing out of the ordinary," he lied to them. He could deceive Paul, perhaps, but not Zhang.

"We'll find the owner of the vehicles through the license plates and check them out just in case. Maybe they noticed something suspicious."

Paul had to go to the toilet. One of the policemen accompanied him.

"There were no number plates on the cars," Zhang said as soon as he was alone with the other policeman.

The police inspector gave him a searching look and dragged at his cigarette in silence. The two men were about the same age and had probably had many of the same experiences in thirty years of police service. Seen too much of the things people did to each other. Heard too many lies. Too many excuses and too little understanding. Stared into abysses without finding a trace of comfort. Judging by the sadness in his eyes, time had made him a melancholy man too.

"What makes you say that?"

"I was a police inspector in the homicide division in Shenzhen for thirty years."

The policeman started. He took another drag at his cigarette and exhaled the smoke slowly through his nose.

"The number plates are not the problem."

"What, then?" Zhang asked, confused.

"Sometimes knowing is a much greater problem than not knowing."

"What do you mean by that?"

"Your friend will not see his son again." After a long pause, he added, "He shouldn't even try to find him. Do him a favor: stop him from doing so."

"How do you think you can do that?" Zhang retorted in annoyance. "Of course he will do everything to find his child again. You would do that too."

"Maybe he has other children who still need him? A wife that he wishes to see again?"

A horrible feeling was creeping over Zhang. He asked if he could see the footage. In confidence, of course.

The policeman shook his head and stubbed his cigarette out.

It would have been a small gesture to make for a former colleague. With his experience, he might have been able to spot something that passed younger officers by.

"It's being erased as we speak," he said. "Be glad that you don't know what there is to see on it."

VIII

No, he did not want to go back to the hotel now. He didn't care what the police inspector recommended. How could Zhang seriously believe that he could rest while the police were looking for his son? Rest! What a ridiculous idea. He wanted to help with the search. He would walk the streets around the Shangri-La in a systematic way, look in every doorway, every courtyard and every building entrance. He would knock on doors and ask other children if they had seen David, he would go to playgrounds. He would not take no for an answer. He had a photograph of David with him. Maybe someone had seen him. A passer by? The sales assistants in the teashop opposite the hotel? In the supermarket. In the kiosk. In the restaurant. In the small row of shops one block away. He would not rest until he had found his son. The policemen themselves said that little children often got lost, more often than you thought; children got lost because they were curious. And they always turned up again.

Or maybe a car had run over him and he was in one of the city's hospitals. They hadn't even talked about that yet – the hospitals. He would ring them up, one after another, no matter if the police were doing the same. Another phone call did no harm. Or was it better to go in person to each of them and ask for information at the accident and emergency departments? He did not care how many hospitals there were in Shi.

Or maybe someone had seen David crying on the street and taken him home for safety. Now they did not know where to take him because David did not know the name of the hotel. Maybe they should make copies of his photo and pin them to trees and buildings near the hotel. Maybe it was possible to ask the local TV stations for help. They could broadcast a photo of David. Is that a good idea, Zhang? They would find him somewhere in the next few hours, alive and well. Children did not vanish without a trace, did they, Zhang? You were a policeman. You know that. Say something, Zhang. Say something.

IX

She had been filled with a sense of quiet anticipation all day. This was the first time since David's birth that Christine had spent two nights without her son. She had not slept more badly than usual as a result; she was not that kind of mother. The two days in the office had been packed with appointments and she had not had much time to think about him at length. So she was looking forward to seeing him all the more. A long weekend just with David and Paul lay ahead. Without rushing between home and work. Without the constant complaints from her jealous mother.

Three days, she hoped, that would do her and Paul good as well. They had neglected each other since David's birth. Their roles as mother and father occupied almost all of their selves. The days were long and the nights with Paul were short. They often got to bed at ten o'clock too tired to talk about the day or to read even a couple of pages of a book. They were parents. They were happy to be parents, but there was little time left for them to be lovers. They had both forgotten or suppressed the memories of how tiring it was to be the parents of a small child.

———

Christine saw at once that something was wrong.

His eyes. The face drained of blood. Skin like ash. No smile at seeing her again.

He must have had food poisoning and hardly slept. He should have said something. She could have taken a taxi to the hotel by herself.

Paul and Zhang. Where was her son?

Was he hiding behind one of the pillars? Behind his father? Christine stood still and looked around her. She did not like his constant hide-and-seek games.

The other flight passengers streamed past her toward the exit. Some of them pushed and swore because she was in their way.

Had he run out in front of a car? Fallen down the stairs? Had an accident in the hotel pool, perhaps? If he was lying somewhere in a hospital, why was Paul not by his side? Why had he not phoned her to give her warning?

Where was David? She felt an ominous foreboding rising within her.

Suddenly Paul was next to her and taking her in his arms. For moment she hoped she had just been imagining things.

David was fine.

He was in the hotel. A babysitter was watching over him as he slept.

Tell me that's where he is, Paul.

He said nothing. He held her tight with arms that had no strength.

They sat huddled in a corner of the terminal and he spoke quietly, avoiding her gaze.

"How could you leave him alone in the foyer?" She grabbed him by the shoulders and shook him. Look at me!

"Why didn't you take him into the toilet with you?" How could he have been so careless?

He had no answers.

"Why didn't you look after him better?" She pushed him away from her, jumped up, and wanted to get away; where to, she did not know.

She screamed a torrent of random words. Within seconds they were surrounded by plainclothes policemen.

Zhang explained the situation to them and tried to calm Christine down. He understood how frightened she was, but the police in Shi seemed competent; they were searching for David far and wide. Everything seemed to indicate that David had run out of the hotel and got lost. It was only a matter of time until he was found.

His body language and the look in his eyes said something different.

———

Christine wanted to see everything. The foyer. The toilets. Tables. Display cabinets. The café. She walked through the foyer and walked every conceivable route that her son could have taken in the hotel. Like a sniffer dog trying to pick up the boy's scent.

She pulled herself together and was functioning again: she downloaded the latest photos of David from her phone for the police and described her son in detail: his height and weight, how shy he was, whether he would go off with a stranger, his favorite ice cream, the kinds of toys he liked. The officials took copious notes. It was long past midnight by the time she lay down next to Paul in bed and could give way to endless sobbing.

He did not try to comfort her. In the last few hours, he had tried several times to take her in his arms, but she had turned away every time. The pain was too great. Her head hurt, as did her limbs, and her stomach. She did not want to be comforted.

She could barely stand the sound of him breathing heavily next to her and she suddenly found his familiar smell, which she usually loved, unpleasant.

Where was David? The fear and the not knowing were driving her crazy. While talking to the police, images had appeared in her head, images that she had immediately suppressed. David lying injured in a ditch. Or bleeding by the side of a road after a hit-and-run accident. He was crying and calling out for her. She had turned her full attention to the official's questions. But in the loneliness of the night she could no longer manage to block out her imagination.

Maybe he had really got lost and was now sitting in a garage or dark basement somewhere he had accidentally been locked into.

Or maybe a pedophile had lured him home. He was easy prey: so trusting and curious. On Lamma there had been no reason to warn him about strangers. She felt ill. There were possibilities that were too huge, too horrific, that she could not allow herself to think about.

Had someone kidnapped him in order to sell him? In the *South China Morning Post* she saw articles from time to time about people smugglers and Chinese parents who were desperately searching for their children and whom the authorities ignored. His kidnapper would at least treat him well, she hoped. He was their contraband.

Her little David. Who was so afraid of the dark. Who had never been apart from his parents for a single day of his life until now. How frightened must he be? Was he crying? Was he sleeping? Was he injured? Was he hurt?

Why was she not with him? Why could she not help him? It was unforgiveable. They had failed as parents. Their job was to protect their child from harm.

She shouldn't have let him travel to Shi alone with his father. Why had she gone to work instead of coming with them? It was all her fault. And Paul's.

Her fault.

Her fault.

And Paul's.

Her fault.

Her fault.

And Paul's.

When she could no longer think of anything else and when these words were the only thing filling her mind, she took two of the sleeping tablets that Zhang had given her.

She felt her body relaxing, letting go, and everything receding slowly into the distance and losing its meaning. Then she fell asleep.

———

The ring of the telephone woke Christine. A gray dawn light was filtering into the room through a crack in the curtains. She looked at her watch. It was just before half-five. Paul was sitting at the desk and he picked up the phone. He nodded mechanically, ended the conversation, and stood up.

"Where are you going?" she asked quietly.

"To the foyer. Someone wants to see me."

"Wait, I'll come with you." She tried to get up, but the sedative effect of the pills was still too strong. She sank back into the pillows.

"I'll be right back," Paul said.

"Wait, wait . . ."

She heard the sound of the door clicking shut.

X

No one was waiting in the foyer for him. The night porter gestured towards the exit with a nervous incline of the head.

Half a dozen luxury sedan cars were parked in the driveway. Paul looked around but no one was to be seen. Suddenly, one of the car windows a couple of meters away from him was lowered by the width of a hand and someone called to him and told him to get in. At the wheel was a pockmarked man with a big black mole on his forehead. Paul recognized him immediately.

"Quick. Close the door," he commanded.

Paul got into the car. He saw a small woman on the back seat.

The man gripped the steering wheel with both hands, looking straight ahead.

"What do you want from me?"

"You must leave Shi today," he said, without looking at Paul.

"Why? My son has disappeared. I'm not leaving Shi before . . ."

"He is lying next to my wife, asleep."

Paul whipped around. On the back seat was a heap covered in a blanket. The woman pushed one corner of the fabric to one side and David's face appeared. Paul looked from the woman to the man. Tears shot into his eyes.

"Who are you?"

"That doesn't matter," the man said brusquely.

"What do you want? Ransom money? I will give you everything I have. I have shares and a house in Hong Kong that I could sell . . ."

"We don't want any money."

"What, then?"

"Nothing."

"Nothing?" Paul was sure he had misunderstood.

"But why . . . I don't understand . . ."

"The less you know, the better for us and for you."

Paul looked at the man and the woman more closely. They seemed to be in their mid-forties and were simply dressed. Both wore necklaces with a gold cross as a pendant.

"Take your child and leave the city as quickly as you can," the man said again.

"But why?"

"Because people will be looking for you."

"Who?"

They said nothing. Paul repeated his question.

"My husband's boss," the woman said quietly. "He kidnapped your child. We're simply bringing him back to you. In the name of the Lord."

Paul did not immediately grasp what she was referring to. "Which lord?"

"Jesus Christ, our savior."

"My boss gave your son to his girlfriend as a present. Because she found him so adorable."

"Who is your boss?"

They ignored his question.

"How did the girlfriend see David?" Paul asked, beginning to feel suspicious.

"She saw him yesterday at the panda zoo, and expressed a desire to have him," the woman said. "My husband recently started work as one of his boss's drivers, and I was supposed to be your son's nanny. If the boss realizes that we and the child are no longer there, it won't be long before he realizes that your son has been reunited with his parents. He will do everything to get hold of him again."

Paul shook his head disbelievingly. "She expressed a desire to have him? A child as a present?"

They nodded.

"I don't believe it. He can't simply take my . . ."

"He can, he can . . ." the woman retorted.

"You're not from here," her husband added. "You have no idea how powerful this family is."

Paul looked from one to the other doubtfully. "But how could he take David . . ."

The man interrupted him. "The police will arrest you on some pretext and find drugs in your room. You will be handed a sentence in court for drug smuggling. That's what happened recently to a businessman from Singapore who got into a disagreement with our boss. He's now in jail for the next nine years."

Paul said nothing for a moment. The scenario the driver was describing was not unlikely.

"What will you do now?" he asked, breaking the silence.

"We have family in Fujian province. They'll hide us for a while."

"Can I help you?"

"How could you help us? The Lord will protect us."

Paul thought about how much money he had with him. "I'd like to give you something . . ."

"We don't want your money," the man and the woman said in unison.

"Why are you doing this?"

The man looked at his wife, as though she alone had the answer.

"We believe in the Lord. My husband has worked six months for his boss. He has accumulated enough sins. Your child . . . that was too much."

"Thank you. I . . ." Paul was lost for words.

"Truly I tell you, whatever you did for one of the least of these brothers and sisters of mine, you did for me. Matthew 25:40," she said quietly. "The Lord shows us the way."

Paul saw fear in both pairs of eyes, but he did not hear it in their quiet voices.

"You now have two, three hours at most before someone notices we're missing. You must have left the city by then. The hotel will be one of the first places they search. Perhaps the hotel will even report this to him. The head of security is in his pay."

Paul turned to open the door, then hesitated.

"Who is your boss?"

"Chen Tian Hao, the son of Party Secretary Chen." The man paused. "Now go."

Paul got out of the car, opened the rear passenger door and carefully took his sleeping son in his arms. "How can I thank you?"

"There is no reason to thank us."

The woman nodded at him. "May the Lord be with you. He will bring you to safety. God bless you."

———

Paul hurried through the empty foyer, watched by the night porter's suspicious eyes. David woke briefly in the lift. He opened his eyes, and when he saw Paul, a smile flitted over his face. Then he fell asleep again.

Christine was sleeping. He put David down next to her and hurriedly packed their things. He wanted to get out of the hotel as quickly as possible. He looked up flights online: the 16:30 flight was full but he got three seats on the later flight.

When he had arranged the flights, he realized that he had no idea where they were to spend their time until then. In another hotel? Too dangerous. Every foreign guest had to be registered with the police. Shopping? In a café? A restaurant? Public places were also too risky, if the couple was to be believed, and Chen was looking for him. The safest place was Zhang's monastery.

Paul sat down on the bed and stroked Christine's face gently. He bent down and whispered in her ear, "Darling, wake up. We have to go."

XI

Zhang had been sitting with the other monks in the hall for two hours now, trying to let go. Trying not to think about his painful knees, not to think about his back, not to think about Paul, David, and Christine.

The more he tried, the more difficult it became. He focused on his breath. Felt the cool morning air rush into his nose and escape, warmed by his body. He chanted his mantra. He kept his eyes on the golden Buddha in front of him. Nothing helped. His thoughts would not stop whirling around his friend. What kind of karma was that? To lose two children? What misdeeds had he done in his previous life to deserve this? Or were the rules of life different from what the Enlightened One had divined and proclaimed? Was it coincidence after all that governed life? A cold and merciless arbitrary force? The power of the absurd?

Just as Paul always claimed.

The hammering of the first construction workers could be heard from the hall. Zhang was pleased about the noise this morning. It was the unofficial sign that the meditation session had come to an end. The abbot and the first few monks rose.

Zhang went into the refectory and was morosely eating noodles when he heard familiar voices. He turned around: Paul, Christine, and David were standing in front of him. Zhang immediately saw from the look in his friend's eyes that it was not just good news that had brought them to the monastery so early in the morning.

He fetched bowls of rice and vegetables and a thermos flask of tea for them and they sat in the courtyard in the first rays of the sun. Paul described what had happened while David ate a little.

He finished by saying, "I've booked the 22:00 flight to Hong Kong for us this evening."

Zhang shook his head vigorously. "You can't go to the airport."

"Why not?" Christine asked uncertainly.

"What can happen to us there? I have the tickets and the boarding passes. We're already checked in," Paul added.

Zhang marveled at their naivety. "You have to show your passports before you board. If Chen is looking for you, and I assume he is, they will stop you then."

"For what reason?"

"They want your child. And they are used to getting what they want. If they don't get what they want from people voluntarily, they take it."

"Who are 'they'?" Paul had still not understood. Zhang could tell by the doubt in his voice.

"Chen. Xi. Wu. Choose a name. The most powerful people in the country. It would be easy to concoct a reason to get both of you locked away for interrogation for months. The resulting trial would not be fair, and the judges would not be impartial. You know all that! This is not your first time in China! Do you think that anyone will take any interest if you disappear for years into a prison in Sichuan? The American embassy would visit you a couple of times at the beginning. Maybe the American government would make a formal complaint. And then? You think a diplomatic crisis would ensue over you? I don't think so."

———

Zhang watched them to see what effect his words had. "And all through that, David would be in a children's home. Or with the Chens – that would be easy to arrange too."

"What else can we do? Is there a train to Shenzhen?" Christine asked.

Both of them had not grasped the seriousness of the situation they were in. "Forget the train. You need ID to buy the tickets.

Apart from that, I wouldn't travel to the south. I don't think they would let you travel onward to Hong Kong. Chen used to be Party Secretary of Guangdong province. He is well connected there. The border would be closed to you."

"Do you really think his power extends that far?"

"I don't know. But that is one of the problems in this country. We don't know exactly how far a person's power reaches. Do you want to come up against it?"

"No, of course not," Paul said. "But where should we go instead? To Yunnan and over the mountains to Burma?"

"No. That would mean hiking in the mountains for days. Not with a four-year-old."

"Where to, then?"

"To Beijing," Zhang said decisively.

Paul looked at him disbelievingly. "Why to the capital?"

"Because the American embassy is there. That's the safest place. You're American. You're not dissidents. The embassy can arrange for you to leave the country. Chen's power ends at their doors."

"How far is Beijing from Shi?" Christine asked, filled with doubt.

"About two thousand kilometers."

"How do we get there?"

Zhang passed both hands over his shaven head. He had not the slightest idea how they could travel to Beijing without being identified. Paul was conspicuous because of his height alone and David's appearance made him no less so. They could not stay overnight in hotels or use any form of public transport.

All it would take was a few phone calls in Chen's name and the police in every province would be on the hunt for them. Who would dare to take them into hiding for even one night? Who would be prepared to endanger themselves taking them from one place to another? And why? The only motive that Zhang could think of was money.

He lit a cigarette, took a couple of drags from it and put it out again. "How much cash do you have on you?"

Christine and Paul thought about this. Not more than six thousand yuan, they reckoned.

"That's not much." Six thousand yuan was not enough to buy them free passage to the capital. Not even sixty thousand would be sufficient. The risk was too great, too incalculable. Chen hunted down his opponents without mercy, and he did not spare their families, friends, and business partners. He was a child of the Cultural Revolution, and proved every day in Shi that he had learned its lessons well. Anyone who was lenient to his enemies would regret it. Anyone who displayed weakness would lose. Zhang looked at them one by one. David had hardly eaten anything and not said a word. Paul looked totally exhausted.

"You look tired. Do you want to rest a little in my room? I'll try to organize something. I still have a couple of relatives in the city."

Zhang wandered the streets aimlessly. He did not want to stay in the monastery. He needed to move in order to get his thoughts in order. But he found it difficult. A child as a present. Like a pet. Even though it sounded absurd, Zhang had not the slightest doubt that it was true. People stopped at nothing nowadays to get what they wanted, and their appetites were insatiable. All sense of propriety had been lost.

Just like before. He had experienced the loss of restraint and the lack of conscience during the Cultural Revolution. No one could understand the excesses of China today without being familiar with the history of those years. They had been at war then. At war against the old world. At war against old ways of thinking. Traditional culture. Traditional customs. Traditional ways of doing things.

Now they were at war again. At war against the memories. At war against the environment. At war against modesty and moderation. Against decency and honesty. Nothing had really changed: once again they were at war with themselves. We are a traumatized people, he thought. Nothing had changed there either.

————

Paul and his family had to leave the city as quickly as possible. The police would turn up in a few hours to interrogate Zhang. In the police station yesterday, he had been careless, telling one of the officers the name of the monastery he lived in.

But where could they go?

Zhang had to seek help from people who had turned their backs on society. They had to be living on the edges of it and have nothing more to lose, yet not be in public opposition to those in power, for political dissidents would be kept under surveillance. But how was he to find people like that in such a short time? And which of them would really be reliable? A betrayal would be well rewarded in such a case.

In China, no organizations escaped the control of the authorities. Apart from churches, nunneries, and monasteries, perhaps. Zhang thought about the couple that had brought David back to Paul.

In the name of the Lord.

Their religion had moved them to risk their lives. There was an underground church with thousands of fearless members, but he had no links to them. And he couldn't get in touch with them so quickly.

Zhang remembered the abbot of a monastery not too far away whom he had encountered often in the last two years. The abbot came from a village a few hundred kilometers away in the northeast, near the border to Shaanxi province. At least that was on the way to Beijing. He probably had family there still or knew other Buddhists who would help. Zhang also thought about his own nephew, who lived in Shi and was the editor-in-chief of a weekly publication that was, as far as it could be under current conditions, mildly critical of the regime. Perhaps he had an idea of how to help. These two men were Zhang's only hope.

———

When Zhang returned to the monastery three hours later, it was just after half-past eleven in the morning. He went straight to the abbot and told him that he had to make an urgent trip to Shenzhen due to a family emergency. His son had been severely injured in an accident and was in hospital. He had a ticket for the flight at eight p.m., but wanted to show his friends around the panda reservation before that. His friends would take the late flight back to Hong Kong, he said several times, very clearly.

It would be easy for the authorities to check on what he had said. With any luck, they would believe him and wait for Paul at the airport this evening. The red herring would buy them a few hours' head start.

He hurried to his room. Paul, Christine, and David were asleep in his bed, more on top of than next to each other.

Zhang shook his friend's shoulder vigorously. "Wake up."

He dragged Paul out of a deep sleep. Paul looked around, blinking, and took a moment to remember where he was. He got up wearily.

"We have to get going immediately," Zhang said urgently.

"Where to?"

"I'll explain everything later."

Christine woke slowly and with great difficulty.

"I'm thirsty," David said.

"Have you anything to drink?" Paul asked.

"Later. You must hurry now." Zhang heard the gong sounding for the meditation session at noon. "If we don't get going immediately, it will be too late."

They left the monastery via the back exit, where the car organized by Zhang was waiting. The last thing Zhang saw before they left was plainclothes policemen on their way to the abbot's office.

Christine looked out of the window. The driver was taking a long time getting them out of Shi. There was a traffic jam on the three-tier highway that went on for kilometers past factories, warehouses, construction sites with half-finished buildings, and rubbish dumps. They left the highway and drove down a country road that twisted and turned. The sky clouded over and the low-hanging clouds cast the hilly landscape of rice paddies in a dull light.

They had to stop every now and then because a horse- or ox-drawn cart was blocking the way, or because farmers were drying their chillies on the road. Each time this happened the driver, who had not said a word to them yet, cursed and swore. Christine noticed whenever he looked at her in the rear view mirror. Their eyes met but it was difficult to read his expression. He probably couldn't wait to be rid of his risky passengers.

David was asleep. His head was nestled in Paul's lap and his feet were in hers. She held them tight with both hands, pushed his trousers up a little, stroked his pale skin and looked at his thin calves. Since he had returned she had had to touch him constantly: smell his skin, stroke him, and cuddle him. She would have preferred never to let go of him, but David made it clear to her that that would have been too much.

David, who usually couldn't sit still for a second and was always talking, had fallen into a deep and strange silence on his return. "Hungry" and "thirsty" were the only two words that they heard from him. As though he was only just learning to speak. He had wet himself twice, even though he no longer wore nappies, not even through the night. He ignored her questions about what had happened in their absence.

She had wanted to know everything, every detail, as though she could regain control over that period in which he had been so defenselessly at the mercy of strangers. Had they locked him up? Had he been alone? Where had he slept?

Paul looked out of the other window. Shortly after Zhang had got out of the car, he had tried to take Christine's hand but she had pulled it away. He had remained silent ever since.

Zhang had given them exact instructions. But no address. No names. They were not to be in a position to give away anything if anyone stopped them. The journey would last several hours. The driver knew where he was bringing them and that was enough. Zhang had given them a mobile phone and told them that they were not, under any circumstances, to make any calls from it, but simply wait to receive calls on it. In the gravest emergency they could send a text message to a number that was saved in the phone. At the place they were being brought to, they would be safe for a couple of days, no more. Zhang would try to get to where they were by roundabout means. If he didn't manage to do that, they would receive further instructions by text message on the phone. If they did not hear from him within a week, they were on their own. In reply to their question of how they were to get to Beijing, he had simply looked at them with his tired eyes and said nothing.

———

"Paul?" It took a moment before he turned his head to her. The exhaustion in his eyes. The fear. She did not know him like this.

What do you think they did with David, she wanted to ask.

"Yes?"

"Do you think they beat him?"

He shook his head. "Why would they have done that?"

His reply annoyed her. "How should I know?" she snapped at him. "Maybe because he didn't do what they told him to do?"

"I don't think so."

"Why don't you think so?" His hesitant manner infuriated her even more. "He was frightened. He cried. I'm sure they beat him. Don't you wonder what they did with him?"

"Yes, of course I do."

"But?"

"He was apart from us for fifteen hours. He probably slept through ten of them. I think ..."

"Paul," she interrupted him in a sharp tone, "what are you trying to say? That everything was really not so bad?"

"No, I don't mean that."

"Maybe he didn't sleep at all. Maybe he spent most of the time crying and there was no one there to comfort him. Can't you see how changed he is? He doesn't say anything any longer. He's wetting himself ..."

"I know," Paul said very quietly. "But is it helpful for us to imagine what they ..." He turned away without finishing his sentence and looked out of the window again.

Christine was too furious to say anything else. She did not want to force herself to imagine what strangers had done to her child. Surely that was the first question to ask. Fifteen hours could be an eternity. Maybe it would help to talk about it? She needed his help, and he was turning away.

The car juddered as it hit a pothole. David woke up and stared at his mother, looking strangely absent. As though he was looking through her. Christine recognized this glassy look in his eyes from the few days that he had lain in bed with a high fever. She put her hand on his forehead; his temperature felt normal.

"Are you all right, sweetie?"

He closed his eyes without replying.

"Are you thirsty? Do you want something to eat?"

Not even a shake of the head.

She pushed his T-shirt up and checked his torso once more

for bruises, scratches, or other signs of maltreatment. He pushed her hands away, pulled his shirt down and turned to one side.

A larger village appeared before them. The car slowed down, suddenly braked hard, turned right and stopped after a hundred meters in a square on the edge of the village. Another car was waiting there. Their driver told them to get into it.

Christine cast a questioning glance at Paul. He shrugged. The driver got out, talked to the other man and passed him some envelopes. Then they transferred their luggage and Paul carried David to the other car. He opened his eyes briefly and immediately fell asleep again.

———

The new driver gave Paul one of the two envelopes and started driving. Paul took the letter out, skimmed through it and passed it to Christine.

> *My dear friend,*
> *Xu, my nephew, is editor-in-chief of a weekly newspaper in Shi. He organized this drive and the first stage of your journey for you. He thought it would be better for you to change cars once; he does not completely trust his driver. You are on the way to a farmer called Luo Jia Ding. My nephew once did a story on him and his family. He thinks you will be safe there for a few days. Luo only knows that you are travelling and that you need somewhere to stay for a few nights. You don't have to pay him; he does not expect money from you, and you will have urgent need of your money later.*
>
> *I'm trying to organize the next stage of your journey, and hope that we will see each other at Luo's place in a few days.*
>
> *Zhang*

Christine passed the letter back to Paul. She felt queasy. Perhaps that was down to the twists and turns in the road or the speed at which the new driver was going. She did not want to think about how much they were at the mercy of strangers. Dependent on them. On their willingness to help. Their honesty. Their decency.

Paul opened a window. She took a deep breath in and out. The fresh air did her good.

The roads they were travelling on got even smaller and were in even worse condition than the ones before. The villages they passed had hardly any stone buildings, only wooden or mud huts. Half an hour later, they stopped in front of a farmhouse. It stood behind a high wall whose red paint had long faded away. Glazed green tiles lined the top of the wall and there was a round wooden gate in the middle that had recently been painted a deep red.

An elderly man stepped through the gate as though he had been expecting them. He walked with a stick and limped heavily. A dog, barking loudly and agitatedly, followed him. The driver got out of the car and passed him a thick envelope. The old man took a letter out of it, read it, looked over to the car and nodded at them.

The Village

I

The farmer was short but thick-set. He wore a greasy blue Mao jacket, had white hair that was cropped short and thin grey stubble. There was a cigarette tucked behind his left ear. It was difficult to guess how old he was. His was the kind of face – with deep wrinkles and tanned, weather-beaten skin – that Christine no longer saw in Hong Kong. He was certainly over seventy and was perhaps already over eighty.

The dog barked more furiously and aggressively. A sharp retort from the man was enough to quieten it. The old man sized them up in silence, then finally inclined his head to indicate that they should follow him.

They stepped into a small courtyard. The driver followed with their luggage, put it at their feet, said a hasty farewell, and left. The farmer closed the gate behind him.

Christine looked around uncertainly. There was a well in the middle of the courtyard and firewood was stacked against the side of a shed; two bicycles were leaning against it. A couple of chickens were running around and red chillies were drying on a large cloth spread on the ground. The chillies were covered in a grayish-brown layer of dust. In another corner was a basket full of corncobs and a wooden wheelbarrow.

A child's voice came from the house. "Grandpa?"

"I'm out in the yard. We have visitors."

A young boy came running out but when he saw them, he stopped suddenly. Christine thought he looked about seven, maybe eight years old.

"Who are they? What do they want?" he asked suspiciously.

"Behave. They are our guests," the old man murmured.

He turned to Paul and said, "My name is Luo. Have you eaten yet?" Without waiting for a reply, he added, "Come in."

The young boy gave them a dark look, turned his back and disappeared into the house.

They followed him into a dim, damp room that reeked of smoke. On the chest of drawers by the door, two black-and-white photographs could be made out in the half-light: one of them was of an older woman and the other was of a young man gazing very seriously into the camera. In front of them was a dried-up cob of corn, two sweets, and a handful of burned-out incense sticks in an old can.

"I'll make some dan dan noodles," the old man said, hobbling into the kitchen.

Christine had no idea what she should do. She could see from Paul's face that he was just as much at a loss as she was. David had laid his head on his father's shoulder and kept his eyes closed the entire time.

The young boy hunched on a chair and stared at them. He had short cropped hair too, a narrow face, and notably large eyes.

They heard the old man clanging pots and cutlery in the kitchen.

"Can we help?" Paul called out.

"Da Lin!" came the reply in a loud voice.

The boy stood up reluctantly. Only now did they notice how gaunt he was. Sticking out of his short-sleeved T-shirt that was several sizes too big for him, his arms looked as thin as sticks.

He went into the kitchen and returned with a tray full of bowls. There was a portion of noodles for everyone. The noodles were covered in a red sauce that was so spicy that Christine's lips were burning after the first bite. The two men ate their noodles in loud slurps, saying nothing. Da Lin looked at his food and did not touch it.

"Eat," his grandfather ordered him.

The grandson remained silent.

"How old are you?" Christine asked.

The boy did not reply.

"What's your name?"

He gazed at her with eyes that were alert but much too wary for his age. How could a child have such shadows in his face already?

He probably didn't understand her Mandarin. She had been learning it for four years in Hong Kong, but still had a thick Cantonese accent. "I'm sorry. My Mandarin isn't very good," Christine said.

"He can speak a little Cantonese," Luo said with his mouth full. "He lived in Shenzhen for a couple of years with his parents. His name is Da Lin and he's twelve years old."

"Twelve? I . . ."

"But he doesn't talk," the old man interrupted her.

"Not at all?" Christine asked. Hadn't she heard him speak in the courtyard?

"Not to strangers." Da Lin gave his grandfather an angry look. "Only to me," the old man continued. "And to his mother."

"Where is she?"

"In Beijing."

"And his father?" Too late, she remembered the photograph of the young man on the chest of drawers.

The old man ignored her question and continued slurping his noodles. When he was finished, he wiped his mouth on his shirtsleeves and said, "You can sleep in Da Lin's room. He can sleep with me."

He showed them the bathroom behind the kitchen. The toilet bowl had neither cover nor seat and had clearly not been cleaned by anyone for years. The sink looked equally filthy.

Da Lin's room was behind his grandfather's, at the end of a dark corridor. Christine had imagined a child's bedroom. How stupid. It was a windowless room with bare, un-whitewashed walls. A lamp without a shade was next to the door.

"Thank you," Paul said.

The old man said something he couldn't make out and left them alone.

The air was humid and smelled as if they were in a musty basement. Christine looked around the cold room again. Several blankets were strewn across the floor, along with old vests, a pair of torn trousers, a few socks, and a dirty jacket. In one corner was a rusty tricycle, covered in a thick layer of dust. Thumb-sized cockroaches were crawling on the ceiling. She felt like screaming.

Christine felt Paul, who was still carrying David, put his arm around her. She let him.

"I want to get out of here," she whispered.

"I know. I do too."

"I want to go home."

He held her a little tighter. She could feel his warm breath on her neck.

Christine fought back her tears. She had had lots of practice with that.

"What do we do now?"

"Wait."

"For how long?"

"I don't know. A week?"

"And then?"

Paul shrugged.

"I won't be able to stand it." As if there were an alternative. As if they had the power to change anything in their situation. She felt her strength slipping away, and started sobbing.

"Christine, please!"

Not in front of David, of course not. She made an effort to control herself. But a reprimand was the last thing she needed now.

"What's wrong with Mama?"

It was the first full sentence David had spoken since he had been returned to them.

"She has a headache," Paul said.

"Is that why she's crying?"

"Yes."

David's little hand stroked Christine on her head, which made everything even worse. She cried with abandon.

Paul led her to the bed, spread the blankets out, sat down next to her with David and took her hand.

"Do you need a plaster?" The concern in her son's voice could barely be borne.

"No, my darling."

"Why not?"

"Because it's Mama's head that hurts. She hasn't cut herself."

David stroked her again, with both hands this time. The thought of losing him was unbearable. Her little David, beloved above all else. She would rather kill herself than hand him over to those strangers.

And Paul.

And him.

II

What did these people want from them? The woman with all the questions got on his nerves. Didn't she realize what a nuisance she was being? Why was the child held by the man throughout, and why didn't it move? And now they were sleeping in his bed too. Why had Grandpa asked them to stay?

Da Lin hated visitors.

The last time there had been strangers in the house they had brought his father. They had come on a horse cart. He had heard the clip-clop of the hooves when they were still far off. He still heard them today, at night, when he was awake and Grandpa was snoring away.

He had been lying in the back of the cart. Wrapped in white cloths. Soaked through with blood.

But Da Lin had not understood that at first.

They had carried him off the cart and into the courtyard and laid him down on the bench in front of the house.

Grandpa had watched the entire time, expressionless, not saying anything. Then they had unwrapped him from the cloths. Or at least what was left of him.

He had not recognized his father.

Grandpa had turned his back, hobbled into the house, and returned shortly after.

Da Lin had not been able to tear his gaze away. As if he only had to stare at the body long enough to bring him to life again. He had even stepped closer to him, hoping to recognize his smell, at least. Nothing was more familiar to him than the warm, comforting smell of his father. For as long as he could remember, they had slept in the same bed every night and woken up together in the morning.

What lay before him now did not smell.

It stank.

That is not Papa, he thought, no way. That is a stranger that they have brought here. But then he had seen Grandpa's face and known that this was his father after all.

When I'm grown up, he had told the strangers, I'll find the murderers. First I'll earn enough money so that Mama no longer has to work in Beijing. Then I'll find the murderers.

The men laughed. A strange laughter. Brief and cold. You don't need to do that, child, they said. We know the murderers. Everyone knows the murderers. There were enough people watching.

Grandpa listened to their story. Da Lin had not understood much of what they said.

When the men were gone, he started retching. The whole afternoon and into the night.

And the next morning too. And the evening.

He had been sick for a month, and grown so thin that the skin stretched over his ribs.

Since then he had been silent. And he hardly ate.

He only spoke to the dog and to Grandpa, who got so worried otherwise. He did not want to worry him. And he talked to Mama of course.

But he had not seen her for a long time.

He did not speak to anyone on the telephone. Not even with Mama.

III

Luo read the letter and looked into the envelope. There was a bundle of red hundred-yuan notes as thick as his thumb. Several thousand yuan: wages for half a year's labor in the fields. At least.

Luo put the envelope away, disappointed. How stupid, he thought. How unoriginal. Everything was about money these days. As though there was no other currency left in the world. As though every human impulse, every helpful deed and every betrayal, indeed, every action, had its price tag and could be bought.

He was helping these strangers because Xu had asked him to. That was enough. He would hide anyone who was on the run from Chen, the authorities, or the government. They were not safe with him for very long in any case. Since Zhong Hua's death the police had been watching him. They dropped by regularly or summoned him to the station to ask him what he and Da Lin planned to do. He asked them every time exactly what they expected from him and his grandson.

Did they think that he would go to the press, who would never be able to write about them anyway? That he would go on hunger strike until his son's murderers were arrested? That he would stand in front of the police station or the headquarters of Golden Real Estate, pour petrol over himself, and set himself alight, like a woman from a nearby village had done a few weeks ago? It would be pointless because it wouldn't change anything.

Once, a few weeks after his son had been murdered, he had travelled alone to the district capital. He had wrapped around himself a white sheet on which he had written details of what had happened, of who was responsible for the murder of his son. All the names. He had limped up and down in front of the Party headquarters. A few passers-by had stopped and read the writing on the sheet but most people had walked past paying no heed or had crossed to the other side of the street, hurrying on fearfully. After fifteen minutes they had arrested him, brought him back to the village and threated to take Da Lin away to a children's home if he did it again.

He could never let them put Da Lin in a home. As long as the boy needed his care, Luo could do nothing.

But the regular interrogations did not bother Luo. Quite the opposite. He enjoyed the time that he spent with the police. That showed him how frightened the officials were, that they feared even a silent twelve-year-old who was in the process of starving himself to death, and a limping old farmer whose days were numbered because his leg was rotting. That they did not feel safe in their high-security mansions.

The thought pleased him.

Paul started awake. He had woken often in the night, drenched in sweat, not knowing where he was at first. This time, he still felt disoriented. Why was he sleeping in such a narrow bed? Why was it so quiet? He listened and heard David breathing next to him. He stretched out to reach for his son in the darkness and felt his hair and Christine's arm.

Awareness returned to him and with it came the fear.

Were they safe with the old farmer? What would the police do with them if they found them? Paul could no longer stand the darkness so he got up.

Christine groaned slightly in her sleep. He felt like curling up close to her but did not want to wake her. He felt his way to the chair, got his things, and searched for the door.

Dawn was breaking outside the house. It was still cool.

Luo was up already, standing next to the well, doing his exercises. He bent his knee, stretched his upper body, raised his arms in the air and lifted one foot after the other, rotating each one. Paul could see the pain in the old man's face when he made certain movements. When he was finished, he limped over to the bench, where a thermos flask and a cup of green tea was waiting, and sat down.

Paul was not sure if he should join him.

"Get a cup from the kitchen. There is tea here," Luo muttered without looking at him.

Paul fetched a cup and Luo poured tea for him, saying nothing. He was breathing heavily. The exercises had clearly been more of a strain than they had appeared. They looked across the courtyard in silence. The rising sun cast long shadows over it and bathed the shed in a warm red light.

"I want to thank you again for helping us. It's very generous of you."

The old man nodded.

"We won't stay long."

"Hmmm."

Paul tried to remain silent too but could not manage it. He felt more and more awkward. "What do you know about us?" he asked, merely to say something.

Luo sipped his tea. "No more than I need to: that you need help."

"That's enough for you?"

"Yes." He lit a cigarette and passed the packet to Paul.

"Thank you. I don't smoke."

He put the packet back in his jacket without saying anything. He was clearly not interested in conversation.

Paul looked around the courtyard. He saw a homemade table-tennis table and a kind of billiard table, small and octagonal, that he had not noticed yesterday. There were a few balls and a cue on it.

"Do you play billiards?"

"Da Lin."

"You don't?"

"No." Luo drew at his cigarette and inhaled deeply. "You're not really safe with us," he said unprompted.

Paul started. "Why not?"

"The police come by now and then."

"The police?" Paul echoed, not sure whether he had understood the old man's thick accent correctly. "What do they want from you?"

The old man replied only after a long pause. "I ask myself that too."

"What do you mean by now and then?"

"Once a week or sometimes only every fortnight. They seldom stay long."

Paul shifted uncomfortably on the bench. "Maybe we should move on," he said, more to himself than anything.

"Where to? What is your next destination?"

"I don't know that yet," he replied quietly.

Luo thought for a moment. "If the police see you here, I'll say that you are related to my late wife. That will make them suspicious of course. You are a Westerner. But it will take them at least one or two days to come again and ask more questions."

"Do me a favor and don't tell my wife about this. She's worried enough as it is."

Luo nodded.

The day had barely begun but Paul already felt as tired as he had been the night before. Even in his exhausted state, he felt gratitude towards this stranger, but did not know how to express it.

"Do you need help?" he asked without thinking.

"Me?" Luo turned his head and looked at him. A brief, mocking smile flitted across his face.

"Why are you laughing?"

"I don't know when the last time someone offered to help me was. Why should you want to help me?"

"No idea," Paul said awkwardly. "I thought perhaps we could help you a little while we're with you." He could hear how clumsy he sounded. "Does Da Lin learn English in school? We could ..."

Luo interrupted. "He doesn't talk."

"I'm sorry, I forgot that."

"Have you any painkillers with you?" the old man asked, abruptly.

"A few aspirin, I think."

"What's that?"

"A painkiller."

"Can you give me some?" He pointed at his leg. The left foot was wrapped in a thick, dirty bandage.

"What's wrong with it?"

"I stepped into an animal trap in the woods. It won't heal properly."

"Have you been to the hospital?"

Luo shook his head. "Is this your first time in China?"

"Have you been to the doctor?" Paul asked, undeterred.

"There is no doctor here. And even if there were, I wouldn't have the money to pay one. I treat myself. But the pain is too great. My ointments don't work any longer."

With a swift movement, he put his cigarette out, shook the ash off and put the stub back in the packet. "You can mend the roof for me later if you want to make yourself useful. It's been leaking in the kitchen, in Da Lin's room and in my room for a long time. I can't get up the ladder any longer. Da Lin can't help with such things."

V

"Where is Papa?"

The same question every morning. Whether he woke next to only her because Paul was already up and about in the house or he called for them from his room and she was the one who came.

Where is Papa?

Not that it bothered her. Quite the opposite. She was glad that David was so close to his father and wanted to be near him.

But it hurt her to see how Paul sometimes reacted to it. His hesitation. His indifference.

In those moments she feared for her son. His father was a difficult person. Loving him did not come without risks. She had a choice. She could protect herself. She hoped. David could not.

Loving always comes with a great risk, Paul had said to her once when she had spoken to him about it. Love can be un-reciprocated. People can be disappointed. Betrayed. Abandoned.

Yes, Paul, that's right, she had said. But that doesn't apply to children. Loving shouldn't hold any risks for them. He had looked at her and not said anything. He had understood. She could see it in his eyes.

"Where is Papa?" David repeated his question. His voice sounded fearful, not curious.

"Outside. He's up already." Christine raised herself a little and realized how unwell she felt. She was hungry and her whole body ached, especially her head. A piercing pain that tugged at her from her neck to her forehead and her eyes. She leaned forward and reached out for her son. Something rustled somewhere in the room. Christine drew a sharp intake of breath.

"What was that?" David wanted to know.

"I don't know. Most probably a mouse."

"Why is it so dark? I can't see anything."

Paul had closed the door. Not the slightest ray of light entered the room. "Wait. Let me turn the light on."

She tried to get up but David held on tight to her. "Don't go. I'm frightened."

"How am I supposed to turn the light on?"

She took him into her arms and he clung to her body. She got up, lost her balance, and fell back onto the bed. She tried again, carefully, feeling her way through the darkness. A sharp pain shot through her foot. She had stepped on something sharp.

"Mama?"

"Everything's fine, my darling."

It was so dark that for a moment she thought she might start panicking. Her feet got caught in a piece of clothing and she stretched her arm out in order not to walk into a wall. Where was the door?

"Paul?" Why had he left them in this miserable hole? He should have waited until they were awake too or he should have woken them. How could he have been so inconsiderate?

"Paul," she shouted angrily. "*Paul!*"

Suddenly the door opened. She nearly lost her balance again from the shock. She saw the silhouette of a child in the light pouring in.

"Thank you," she said, relieved.

Da Lin switched on the light. He watched the two strangers in his room with an expression that Christine could not read.

"Do you know where my husband is?"

Instead of replying, he stepped into the room and starting gathering his things from the floor.

———

The bright sunlight in the courtyard made her headache even worse. Paul and the old man were sitting in front of the house drinking tea.

David slid from her arms and scrambled onto his father's lap.

Christine felt faint. She urgently needed something to eat and drink.

"Are you hungry?" Luo asked when he saw her.

She nodded. "And some tea or water would be very good."

A few minutes later they were seated at the table in silence eating dan dan noodles. She would have liked to have had some rice or soup but had not dared to ask. The noodles were even more spicy than they had been the previous evening, even though Christine had asked for them to be less spicy. David had been given a portion without sauce. He plunged his chopsticks into the noodles and moved them around, but did not eat.

Da Lin devoured his noodles quickly and watched David all the time.

Christine admonished her son to eat at least a couple of bites.

"I'm not hungry," he whispered back.

"Now then," she said sternly.

"No."

"Just a little."

He shook his head and pressed his lips together.

"Your child has a fever," Luo said with his mouth full.

"How do you know that?"

"I can see it."

"Are you a doctor?"

"I used to be."

"You?" It had slipped out of her. It shouldn't have sounded so derogatory.

Luo had either not noticed her incredulous tone or was not interested in her doubts in his ability. She pressed her lips to David's forehead. It was hot.

"A barefoot doctor, if that means anything to you." He slurped up the rest of his noodle sauce.

He pulled his chair up to her, inspected David's tongue, felt his pulse with some concentration and felt his throat and feet.

"If you like I'll make him some tea, then he'll be better tomorrow."

"What does he have?"

"A fever."

"You said that already. But why? He doesn't have a cold."

Luo sighed. "Tea or no tea?" He clearly had no desire to elaborate on his diagnosis.

Paul chimed in. "Tea would be very kind, thank you."

Luo got up and limped to the kitchen. Christine followed him with a mixture of suspicion and curiosity. He put some water on to boil, cut a few slices of a moist brown root and fetched a handful of leaves, dried berries, and fungus from various cans, adding everything to the water.

"You don't believe in Chinese medicine."

"I do," Christine said. "I have a Chinese doctor in Hong Kong."

"Why are you so suspicious, then?"

"I'm not. Just curious."

Luo shook his head and rummaged around on the shelf for another can. "Shall I give you something for your headache?"

"How do you know that I—"

He pointed at a stool. "Sit down."

Christine sat down gingerly on a rickety three-legged stool. He stood behind her, put his hands on her shoulders and pressed down firmly with both thumbs.

"Ouch!" she cried. "Not so hard."

Luo ignored her protest, took hold of her arms and pulled them back behind her head until there was a cracking sound. He massaged her neck and the back of her head. His skin was rough and his grip was firm, but it did not take long before she felt her shoulders slowly relaxing. She closed her eyes. A leaden heaviness overcame her and for a moment she feared she might fall off the stool from sheer exhaustion. Luo took a small tin out of a container and rubbed her neck and her shoulders with some pungent ointment that made her nose tingle.

"Your skin will feel warm in a moment."

A few seconds later, she felt as if she had a bad sunburn.

"That hurts."

"It will get better soon."

But it got worse instead. "When?"

He did not reply but simply put the containers back on the shelf.

Her shoulders were burning up. She was on the verge of grabbing one of the dirty teatowels and wiping the ointment off.

Paul came to the rescue. He suddenly appeared behind her, took her head in his hands and massaged her temples. Gradually, the burning pain eased.

———

The tea was dark brown, almost black, and it smelled of damp, rotting earth. David looked at it suspiciously, sipped it and turned away, repulsed. Christine tried a sip, and nearly spat it out immediately. It was much more bitter than the concoctions that the Chinese doctor in Hong Kong had brewed for her from time to time.

"Do you have some sugar, perhaps?"

Luo looked at her as though that was the first time he had heard the word.

"Or a little honey?"

No reply. In his eyes she thought she could see what he thought of her: weak, spoiled, decadent Hong Kong Chinese.

"No," he finally said brusquely. "It's not Coke. But it will help."

She offered the cup to David again but he put both hands over his mouth.

"Come on. It doesn't taste that bad."

A vigorous shake of the head was the reply.

"Two mouthfuls. Then you'll soon feel better. I promise."

David buried his head in her chest.

"Paul," she said, annoyed, "can you please –" She stood up and placed David on his father's lap. Christine heard a giggle and she turned round. Da Lin was standing behind her. He had followed them into the courtyard, back into the house, into the kitchen and back into the dining room, and watched them the entire time. Now he seemed to be laughing at David.

"What are you looking at?" she snapped at him.

Startled, Da Lin took a step backwards. For a moment she had the feeling that he wanted to say something in response. Before she could apologize, he had turned away and run out of the house.

VI

Da Lin sat on the dusty ground with his legs outstretched and his back leaning against the well, waiting. It was all a matter of patience, Grandpa had told him. He had been right. Patience and concentration.

The rat had disappeared into a hole in the wall of the shed. It would emerge at some point. He had been watching it for days, and he knew that, for some reason, it had a liking for the oval-shaped gap between the piles of wood. Before it went back there, it would stick its head out, sniff the air and look around – he didn't know what or how well it could see – and when it felt that it was not in danger, it would dart across the courtyard in a couple of seconds. That was his chance.

Everything would have to happen quickly when it appeared. Raise the catapult.

Pull.

Aim.

Let go.

One shot. That was all he had.

He noticed the woman, her husband, and the child watching him. He considered abandoning the hunt for a moment; he did not want any onlookers. Then he decided to simply ignore them. The most important thing was not to be distracted by them. If his thoughts wandered off elsewhere, to Papa, for example, or to Mama, then the stone would miss its target or only hit the tail or the back and the rat would merely squeal in pain and keep running. He had experienced that often enough. There was only one spot to hit in order to kill. The head – and it was small.

Grandpa had promised him one yuan per rat or mouse. Because they ate their rice and corn. And gnawed holes in the baskets. And in the roof.

One yuan. He had eight already.

There was no sign of the rat. He hoped that it would stay a while longer in the shed and that the visitors would lose interest in him.

Against his will, his thoughts turned to his mother once more. He wondered where she was. What she was doing there. Whether she thought about him. And why she had not come home for Chinese New Year. She had rung one day before. One day.

She was sorry, she had said to Grandpa. She had to work. She wanted to explain it to him. He had not believed a word. The parents of the other children had all come home for Chinese New Year. From Shenzhen. From Shanghai. From Guangdong. From Beijing. One mother had even come from Harbin. All the factories in the country closed for the entire week. Everyone knew that.

He was not interested in her explanations. She had promised, and promises weren't to be broken.

Why isn't she coming? he had asked Grandpa. But the old man had only given him a sad look and said nothing. Then Da Lin had thought that maybe there were questions to which it was better not to have any answers at all.

The first thing he spotted was the two tiny black eyes. The rat was sniffing the wood, looking around uneasily, as though it could smell the danger. It turned round quickly and disappeared again. It must have smelled the strangers. But then it reappeared again. Da Lin could tell from its movements that it wouldn't turn back again. A quick glance to the left and to the right, then it was set for its dash.

He whipped his catapult upright, pulled the rubber band back as hard as he could, took aim, and let go. The rat rolled over and lay still.

He got up and took a good look at his victim. He couldn't have been more on target. The head was nothing but a fleshy pulp; the rat must have died immediately.

Once the stone had been too small, or he had not been strong enough. He had hit the target well, but the rat was still moving. It clawed at the ground and tried to crawl to safety. He had started crying. If he really felt sorry for it, Grandpa had said, he should help it along with a heavy stone.

He had done so.

He had not hunted for weeks after that.

VII

Paul climbed the ladder rung by rung, uncertain of whether this incredibly wobbly home-made bamboo construction would support him. He stepped gingerly onto the flat roof, which had only a slight pitch to it. The weatherworn tiles were porous and broken in many places. Every time he moved there was a loud cracking or crunching sound. With his second step, he broke a tile, and with his third. In the courtyard below were Luo and Christine with David in her arms. They watched him with doubtful looks.

"I don't know if it will take my weight," Paul called out.

Luo directed him to the place in the roof where he thought the first leak was. All the tiles there were indeed broken. Paul could see down into the kitchen. He pushed the rubble aside and inspected the wood. It was still in surprisingly good condition. It had to be possible to make the roof here watertight with a dozen new tiles. The same went for the roof over the other rooms.

Luo wrinkled his brow in thought when Paul told him about the state of the roof. "We have enough tiles," he said. "Do you think you can do it? With our help?"

Paul nodded, even though the thought of having to climb up onto the roof and move around on it again made him feel uneasy.

Luo led him to one of the sheds, in which there were two large piles of new roof tiles.

"Da Lin!" he shouted across the courtyard. Soon the boy was standing sulkily next to them.

"Help the man to mend the roof, do you hear me? Do what he tells you." Then, turning to Paul, Luo added, "Talk to him. He understands you even if he doesn't reply. Give him something to do. You may not think it, looking at him, but he's tough."

Paul lifted one of the tiles. It was much too heavy for the slight boy. "Thank you, but I can manage on my own."

Da Lin stayed by his side and Paul found it impossible to read the expression in his eyes no matter how hard he tried. It changed too quickly. Sometimes he had the feeling that they showed nothing but indifference and boredom, but then in the next moment he thought he could see suspicion and a burning rage.

The boy bent down, picked up one of the tiles, hefted it onto his narrow shoulder, cast a defiant look at Paul and carried it to where the ladder was. He laid it carefully down on the ground and walked back to the shed to get another.

"Wait, let me help you," Paul said.

They carried the next roof tile over together. And the third. Paul hurt himself with the fourth. A splinter of ceramic got into his hand. It was an unpleasant, stinging pain, and Paul couldn't tell where it came from. All he could see was a reddish line on his right thumb. He wanted to ask Christine for help – her eyes were better than his. Then Da Lin reached out for his hand, pulled it to him, had a good look at it, and gestured to Paul to wait. Soon he returned with a pair of tweezers, a needle and a pair of shabby gloves. Carefully, he slit open some skin with the needle and pulled a centimeter-long splinter out with the tweezers. Then he gestured to Paul to disinfect the wound with some spit.

"Thank you."

Da Lin passed him the gloves and smiled briefly.

They carried the first pile of tiles over, then the second. When they broke out in a sweat, they stopped to rest. Da Lin went into the house and returned with two cups of boiled water.

"Thank you very much," Paul said, taking a big mouthful. "You're really quite strong."

Da Lin picked up a stick, twiddled it in his fingers for a moment and then drew two Chinese characters in the sand. Paul looked at the writing from all sides but could not decipher it. "What does that mean?"

Da Lin scratched the strokes of the characters again, impatiently. He looked at Paul expectantly.

Paul could not make out the characters, no matter how he tried. "I'm sorry, but I can't read that. Can you say the words to me?"

Disappointed, the boy rubbed out the words with his feet.

"What a strict teacher you are," Paul said, smiling at Da Lin. "Your grandfather told me that you like playing billiards. Would you like a game?"

Da Lin shook his head.

"Or a round of ping pong? . . . No?"

Paul walked over to the billiard table, tugged the gloves off, picked up a cue and held it out the boy. Da Lin did not move.

The table was a little lower than usual. It was a good meter wide, with eight corners, each with a hole at the edge hung with netting. Instead of felt, someone had tacked a worn piece of green cloth to the surface. In the middle were six colored balls and one white one. Paul picked it up, placed it at the edge of the table, gave it a sharp tap with the cue and watched it crash into the others, scattering them across the surface. Two balls landed in the pockets. One by one, he potted the rest of the balls. They rolled surprisingly well on the improvised surface.

Da Lin was suddenly standing right next to him with his hands buried in the pockets of his sweatpants, staring at the table.

Paul stopped playing and handed the cue to him.

No reaction.

"Come on."

Now they were looking each other in the face. The boy hesitated. He clearly wanted nothing more than to take the cue, but something held him back.

"Come," Paul repeated, and smiled at him encouragingly. "We've worked together, now we can surely also play together."

Da Lin pressed his lips together.

Paul waited patiently. "Did you make the table?"

Silence.

Paul looked more carefully at the netting, the table legs, and the cloth. He passed his hand over it, rolled a ball against the edge and caught it on the rebound. "You really did quite a good job. Well done. I couldn't do it. Did your grandfather help you?"

Da Lin trembled. At first it was only his lips that shook, then his whole body. He turned away abruptly, ran into one of the wooden sheds, and slammed the door shut.

"His father made it for him. It was a surprise present for his birthday."

Startled, Paul turned round. He hadn't noticed Luo joining them.

"My son worked on it every evening for almost six months while Da Lin slept. Da Lin wept with joy when he received it. I think it was the first time I saw the boy cry. Both of them played together every day."

Paul nodded.

"You can carry on talking to him. He won't reply. And he won't play with you either. He doesn't even do it with me."

"Why not?"

"Because he only plays with his father."

"Where is he?"

"He's dead."

Paul swallowed. "I'm ... I'm ... I'm ... sorry," he said quietly.

"It's OK. You couldn't have known."

"How long has it been?"

"Two years."

"An accident?"

"No. He was murdered."

"By whom?"

The old man shrugged.

"Is that why the police visit?"

"Hmm . . . In a way, yes."

"Why is his mother in Beijing and not here with him?"

"Why indeed?"

Paul felt annoyed with himself for asking stupid questions. He walked straight over to the shed without thinking about it, opened the door carefully, and stepped in.

VIII

It was warm in the wooden shed, and smelled of dried grass.

Dust motes danced in the beams of sunlight that streamed in through the gaps between the planks. Da Lin was crouched in a corner with his arms around his knees.

Paul made his way past baskets, rakes, and spades and sat down next to him on the floor.

"I'm sorry."

Tears streamed down Da Lin's cheeks. Paul could see how quickly his chest was rising and falling under his T-shirt and how fast his heart was beating.

"I didn't know any of that. Otherwise I wouldn't have asked you if you would play with me." He wished he could take the boy into his arms and just hold him.

"Can I help in any way?" Paul thought he detected a slight shake of the head, but perhaps he was just imagining it.

"Of course I don't know how you feel, but I'd like to tell you a story about me." Paul spoke calmly and slowly, pronouncing every word carefully. "I had a son who was your age. He was called Justin." He paused, not sure if Da Lin was listening to him. "One day, he fell sick."

Pause.

"Soon after that, he died."

Pause.

Da Lin cast a sad glance at Paul. He seemed to be about to say something but then changed his mind and stared out of the shed through a gap in the planks. Luo was still standing in the same spot leaning on his stick, his face etched with pain. A gust of wind raised a brown dust cloud that surrounded him for moment before it continued across the courtyard and past the well.

"After that," Paul continued, "I didn't speak to anyone for a long time. Just like you. It was so painful that I thought I would not survive the loss. My wife could not stand my silence so we separated. I moved to an island where not many people lived because I wanted to be on my own. I could not stand having anyone around. A day on which I did not exchange a word with anyone at all was a good day. I wanted to have nothing more to do with the world. You must know that feeling. All that was left of my son was memories, just like you have of your father, and I had the feeling that if I spoke, my memories would fade until nothing was left of them. Do you understand what I mean?"

Paul repeated his question. "Do you understand what I mean?"

The reply was a slow, but decided nod.

"I think I spoke to almost no one for two years, apart from my friend Zhang, of course. Everyone must have *one* friend, mustn't they? I was silent until I realized that life went on whether I spoke or not ..."

Paul saw that the boy's attention was elsewhere once more, that the tentative interest had turned to indifference. What had he done wrong? Da Lin sat up, as if nothing that had been said mattered to him. He pushed his thin legs downward and his body up against the wall of planks, stood up, and took a step forward.

"But of course that doesn't mean that my memories of Justin, of my son –"

The boy stepped over Paul's outstretched legs without taking any further notice of him. Paul reached out for his arm and stopped him.

"Don't run way," he said calmly. "Stay here."

Da Lin stared at him, surprised and shocked. He tried to free himself from Paul's grip but Paul did not let go.

"Please. I'd like to talk to you. I haven't finished my story."

Nothing happened for a few seconds, then Paul gently pulled the boy towards him.

"Let me go!" An angry hiss. A movement as though Da Lin wanted to hit him.

Paul let go.

IX

"Mama, are we here on holiday?"

"No."

"Why are we here, then?"

"We're visiting."

"Are the man and the boy our friends?"

"No."

"But Papa said they were."

"What?"

"That they were our friends."

"Then that's right."

"But if they're our friends, why doesn't the boy speak to us?"

"I'm sure he will soon. You can ask him questions. Maybe he'll reply to you."

"I did. But he doesn't."

"What did you ask him?"

"Where his papa and his mama are."

X

"Eeeight . . . niiine . . . teeen . . . Right, I don't want to see anyone now. I'm coming." Christine took her hands from her eyes, dropped her arms by her side and turned around slowly and deliberately. She mustn't be too quick or David would object. She glanced around the courtyard in search of them. The two sheds, the wheelbarrow, the baskets, and the open door to the house. The place looked much more abandoned than a few seconds before when Paul and David had been there.

Da Lin sat on the well and watched her.

The lonely scene in the courtyard made her feel frightened.

"Paul!" she called. "David! Where are you?"

Silence.

"Darling boy, give me a little clue."

Silence.

She grew warm and began to feel that she could hardly breathe. She did not want to look for her son. Not to know where he was seemed suddenly unbearable, even if he was only crouching behind a pile of wood and feeling glad that she could not see him. She wanted to have him by her side and hold him tight.

"Where are you?"

Christine tried not to show how she was feeling. Hide-and-seek was David's favorite game; it was a ritual. They played it almost every evening in the garden in Lamma when she came home from work. She had to seek first, then Paul, then David. And she was never supposed to find him. Until he crept out of his hiding place of his own accord, she always had to pretend that she was completely at a loss and despairing over his sudden disappearance.

She walked across the courtyard and looked on the other side of the well. And behind the bench. Into the wheelbarrow. And between the stacks of wood.

"Where are you?" Her voice ought to have sounded playful; she had tried her best, but she didn't sound in the least light-hearted. She did not want to search any longer. She did not want to be alone.

"Paul, where are you? Come out."

Nothing moved.

Why were they doing this to her?

"Paaaul . . . ?" Why didn't he hear the fear in her voice? "I can't find you. Please come out."

Da Lin had been watching her the entire time. Their eyes met and he seemed to feel that she was becoming more and more frightened, for he inclined his head toward the second shed. She took a few steps in that direction and he nodded in confirmation. She stood in front of the door and listened. All was quiet. Da Lin gestured to her impatiently to open the door.

Christine pulled the door open. The two of them were crouching inside.

"That's very mean!" David complained. "You weren't supposed to find us."

Paul gave an uneasy laugh.

XI

Christine stretched out both arms. No matter which direction she turned in, her fingers could feel nothing but cold, damp stone. She was standing at the bottom of a dried-up well and faint light was streaming down the shaft. Far above her, she could see a round patch of blue sky. There was no ladder and there were no steps built into the walls. She knew neither how she had got into the well nor how she was going to get out of it again.

Suddenly, earth and water rained down on her.

She screamed for help but no one answered. The shower of earth and water increased in intensity. Her dress was soaked and her hair was filthy. Soon she was up to her ankles in mud. Before long she was up to her knees in it. She took as deep a breath as she could and held it in. Her inflated lungs gave her buoyancy. She began to float like a balloon, but after a few seconds up in the air she had to exhale, and fell back into the swamp. She tried again, but in vain. The mud was now up to her hips.

Then up to her chest.

She pushed her arms to the sides, trying to cling to the walls, but the stones were too smooth to climb up them. When her head was the only part of her body left above the mud and she was on the verge of sinking, she woke.

Christine touched stone with her fingers. She was lying next to a cold, damp wall. She heard David and Paul breathing next to her.

She reached out for her son under the blanket, stroked his tummy and chest and pulled him closer to her. The smell and the warmth of his small body calmed her a little.

"Christine," Paul whispered suddenly. "Are you awake?"

"Yes, I thought you were asleep," she replied.

"I can't sleep."

They lay next to each other in silence for a few moments.

"You were whimpering in your sleep. Did you have a nightmare?"

"Yes."

"I'm sorry."

He was sorry. How easy it was to say the words. He should have taken better care of David then. How could he have taken his eyes off him for even a few seconds in a strange place? In a hotel foyer. Irresponsible. Her accusations might be unjustified, but she was unable to quell the rage she felt towards him. It was his fault.

Christine felt old fears, ones that she had thought long dead, rising from their graves. Once more she saw the five-year-old cowering under the kitchen table while the Red Guards stormed up the stairs. Her father crouching on the windowsill. Like a fat black crow about to stretch its wings. He leapt before they could grab him.

She saw herself swimming in the sea by her mother's side, escaping to Hong Kong. Six adults and four children. The youngest of them disappeared first. The child simply went under without making a sound. And the parents kept on swimming. Then the second youngest went. She would have been the next in line. Her strength was ebbing. Some of them were praying out loud as they swam. She wasn't.

A fishing boat rescued them.

Over the years the memories had faded, but what remained was the feeling of boundless fear and loneliness.

And now it had returned: the totality of fear. There was no other feeling that consumed a person so completely, she thought. Nothing that makes slaves of us like fear does. Not grief. Not joy. Not even love.

Christine wanted to get out of this room, to get out of this village. She should never have come to this farmhouse. This was a trap. How long would it take before the police found them?

One more day? Two more? Then what? What would happen to David? Would they be able to defend themselves? Her mind circled round and round these questions. She grew dizzy, and felt like throwing up.

"Where are you going?" Paul asked, concerned.

"I can't stand the darkness any longer," Christine said. "I'll sit in the living room for a while."

"Shall I come with you?"

"No," she said curtly. "Stay with David instead, in case he wakes."

XII

Da Lin was woken by the sound of his grandfather's snoring. He turned him onto his side; that normally helped, but it made no difference tonight.

He heard the woman crying in the next room. He waited to see if his grandfather would stop snoring. After a while, he picked up his blanket and slipped into the living room to lie down on one of the sofas.

The woman was huddled on one of them.

"I'm sorry. Did I wake you?" she asked in a worried voice.

He shook his head. "My grandpa snores so loudly."

She answered with an exhausted smile.

Da Lin was amazed at how easily the sentence had come to him.

My grandpa snores so loudly. Five words that had slipped out of him. Just like that. He wondered if he should regret it, but strangely he didn't. Maybe he even felt quite the opposite.

He still had no idea who these strangers were, what they wanted or how long they were staying. Grandpa had said they came from Hong Kong and needed help urgently. The rest didn't concern him.

He had been asking himself why they had to come into hiding here. They must not have many friends, since they needed help from Grandpa and him.

The woman was constantly worried about her child. Even while playing hide-and-seek! She had grown almost hysterical because her son had disappeared. That was the point of the game. She had really thought she wouldn't see him again. He had no idea why she burst into tears when she found her son. He didn't care anyway, but he had felt sorry for her. He didn't know why, but from that moment on, he had begun to like her. He was still not sure about the man.

He sat down on the other sofa and noticed that the woman was shivering.

"Are you cold?"

"No."

Da Lin could see that was not true. He got up and fetched a blanket from the closet in the hall. It was so dirty that he put it back and offered her his blanket instead.

"No, thank you. I'm not cold."

He continued holding the blanket out to her.

"Don't you need it?"

"No," he said, gesturing at the long trousers and long-sleeved jersey that he wore to sleep.

"Thank you," she said. "You're very kind."

Da Lin could not remember who had last called him "kind". Probably not his mother; she seldom used the word. Certainly not Grandpa; he never said it. Maybe Grandma or his father. He was not sure.

"Don't you go to school ever?"

He shook his head.

"Why not?"

He could tell her about Mr. Wang, Da Lin thought, the teacher who hit his hands with a ruler until they bled whenever he wrote a Chinese character incorrectly. That happened often. Or he could tell her about the forty other children in the cramped classroom, who made fun of him at break time because of that, and boasted about their fathers beating his father to death.

He could not stand being near them. He found them all horrible, without exception. He had thrown up every day in school. One day he simply stopped going, and no one had asked after him. They were probably as happy not to see him as he was not to see them.

Instead of replying, he shrugged and hoped she would stop asking questions.

"I didn't like going to school either." It was cold, so she pulled the blanket up to her chin.

"Why not?"

"Probably for the same reasons as you. I didn't like the teachers and they didn't like me. Also, I had no friends."

"None at all?"

"No."

"Why not?"

She gave him a pensive look and repeated his question. "Why didn't I have any friends? I've often thought about that. I always had the feeling that there was an invisible wall between me and the others, separating us. We saw each other but we never touched each other. We heard what each other said, but we didn't understand each other. People were around me but were not close to me. Do you understand what I mean?"

Da Lin nodded. If only she knew how well he understood what she meant. He had just not been able to put it into words.

"Is it still like that?"

"What?"

"The wall."

She hesitated before replying, looking at him closely. "No, it's not like that any more. The feeling passes."

"By itself?"

"You're a clever boy," she replied.

Da Lin laughed shyly. No one had ever said that to him, and he did not know what she meant exactly by it, nor if that was the answer to his question.

"By itself? I'm not sure," she said. "I haven't thought about it before. I think with some people, yes. But not with others."

He would have liked to ask if her wall had disappeared by itself or if she had done something to make it go away, and if so, what that was, but he didn't dare to. He was gradually feeling the cold too, and feeling tiredness seep back into his body. But he didn't feel like sleeping.

"You're feeling cold," she said. "You'll get a cold. We'd better go back to bed."

"No," he said.

"Then come here and have a bit of blanket."

Da Lin hesitated for only a moment. He got up and sat at the other end of the sofa.

"Come closer. The blanket isn't that big," Christine said, laughing.

Da Lin had forgotten that even a smile could be warming. He slid closer, and she covered his legs and feet with the blanket. It was cozy and warm beneath it. And it smelled good. His foot touched her leg and he drew it back, startled.

"I didn't eat much when I was a child either," she suddenly said, without looking at him.

"Why didn't you want to eat?"

She thought for a moment. "I felt queasy all the time. I threw up often. Eating felt disgusting. Maybe for the same reasons as for you?"

"Didn't your parents scold you?"

"My father died when I was little."

Da Lin shuddered. He grew hot and then very cold. He was afraid that she was about to tell him a story about how she had stopped speaking when she was a little girl, and how sad she was, and that she knew exactly what he was feeling. No one knew how he was feeling. But Christine merely tucked the blanket under his legs and said nothing more.

"Was he sick?"

"No. He wasn't the one that was sick."

Da Lin didn't understand her reply. "If someone else was sick, why was he the one who died?"

"The country was sick."

He understood less and less of what she was saying. "A country can't be sick. Only people can be sick. And animals."

She inclined her head from side to side, as if she had to thoroughly weigh up what he was saying. "You're right. I used the wrong words."

He waited patiently for her to use the right words, but she remained silent. He heard mice or rats rustling in the kitchen. She yawned and he grew afraid that she would fall asleep without going back to bed.

"Did you know Grandpa before?" he asked, just to say something.

"No."

"What do you do in Hong Kong? Are you a teacher?" He simply wanted to hear her voice; the more he listened to it, the more it sounded like a long melodious song, like one of those Grandma had sung him to sleep with. He hoped that this stranger would simply keep talking and never stop. When she replied, his eyelids drooped; he opened them again, but they grew heavier and her voice seemed very far away, looping back round again. He drifted back and forth between the world of the sleeping and the waking and could not decide which he wanted to belong to.

XIII

It was his fault. Of course it was his fault. He knew it and he would never deny it.

He had been careless.

He had neglected his first and foremost responsibility as a father: to protect his child from harm. And Christine was telling him that. With every gesture. With every look. With every word.

He had already lived through all that once with Meredith, his first wife.

The fear. The despair. The guilt. The inability to share these feelings with each other.

Paul had observed two kinds of couples at the children's cancer ward. The first kind still looked each other in the eye. Their child's illness had welded them together. They supported each other, gave each other strength, or clung to each other. The other kind crept down the hospital corridors with their heads lowered, staring at the floor. They were afraid to look into their husband's or wife's eyes because they would find there reflections of what they did not want to see: their own fear, their anger, and their boundless grief. They grew mute and turned away from each other, retreated back to a place where pain would no longer find them. The illness pushed them apart. Paul and his wife had been one of those couples.

He was terribly afraid that history was repeating itself and that the same thing was now happening with Christine. He had thought that with her and her help, he had come a long way away from all that.

But maybe we don't really change at all, he thought. Regardless of what efforts we make. Maybe we are cursed to remain who we are. A lifelong sentence, condemned to live within our narrow boundaries, to repeat our mistakes, to keep making the same errors over and over again.

In times of crisis we are thrown back on our true selves and cannot escape our skins. Everything else is an illusion.

Why else were they not able to draw strength from each other? Was it his fault? If so, it had been his fault before as well, not Meredith's. But he didn't want to retreat into himself now. He wanted to share the fear and the guilt with Christine. Why couldn't he do it? Why was she turning away from him?

Paul could see how unwell she was. How tense she was, how she was getting headaches.

He was sorry.

He saw how angry these words made her, every time. What else was he to say? He couldn't make anything that had happened not happen. He could only plead for her forgiveness. It was up to her to forgive him.

They had to hold fast together. If they were to make it to the embassy in Beijing it would only be together.

Last night he would have liked to follow her into the living room. Maybe they would have had a chance to talk there. Or they could at least have hugged each other.

Why could she no longer stand being close to him?

Where was the Christine who had drawn him out of his hermit existence?

Who had showed him, with her patience, her understanding, and her love, that there was a way back to life after Justin's death. Without her he would still be living alone on Lamma. Without friends, without any interaction with his neighbors. He had felt free but had been a prisoner.

He did not want a life like that any more. But he had the feeling that it was exactly that loneliness that was returning to him now.

Paul heard his son crying in the courtyard. He had fallen, and scraped both knees. Christine tried to comfort him, and wanted to clean the cuts, but David insisted on Papa doing it. Paul cuddled him and looked at his knees. The grazes were not deep, but full of sand and dirt.

"Does it hurt there too?" Paul asked, stroking David's forehead.

"No, Papa. My knees do."

"And there?" he pointed at his son's hands.

"No."

"There?" he stroked his tummy.

"No."

"On your back?"

"No." David laughed.

"Then we've been lucky. Now let's clean your knees up and put plasters on them."

Paul fetched a bucket of cold water from the kitchen – only a drop or two had come out of the hot water tap – and a small plastic bowl. David dipped a hand into the pail. "That's much too cold."

Paul felt the temperature of the water. It really was quite cold. "It's not thaaat cold."

"Yes it is, " his son said, holding his hands protectively in front of his knees.

"No. I'll show you. You give me a wash first. After that I'll clean your knee. OK?"

David nodded. Paul stripped to the waist and kneeled in front of him. "Face and hair first."

His son scooped a bowl of water and poured it over his head. It was colder than he had feared.

"Again."

It did not get any more pleasant the second time.

"Now it's my turn." Paul picked up his vest, wet it and carefully wiped the scraped knee clean.

"That hurts," David whined, pulling his leg away.

"I'm being very careful."

"But it still hurts."

"When I'm done you can make a wish."

"I want to dance with you."

"Where?"

"Here in the yard."

"But we don't have any music."

"That doesn't matter. We can sing something."

After Paul had washed the dirt out of the cuts, he stuck two plasters over them, lifted his son onto his shoulders and started dancing. He took one step forward, one to the side, and one backward. He rocked back and forth on his knees and turned with a flourish. David sang a hiking song.

He held onto his child's legs tight with both hands. No, Paul thought. He was wrong. He would never again feel as lonely as before.

XIV

They did not speak while eating. The only sounds were of lips smacking and of slurping, along with the occasional fart by Luo.

Christine was used to silence at the table. As a child and then as a young person, she had sat together with her mother at meals for years, only rarely speaking. Later, the television had taken the talking away from them. She had not found it depressing then; she knew nothing else.

The silence in this house was different. Sadder and lonelier. But maybe she was mistaken. Maybe the wordlessness between her and her mother had been just as bleak, and she either did not want to acknowledge it or was repressing the knowledge of how oppressive it had been.

David tore her away from her thoughts. He sat on her lap and wanted more noodles. Now. Right now. Feeling relieved, Christine put some noodles in his bowl. His fever had gone, just like Luo had said it would.

Da Lin got up from the table first. He picked up his own and his grandfather's chopsticks and empty bowl and brought them into the kitchen.

He had not responded to her friendly "Good morning," and was silent, just like he had been on the first two days. She feared that it was only the unusual situation they had been in and the feeling of protection given by the night that had made him start talking. Or perhaps he didn't dare to speak in front of the others.

"Do you have a large basin? I'd like to do some laundry."

Luo cleaned his teeth with a toothpick. "In the kitchen."

Christine took David with her to the kitchen and looked around the room. It was the dirt that was hard to put up with, she thought, not the poverty. The floor had rubbish and food remains stuck on it, with dozens of flies hovering above. The plates, bowls, and cups were covered in a layer of grease and dirty dishes were piled high in the sink and on the shelves. The pots and pans were blackened and had a thick coat of rust.

She found a plastic basin under the sink, filled it with water, and carried it into the courtyard.

Da Lin followed her, curious. She was touched by the way he looked at her. Since she had arrived he had hung around her, wanting to be close, but had been too shy, too frightened, to really be near her.

"Might you have any soap?" she asked him.

He hesitated, then ran into the house and returned with an old cardboard box. The cardboard must have got wet before; it was stiff and crumbled easily. The soap powder inside was a solid mass. Despite every effort, she could not manage to break any of it off. Da Lin fetched a stone and pounded the package with it until the powder disintegrated into smaller lumps.

"Thank you. Do you have any dirty laundry?" What a stupid question, she thought. Everything he was wearing was dirty, covered in stains, and full of holes.

He shook his head.

She went to her room and picked up two of David's sweatshirts and vests.

"Come, give me your T-shirt," she said to Da Lin. He hesitated for only a moment, then pulled his T-shirt over his head and gave it to her. The sight of his bare torso shocked her. Every single rib was visible; the skin stretched over his collar bones and his shoulders.

Christine put his T-shirt in the basin. The water turned black in a matter of seconds. David laughed. Da Lin looked uncomfortable, so she quickly added her son's clothes to the basin.

"You can help me," she said to the boys. "I'll wash the clothes. Da Lin can wring them out, and David can drape them over the bench. OK?"

Both of them nodded.

They started washing together, and because they were having fun, David fetched more of his clothes. When everything had been washed, Da Lin brought one T-shirt after another and one pair of trousers after another. Christine had to change the water twice. By the end, the bench, the fountain, and the drying rack they had cobbled together were all draped full with laundry.

———

Christine and David were sitting on the step in front of the house. Paul joined them. Da Lin disappeared into the shed and returned with two bricks and a plank. He made a little seesaw and gestured to David to play with him. But their weights were too unequal and the plank did not move. Da Lin moved towards the center a little, then a little more, and the plank finally sank on one side. The sudden movement startled David. He got off the seesaw and ran back to his parents.

Da Lin took the bricks and the plank back to the shed and walked out of the courtyard without waving goodbye.

"Where's he going?" David wanted to know.

"I don't know," Christine said.

"I want to go out too."

"That's not possible."

"Why not?"

"Because it's not possible."

"Why not?" David repeated his question.

"I said so already. Because it's not possible."

"But why not?" David insisted.

"Didn't you hear what I said?" Unlike Paul, Christine found these constant confrontations with her son difficult. Paul liked these conversations. He was convinced that it was never too early to teach a child how to have a discussion. She thought that a four-year-old didn't need to have everything explained to him.

He should obey without talking back constantly. And that was that.

"Wh –"

"Because I say so," she interrupted him. "And that's enough."

David climbed off her lap in a rage, sat down on the step and crossed his arms over his chest. "That's not enough at all."

Paul was about to join in when Da Lin walked through the gate. He was pushing a small bicycle. It was a narrow bicycle frame made out of old pipes, with a saddle and wooden wheels, and a rusty chain, all held together with wires.

David looked at it with intense curiosity.

"Thank you very much," Christine said. "That's very kind of you, but David can't ride a bicycle."

Da Lin nodded encouragingly anyway.

"David doesn't know how to ride a bike," she repeated. "He has to learn first."

"I can teach him," Da Lin said.

Christine was happy to hear his voice. "That's really kind of you, but –"

"Yes, please," David said. "Please, please, please."

She thought for a moment and finally nodded. "Try it, but be careful."

Da Lin held the bicycle firmly with one hand and helped David onto the saddle with the other. He told him how to steer, how to push the pedals, and how to brake. Then he stood behind the bicycle, gripped the luggage rack, and pushed.

The bicycle was very wobbly. David cycled in a crazy zigzag across the courtyard, but after a few meters the look of fear in his face gave way to one of pride. They cycled round and round the fountain. David grew more and more confident with each round and he was laughing as she had not heard him laugh for a long time.

XV

Luo crouched next to the laundry drying on the bench and sharpened a saw. It was tedious work. The whetstone was worn out and the saw-blade was old and rusty. He slid the metal over the whetstone several times and tested the sharpness of the edge. It remained as blunt as before. Perhaps it was because his heart wasn't in it. Instead of concentrating on his task, Luo was watching his grandson. Da Lin was talking to strangers. He had had a second helping at lunch! He was playing with a child. Like a child. Luo wondered how the woman had managed to get through the wall. Was the presence of a woman enough? Maybe he underestimated how much Da Lin missed his mother. But what was he to do? He could not force Yin Yin to visit them at least once a year. He could only try to lessen the pain that life had doled out to his grandchild. Their guests had no idea what a miracle they were working. He hoped they would stay a little longer.

———

"You dirty little scumbag."

Deng, the neighbor, was standing at the gate with his fists on his hips. Deng of all people, Luo thought. They had never been able to stand each other. Deng had been the Party Secretary of the village until a few months previously, and had often harassed him. Luo had often had to practice self-criticism because of him.

He was a tall man with thick white hair and a deep, impressive voice. Since Zhong Hua's death, neither he nor any of their other neighbors had entered their courtyard. The neighbors also avoided Luo and Da Lin in the village, as though the old man and his grandson had an infectious disease.

What did he want from them now?

Da Lin stopped immediately and let go of the bicycle, frozen in shock. David continued cycling for a little bit, lost his balance, fell over, and started crying. Paul jumped up, gathered his son in his arms and comforted him.

"This filthy rat stole our bike," Deng shouted, pointing at Da Lin.

Da Lin lowered his head in acknowledgment of his guilt and stared at the ground.

"Is that true?" Luo said in a stern voice.

A tentative shake of the head in reply.

"And now the brat is lying as well!" Deng took a couple of steps towards Da Lin and lifted his arm as though he was about to hit him, but changed his mind and looked suspiciously around the courtyard instead.

"You have guests," he said, surprised.

"My wife's relations," Luo said.

"A foreigner?" the neighbor asked in a mocking tone. He might as well have said: you don't even believe what you're saying yourself.

"One of my wife's sisters lives in Hong Kong. This is her daughter."

Christine nodded shyly.

"That's her son," Luo said, pointing at David. "And this is her husband."

Paul also nodded in greeting.

"I never knew that your wife had family in Hong Kong," Deng said, smirking.

Luo couldn't think of anything to say in reply.

"She never spoke about them."

Luo was still lost for words. The situation was growing more and more uncomfortable with each passing second.

"Do you like it here in our nice village?" Deng asked, staring boldly at Christine.

She looked over to Paul for help.

"My wife doesn't speak Mandarin very well," he said.

"But you certainly do," Deng said, growing more suspicious. "Where are you from?"

"Hong Kong."

Luo fidgeted. Why did Paul have to provoke the uninvited visitor? The quicker he left the better it would be for everyone.

"I've just heard that," Deng replied, his voice growing sharper. "I wanted to know which country you're from."

"Does that matter?"

This argument must not escalate. Luo intervened. "They're not staying long," he said.

"How long?" Deng wanted to know.

"Just a few days. They'll be leaving tomorrow."

"Foreigners don't often make their way to these parts," Deng said pointedly, looking at Paul.

"That's a shame," Paul said calmly. "It's very nice here and the neighbors are so friendly."

That was the wrong tone to take. Irony did not go down well with Deng. Luo had often seen how, as Party Secretary, he had put down and humiliated supposed enemies of the Party in the most abhorrent way at public tribunals. Nearly every one of his victims had broken down in tears; one young woman had even killed herself by swallowing weed killer one night two years ago.

"Da Lin, apologize and give him the bicycle back."

The boy stood in the middle of the courtyard as if paralyzed.

"Da Lin!" Luo shouted. "Didn't you hear what I just said?"

He still did not move.

To appease Deng, Luo had to punish his grandson for his misdeed, preferably in front of the neighbor. He walked over to Da Lin, raised his arm and struck him soundly on the cheek. "Apologize! Now." He slapped him again. Blood trickled from Da Lin's nose. But he remained completely silent.

Paul lifted the bicycle and held it out to Deng. "Thank you for letting my son use it. It was really very generous of you."

Deng's lower lip trembled with rage; he was on the verge of losing control of himself. He tore the bicycle from Paul's hands and left the courtyard without another word.

Luo turned on Paul. "What kind of fool are you? Provoking my neighbor like that. Do you want to get us all into prison?"

Paul was too startled to reply.

"You idiot," Luo hissed at his grandson. "Why did you steal Deng's bicycle?"

Da Lin lifted his head. Blood was still dripping from his nose. "I didn't steal it. I just wanted to borrow it," he whispered. "I would have taken it back later."

"Borrow it?" Luo exclaimed. "Then you ought to have asked first and not simply taken it."

Da Lin wanted to say something, but kept silent instead.

Luo was beside himself with anger.

"He was only trying to do something nice for us," Christine said in a conciliatory tone.

The woman had clearly understood nothing. "Then the idiot should have thought about it first. How long do you think it will take Deng to tell the police about what he's found here? Will he do it today or only tomorrow morning? And how long after that until the police are standing here in this courtyard? What do you think? An hour? Two? How much longer are you safe here?"

The woman said nothing so Luo answered his own question. "Not at all. You are no longer safe here. You must leave. Where are you meant to go next?"

The woman and her husband looked at him helplessly as though he ought to know where they should go to next.

"We don't know," Paul said in a low voice.

"What do you mean? How long did you think you could stay with us? For weeks? Months? The letter said a few days."

"We're … we're … we're waiting for a message to arrive any day."

"What kind of message?"

"Telling us where to go to next. Who the next person to help us will be."

Luo turned away, hobbled a few steps across the courtyard and out of the gate. He needed a few minutes alone to calm himself down. His foot had grown more painful than in previous days; it was more swollen and was hot to the touch. He sat down on a sawn-off tree stump, lit a cigarette, looked at the dusty fields – much too dry for this time of year – before him and composed his thoughts.

This family was in a more desperate situation than he had previously thought. He was no longer in a position to offer them security but he had no idea who else could help them. No one in the village. The police would be turning up here in the next few hours; of that he had no doubt. He could only hope that they would believe his story about relatives visiting from Hong Kong long enough until the next refuge was found.

He felt sorry for the family. He had started to like the three of them, especially the man. He did not talk much and, when he asked questions, he did not expect a long reply. Luo heard someone coming, and turned around. Paul was standing in front of him.

"I don't want to disturb you," Paul said awkwardly. "May I sit with you for a moment?"

The tree stump was big enough for two.

"I behaved very stupidly earlier. I'm sorry about that."

Luo did not like apologies. They made him feel uncomfortable. Apologies did not diminish his anger in any way. But he had calmed down now, and all that was on his mind was how to bring these strangers to safety. But he could not think of anything.

"You really have no idea where to go from here?"

"No. I can try to ask my friend. He told me only to contact him in the most dire emergency."

"This is an emergency."

Paul got every second letter of his text message wrong. When he had finished, he showed the short message to Luo:

we have to leave. where to? urgent!

He pressed 'send' and put the phone back in his pocket.

"I'd like to ask you something."

Luo could tell from his voice that he felt uncomfortable about the question.

"You know who murdered your son, don't you?"

The right question. The wrong time.

Everyone knew who had murdered Zhong Hua. Beaten him to death with wooden clubs and iron bars. Like a dog. Ten against one.

And the whole village had watched.

Like before.

The soul of a people did not change so quickly.

If it did at all.

Beaten to death for a few square meters of land. As though there was not enough of it. But there was nothing more precious than a human life. Why was this most irreplaceable of all gifts worth so little? Why was it given no respect, trampled on and thrown away?

Because we have enough of them, a cynical policeman had told him in reply to this question.

But I only had one Zhong Hua, he had retorted.

His son had not believed that they would go so far. That had been his mistake, and Luo himself had strengthened his son's mistaken conviction.

They had acquired the land and the small building on it legally.

Zhong Hua, who had liked helping in the kitchen even as a child, wanted to open a noodle restaurant. He set to it with a single-minded passion, getting up before dawn and working into the night. Preparing hand-made noodles that attracted queues after a few weeks. Soon people were coming from the entire district for his soup and his dumplings.

Zhong Hua, a shy man of few words, flourished among his woks, pots, and pans in a way his father would never have thought possible.

He had brushed aside the first announcement that all the buildings in the street would have to make way for a new settlement. The amount offered by Golden Real Estate sounded more like a charity handout than serious compensation. Zhong Hua did not budge even when the first of his neighbors had sold their properties for a slightly improved offer.

His restaurant was worth a great deal, and he had all the papers and stamps, all the documents and certifications. He was convinced the law was on his side.

How foolish. How simple-minded.

As though the law had ever been on any side other than that of those in power. As though that would ever change.

Why did Zhong Hua have to die?

Why does a person kill another?

His visitor was waiting patiently for an answer. He would wait in vain.

Just like me, Luo thought.

Just like us all.

XVI

Christine crawled carefully out of the bed. On no account must she wake Paul or David. She opened the door carefully. Da Lin and his grandfather were also sound asleep. Only the dog lying in front of their bed lifted its head once. She crept past them into the living room and into the kitchen. The stillness of the house at night made her nervous. But she had had an idea, and she had to know if it was possible to make it happen. It would reassure her.

It did not take her long to find what she was looking for. Christine laid out half a dozen knives on the table before her. The handles were worn and most of the blades were blunt and rusty. But two of them were long and sharp. That was important.

Did she have the courage? To end three lives? To stab into the darkness. Once. Twice. And many times more, if necessary.

First the large and heavy body.

Then the small, light one.

Then her own.

It would have to be quick. She must not think while doing it. She would have to be out of her mind. In a frenzy.

Or cold as death. Not feel anything. Make the movements mechanically, as if she were a machine. She could not think of a better way to kill herself, her husband, and her son.

She had immediately discarded the idea of using a pillow. Paul would wake up and defend himself. And even if she secretly slipped one of the sleeping pills that Zhang had given her in Shi into his tea, it would take too long. She did not have the strength to hold a pillow down on a face for several minutes. She imagined how David's body would writhe beneath her as he was suffocating, and knew that it was impossible.

Yesterday she had found a packet of weed killer in the shed. In Hong Kong she had read a newspaper article about the increasing number of farmers who were taking their own lives this way.

It was meant to be highly effective, but a miserably painful death. Some of those who killed themselves this way suffered for hours before they finally died.

Christine ran her fingertips over the tip of the knife. All it would take would be a little pressure and the metal would pierce the skin and bury itself deep in the body. If she got it right, once would be enough.

She would not allow anyone to take their child away from them.

XVII

They were in luck. Even though Zhang did not reply to the text message and Luo could not think of anywhere safer for them to go, two days after the neighbor had come, the police had still not appeared. Luo now believed that Deng had not reported his meeting with them to the police at all.

It was a mild evening. Christine and Da Lin put David to bed and Luo was sitting in front of the house smoking, with the dog at his feet. Paul walked over to the well, leaned his head back and looked up at the cloudless and moonless night sky. Apart from the small strip of light that the dim light bulb above the dining table cast into the courtyard, it was pitch black. It had been a long time since he had seen so many stars. He remembered his voyage from Hamburg to New York. He must have been about Da Lin's age. His parents had been fighting in the cabin again, and he had escaped to the deck to get away from the endless stream of accusations and counter-accusations.

He had been alone there. The wind, the waves, and the silence as the ship made its way through the darkness had cleared his head. Stars twinkled above him: the Milky Way, the Plough, and the Little Bear, the Pole Star, which shone brighter than everything else.

But the longer he had stared into the night sky and at the sea, the stranger he began to feel about the vastness that surrounded him on all sides, about the idea that thousands and thousands of meters below him was nothing but cold deep black water. Instead of going below deck once more, he stayed by the railing and felt an impulse to jump into the water. No one would ever find him. It would be as though he, Paul Leibovitz, had never existed. He put a foot on the lowest iron bar. Then the other foot on the next one. It was like a pull that increased with every minute. Two or three rungs more. No higher than a garden fence.

Even though the wind was mild, he stood freezing on the deck, paralyzed with horror at his own thoughts. Both hands gripped the rusty railing.

Then his father came looking for him and took him into his arms. The smell of him and the warmth of his body, the touch of his hands and, above all, the familiar sound of his voice, released him from his trance.

That night he realized for the first time that you can feel fear not only because of other people.

———

"Sit down." Luo's deep voice brought Paul back.

The old man looked more exhausted than he had done in the last few days.

"Are you unwell?" Paul asked, concerned.

"No worse than usual," Luo said, pulling at his cigarette.

"Your foot?"

"Yes."

Paul sat down next to him on the bench.

After a pause, Luo said, "You must take him with you."

"Who?"

"Da Lin."

"Where to?"

"To Beijing. To his mother."

Paul buried his face in his hands. Why was Luo asking him for a favor that he knew was impossible for Paul to promise?

"I don't know if that's a good idea," he said evasively.

Luo interrupted him. "He has to get away from here. I'm a sick man. Who knows how much longer I have. Three months? Six? There's nobody in the village to look after him when I die."

"I'm sorry about that," Paul said quietly. "Wouldn't it be better if his mother came to get him?"

"Of course that would be better. But she didn't even visit at Chinese New Year."

Paul hesitated before he said what he was thinking. "Then ... then perhaps she doesn't want to have her son with her at all ..."

Luo gave him an angry look. "He's starving himself to death here. You can see that. As soon as you're gone, he'll stop eating again."

"Are there no other relations he could live with?"

"No."

"We could pay for his train ticket to Beijing."

"He's never left the village on his own before. He wouldn't be able to do that. Impossible."

"Then you can go with him. We'll give you the money for two tickets."

Luo was silent for a moment, thinking. "It's a three or four-day journey by train. And then back again. I can't manage that any more."

Paul was unable to stay sitting on the bench. He got up and walked around the courtyard. He wanted to help. Of course he did. He understood what Luo was asking; in his position he would probably do the same. But he had to think of Christine and David. Another person would make their already difficult escape more difficult and dangerous. He sat down next to Luo again.

"How do you think it would work? We are wanted by the police. We don't even know where we're going next, who is going to help us after this, or how we're going to get to Beijing. We are the worst travel companions that you could have chosen for your grandson."

"Yes. If I had a choice I wouldn't be asking you."

Paul shook his head. "I would love to help you. We're incredibly grateful to you and we owe you a lot."

"Da Lin trusts you."

"But—"

Luo did not let him continue. "He plays billiards with you. He talks to you. He talks to your wife. He plays with your son. You have no idea what that means for him."

"Yes," Paul said. "I do."

"Then take him with you. He will waste away here."

Paul said nothing.

"Please."

He could only guess how much strength it cost Luo to say this word. He hesitated before replying, but the longer he was silent, the more oppressive the silence grew.

"I wish I could help you."

"Please!"

The pleading in his voice. The desperation. Paul felt incredibly uncomfortable. He would like to have spared the old man this scene. And himself.

"No."

Luo threw his teacup across the courtyard and it shattered against the wall of the well. The dog jumped up, startled, and started barking.

Suddenly Christine was standing next to them. "Can I help?"

Luo got up from the bench with some effort and gave Paul a look of contempt.

"Coward." He limped to the gate, opened it, and disappeared into the darkness.

Paul looked helplessly after him. "Did you hear what he was asking us for?"

"Yes."

"And?"

Why wasn't she saying anything?

XVIII

"Paul?" She could tell from his breathing that he wasn't asleep.

"Paul?" she said again, a little more loudly and decidedly.

"Yes?"

"Are you asleep?"

"No."

"Could we–" She hesitated. She had carried the thoughts around with her the whole day, cast them aside, weighed them, and waited for the right moment to discuss her idea with him. They had not been on their own together for a second.

"Couldn't we take Da Lin with us?"

He waited before replying. "Do you really mean that?"

"Yes."

Instead of saying anything, Paul sighed.

"Why not?"

"How do you think it will work?"

"Do you think it really makes a big difference whether we travel on as a group of three or four?

Christine could feel him sitting up in bed. It had been a good idea to discuss this in darkness. She could not see his face or his gestures or the hidden meanings behind the words he spoke. With Paul especially, his eyes and the set of his mouth often told you more than what he said.

"Of course it does. It will put us in even more danger. And him too."

"It's not safe here either."

"Why not?"

"You can see how Luo is."

"Then his mother must come and get him."

"She hasn't been here for a year and a half. He needs us."

"We have to think about David."

To Christine, this was the one factor that weighed against

taking Da Lin with them. But after long consideration, she had come to the conclusion that he was not an additional risk to them.

"You don't have to tell me that," she said with an edge to her voice. "I just don't see how it would be more dangerous to travel on in a group of four. Tell me why. Please."

"Let's say you're right. Have you thought about what we would do if we don't find his mother in Beijing. Or, worse still, if we find her and she doesn't want to have her son with her at all. Are we to leave him on the street then?"

"No."

"Take him with us to Hong Kong?"

"No, of course not."

"What, then?"

She had no answer to that.

"Christine, I feel bad about it too. I'd like to help, but taking him with us is not a good idea. We can't." His tone of voice made it clear to her that he wanted to end the discussion there.

"Perhaps he could be of help to us."

"How could he be?"

"David gets on well with him. Maybe we'll be less conspicuous if there are four of us?" Christine herself felt that this sounded unconvincing. She had conducted this conversation with Paul in her head many times during the day and she knew that he was right about one thing: who would look after Da Lin if they didn't find his mother? But she still did not want to accept the logic of this argument. Why wouldn't they be able to find her? Luo had her address and they were in touch. If she had moved or was no longer in Beijing, she would have told him. And why wouldn't a mother want to have her child with her?

She was disappointed in Paul. Treating her as though she was being silly and was taking their safety less seriously than he was.

"We can't even take care of ourselves," she heard him say in the darkness. "We don't know where we're going next or who will help us. Or if Zhang will find anyone at all. We've been waiting two days for a reply from him."

Christine said nothing in reply. She would not be able to change his mind.

———

The text message came in the middle of the night. They were both woken by the buzzing of the phone.

on my way to you. next stop: hongyang new town, shanxi province. exact address to come.

At dawn they received a second text message.

if i'm not there by tomorrow morning, travel on without me. it's urgent. avoid cities. go to pastor lee on beijing lu in hongyang, block 4, building no. 3. do not stay overnight in monasteries.

XIX

Da Lin heard them first. A car drawing closer, braking and then coming to a stop. The stilling of the engine. Two car doors opening.

"The police."

They started, too shocked to say anything.

"The police," he said again. "You have to hide."

Paul leapt into action. He jumped up from the table and swept David into his arms. "Where?"

Now they could hear the voices of two men, coming closer.

Da Lin ran to one of the sheds, wrenched the door open and practically pushed them in. He had barely closed it when two policemen stepped through the gate.

"Where is your grandfather?"

Da Lin gestured with his head toward the house.

"Then tell him that we want to speak to him."

Da Lin trotted across the courtyard reluctantly.

Christine hardly dared to breathe. They were crouched right next to the door. If anyone were to look in the shed, they would be discovered immediately. Paul held David tightly and put a finger on his lips to show that he had to be quiet. Through the narrow slits between the planks of the shed they could see what was going on outside. The police were about ten or twelve meters away. They heard one of them snuffling. The tiniest noise would betray them. A cough would be enough. A sneeze. A word from David.

The policemen looked around the courtyard. One of them walked over to the billiard table right in front of the shed. He picked the cue up and put two balls in the middle of the table. Christine could see the dirt under his fingernails. David looked at his father in alarm. Paul tried to smile and look relaxed, and winked at him. He might be able to reassure his son that way but not Christine. She could see the fear in his eyes, and only hoped that it remained hidden to David. What would happen if the policemen found them? They absolutely could not follow them back to the police station. Once they were in the hands of the authorities they had no chance of keeping David. Zhang had impressed that on them.

They heard the clicking of the billiard balls and Luo's deep voice. "Put that cue down immediately. It belongs to my grandson." He stepped out of the house. Da Lin was nowhere to be seen.

The policeman continued playing as though he had not heard anything.

Enraged, Luo limped across the courtyard as quickly as he could. He drew himself up to his full height in front of the policeman, who was more than a head taller than him. "Did you not understand what I said?"

The impassive policeman took another shot, vigorously.

Luo wanted to rip the cue out of his hands, but he wasn't quick enough. He swung forward in a violent motion but snatched at thin air, lost his balance and fell. He landed in the dirt two meters in front of the shed. They saw his hands claw at the ground to begin with, and then close into fists. David opened his mouth to say something, but Paul held his hand over him just in time and shook his head forcefully.

"Get up, old man."

Luo did not move.

"Come on." The policeman hit Luo lightly on the back with the cue.

Luo got up with a great deal of effort.

Da Lin was coming out of the house. He stopped at the doorway, observing the scene in silence.

He had a catapult in his hands.

XX

Luo slapped his jacket a couple of times to get the dust off it. He had allowed himself to be provoked. That had been his mistake. He knew this policeman well. He had interrogated him many times at the police station, and had been a frequent visitor to the house. In the last two years, Luo had learned to put officials into different categories. There were the indifferent ones, the largest group, who just tried to do their job without any particular distinction. There were a few sympathetic ones, who had indicated to Luo that they condemned the murder of his son, but sadly could do nothing. There were the many eager ones who took their duties seriously, and held Luo and Da Lin to be threats to public order and security. Or at least they behaved that way.

And then there were the sadists, who clearly took pleasure in the power they had over other people. This man was one of them.

Luo limped hurriedly to the bench in front of the house. He did not know exactly where Paul and Christine were hiding with their son, but he wanted to lead the policemen away from the sheds, for they were probably hiding in one of them.

"What do you want from us?"

"We came to find out how you were," said the second policeman, who Luo had never met before. He spoke so politely that Luo did a double take. He was much younger than the other man and his uniform was at least two sizes too big; extra holes had been punched in the belt for him. The pimples on his face and the hint of down on his upper lip made him look like a boy.

"Thank you. We're fine," Luo said coldly. "Tell your superior that and leave us now."

"We're not in a rush," the other man said. He walked up to Luo holding the billiard cue in his hand. "What do you intend to do in the next few days?"

"What could we possibly be doing? Working in the fields. Harvesting. Repairing the roof. Chopping wood."

"A hell of a lot of work for an old man." The derision in his voice was unmistakable. "And for a sick one too."

"I'm not on my own."

"You can't be telling me that this skeleton is of any help to you."

Luo pretended not to have heard this.

"Or might you have some visitors who are helping you?"

Luo's stomach clenched. If the police were already looking for Paul and his family, all was lost. There was no way to escape from one of the sheds without being seen. And even if they did escape, where were they to go? How far could they get?

"What makes you think we have visitors?"

"A farmer in the village saw a stranger, a Westerner, apparently, walking with a child in front of your house."

"I don't know any Westerners."

"No?"

"No!"

"And what if I told you that this man had been tiling your roof?"

"Are you having us spied on? Are you paying the neighbors to inform on us? What a safe and prosperous country we are, that the police have nothing better to do!"

"Don't talk nonsense. We want an answer."

"If someone says that, he's wrong."

"And if someone tells us he has stood here in your courtyard and seen a foreigner here with his own eyes?"

"Then he's lying."

"Why should he do that?"

"How should I know?" Luo hoped that the policemen could not hear how rattled he felt. "Perhaps he has something to hide himself?"

The older man wrinkled his brow and looked suspicious. "And who did the little rascal here borrow a child's bicycle for?"

Of course the neighbors were spying on him. Of course Deng had reported his encounter with them to the police. How could he ever have thought otherwise? This had happened before and it was happening again now. They probably didn't even have to pay anyone. Denouncing Luo came free of charge. It couldn't hurt to curry favor with the police.

"No idea. Ask him."

"But the little shit doesn't speak." The policeman took a couple of steps towards Da Lin anyway and towered over him. "Who did you borrow the bicycle for?"

Da Lin was impassive. He turned his head calmly to one side, as though all this had nothing to do with him.

"Do you know, boy? If I wanted to, I could get you talking in a matter of seconds. Do you believe me?"

The policeman signaled to his colleague. "We're going to have a look round."

Luo started to get up to stand in their way, but quickly changed his mind.

"Do you really have nothing better to do than to watch an old cripple and a small child?"

Perhaps he could distract them by provoking them.

"How much are they paying you to do this shit?"

The policemen walked past him into the house.

"Do you have no respect whatsoever? Even for yourselves? Why are you not above doing this shit? How much is Golden Real Estate paying you in order to let my son's murderers run free?" he called after them in utter contempt. "Tell me! How much?"

XXI

Christine clung to him from behind. Paul knew what she was thinking: all was lost. It was the end for them. It was all over. They hadn't cleared the lunch dishes from the dining table yet. The police would find their suitcase and books in the bedroom, and would not stop until they found them.

They crawled deeper into the shed and hid behind a tall stack of chopped firewood. Paul looked around him for a weapon. He would not be arrested by the police. He had promised an anxious Christine that last night. No matter what happened, they would not give themselves up. They would not be separated from David. He had made his promise to reassure her, even though he did not feel comfortable with it. He thought that they actually stood more of a chance in court than by resisting with violence. He saw a sickle by the wall. Christine passed it to him. As far as they had been able to tell, the policemen were not armed.

They heard the two men come out of the house.

"And who do these knickers belong to?"

Paul was afraid that they had found Christine's underwear.

"Do you run around in these?"

"They belong to my daughter-in-law," Luo said. "She left them here on her last visit. Or do you really think that a Western man would wear women's red pants? What do they actually teach you in police training?"

The policemen did not reply but walked over the courtyard to the outbuildings. Paul lowered his head and he and Christine crouched closer together with David between them. Someone opened the door of the other shed. And slammed it closed again.

Their door was opened.

They held their breath. David's eyes were full of fear. Paul gripped the sickle more tightly.

The door closed again.

Silence.

Steps going off into the distance.

Paul slid back to the wall to see out better.

Luo's voice was almost shrill with relief. "What did I say? Are you happy now? Do you believe me now?"

"Shut up," the older policeman said. "Do you have any idea where the foreigner could have gone?"

"No. Ask your spies. They must have some idea."

"We want you to think about it."

"Why? Even if I knew something, do you really think I would tell you?"

For a moment it looked as if the policeman was about to hit him. He had already raised his arm and his hand was balled up in a fist. But he dropped it and turned away. "Asshole. Be careful or you'll end up like your son."

The policemen walked over to the gate. Suddenly, a loud cry was heard.

"Stop!"

It was Da Lin. "The cue! It's mine!"

Later, when Paul remembered this moment, in which several lives took a tragic turn, he sometimes thought that things might have been different if Da Lin had been more polite. Asked for his cue in an obsequious manner. And if Luo had chimed in with two or three sentences about how much the cue meant to his grandson. Pleading looks. A few tears from the boy. Perhaps the policemen would have had sympathy then. But that was probably too much to ask from them, and what happened was the unavoidable ending to a drama that had begun two years earlier with a disagreement over a piece of land. Or perhaps much earlier than that.

Perhaps, thought Paul, we are all too much like prisoners for the story to have ended a different way. Just like most stories carry their endings within them from the start.

The policemen stopped in their tracks and the one holding the cue turned round.

"So you can speak after all," he said, shaking his head in amazement. "That is good to know."

He lifted his leg, snapped the wooden cue against his thigh with a mighty crack and tossed the pieces in the boy's direction.

"You can keep those," he said, smiling.

Before he had reached the gate, he collapsed with a short, shrill cry.

XXII

He was usually overcome by a wave of nausea whenever he saw policemen. Whether they came to the house, or he had to go to the police station with Grandpa, or if he saw them in the town. The sight of them made his stomach turn, and he felt like throwing up. There was nothing he could do to prevent it. It was just like when other children felt ill if they saw a dog or cat that had been run over on the street, with its entrails bursting out of its body.

But today everything was different. Instead of freezing in fear, he knew what he had to do. Hide the visitors. Fetch Grandpa. Clear away things in the house.

While his grandpa had been arguing with the policemen in the courtyard, he had erased all traces of the guests. He had hurried to put the dirty dishes in a cupboard, hidden the toothbrushes behind the toilet bowl, tossed the toys and books into the suitcase and pushed it far under the bed. He had spread his dirty clothes all over the floor, with his unwashed underpants right by the door. They would have to search thoroughly in order to find any evidence of the visitors. He picked up his catapult and a couple of stones and stepped outside.

How could he have overlooked the red underwear?

When one of the policemen opened the door of the second shed, he put a stone in the sling of his catapult. He would not allow them to take Paul, Christine, and David away with them.

He knew how it would all end.

Wrapped in white cloths. Soaked with blood.

Then everything happened very quickly.

The cue. The sound of splintering wood.

He did not need patience or concentration for this shot.

Lift.

Pull.
Take aim.
There was only one place. The head – and it wasn't small.
Release.

XXIII

The shot hit the temple above the ear and drilled into the head. Blood streamed from an open wound and ran down the neck, trickled onto the ground and was absorbed by the sand. The policeman groaned in pain a few times before he lost consciousness.

The young man next to him stood there, pale with shock. He looked around the courtyard in confusion to see what had hit his colleague, but could see nothing. "Stop!" he screamed into the silence. "Stop!"

Luo thought he had heard the stone fly past his ear. A light hiss. A dull thud. At first he was gripped by the same panic he had felt when they had brought the body of his son to the courtyard. A few seconds later, all he could think of was what had to happen now. He had to get the policeman out of the courtyard and make arrangements for Da Lin's escape.

He leaned over the man. It looked as though an artery had burst. "He needs a doctor, otherwise he will bleed to death."

———

The young policeman grew even paler. "What has happened?"

Without answering the question, Luo picked up one of the unconscious man's arms. "Help me. You have to take him to town."

The two of them carried the man to the car and, with great effort, heaved his motionless body onto the back seat.

"Do you even have a driving license?"

The policeman nodded.

"Then drive as fast as you can to the nearest hospital."

Luo hobbled back into the courtyard, where Da Lin, Paul, Christine, and their son were waiting for him. Their questioning looks.

"Pack your things," he commanded. "The police will be back in two hours at most. I'll try to find someone in the village to drive you."

There was only one man there who was fearless enough to accept the request. Luo didn't trust him, because he was more in thrall to the lure of money than everyone else in the village. But he had no choice.

The Monastery

I

The car was a run-down Volkswagen Passat that stank of stale cigarette smoke. None of the displays on the dashboard worked, and there were loose leads dangling everywhere. Wires held the panels and the glove compartment together. The windscreen had two cracks in it.

The driver gave them a suspicious look and insisted on Paul sitting in front next to him. He opened the trunk with a claw hammer and put their luggage in. He said it would take him sixteen to eighteen hours to take them to Hongyang, depending on how many breaks they took.

Payment in cash upfront. That was non-negotiable.

Paul made attempts to strike up a conversation at the start of the journey. He found out that the man had been a seaman before, and had opened a restaurant in the village with his savings. But he had gone bankrupt shortly after and his wife had left him, taking their daughter too. Since then, he had lived with his parents and did odd jobs such as this one. He had not married again, and was not in contact with his child. He did not even know where she lived. He didn't think much of the government. Nor of the Party. And even less of the police. They were all corrupt. He had nothing against a return of Mao.

The conversation died away after that.

The driver lit himself one cigarette after another. He ignored their requests for him to stop or at least to smoke less.

Paul thought about Luo, about the few words in which the old man had made it clear to him there that was no other choice but to take Da Lin with them. He and Christine had merely nodded silently and gathered their things hurriedly.

Luo had taken him aside at some point and pressed a black and white photo of his wife into his hand. "Can you take that to Beijing for me?"

"Yes, but why?"

"She always dreamed of going to Beijing one day. We never managed it."

It had been a strange leave-taking. Luo had pushed his grandson to the car, patted him on the back of the head silently, turned away and limped back into the courtyard. No hugging, no final words. Da Lin hadn't looked around either; he had simply got into the car. When Paul ran back to the house, because he had left their passports in a drawer in all the commotion, Luo was sitting on the bench crying. Paul stopped and wanted to say something but Luo made it clear to him with a gesture that he should go back to the car and leave him alone. He could not get the image of the old man crumpled and crying out of his head.

They had been given Da Lin's mother's address and telephone number in Beijing, and had promised to hand Da Lin over to her there. In person. Da Lin was not to be left in the care of anyone other than his mother. Paul had given his word on that.

Darkness had fallen and it had grown cooler. In the rear view mirror, Paul saw Christine dozing off. David was sleeping in her arms and Da Lin was leaning against her shoulder, asleep too.

Suddenly, the driver braked and turned off the main road.

"What are you doing?" Paul asked suspiciously.

"It's not enough money," the man said firmly.

"What do you mean? We agreed on a price," Paul said, annoyed. "You've got your money. Drive on."

The driver turned the engine off. "The price has changed."

Paul thought this was one of the usual tricks to try to get more money out of a deal. He had experienced these often on his travels in China: fees and prices that doubled overnight; quotes and amounts cut in half. It was a process of haggling and trying one's luck. If he had refused to be cowed and insisted on the terms of the original agreement being met, his opponent had always given in eventually.

"No way. Forget it. We made an agreement. Drive on, now."

"Pay, or get out."

Was this man daring to threaten them? "Now listen. You want a tip, don't you? It's not far. Drive on."

"Get out," the man repeated calmly, but in a tone of voice that left Paul in no doubt that he was serious.

Paul felt his throat going dry. The children were awake now and Christine wanted to know why they weren't moving. He looked out of the window into the darkness. As far as he could make out, they were by the side of a harvested field and there were no buildings or farmhouses to be seen in any direction. The last village they had driven through had been at least twenty kilometers ago.

"How much?"

"Three times more."

"Are you mad?"

"Not one yuan less."

Paul made his calculations. All the Hong Kong dollars and Chinese yuan they had would not be enough to cover even twice the original sum agreed on. "We don't have that much."

The man shrugged.

"You can't do this. We have two children with us."

"Get out," he said again, unmoved.

"Twice."

The driver drew on his cigarette, blew the smoke in Paul's direction and shook his head.

"Please believe me. That's all we have."

"Then get out now."

"Listen, I would give you more but we don't have it. Search our things if you think I'm lying."

"That doesn't interest me. Get out."

"No." Paul sized up the man properly. He was two heads shorter than Paul but also twenty years younger and had a very muscular build. Paul stood no chance against him.

"I beg you. You can't leave us here in the night, not with children. At least take us to the next village."

"No. Get out now." His voice had a threatening undertone to it now.

Paul knew that there was no more bargaining to be done. "All right. Three times more. Luo will give you the rest of the money."

"Don't talk nonsense. He doesn't have a yuan to his name. Anyway, I won't be seeing him for a long time. He'll be arrested long before I get back."

"Then I'll transfer it to you once we're back in Hong Kong."

"Transfer?"

"I promise. I give you my word."

"Your word?" The man looked at him as though Paul was making a bad joke. "How stupid do you think I am?"

With a quick movement he took a switchblade out of the side compartment in his door and flicked it open.

"Get out of the car."

II

Da Lin watched the two men in the front seats. They were arguing over money. The tone of their voices told him that the journey would end here. He held his catapult more tightly in his hand. He wanted to help Paul but at this distance and in the confined space of the car he could do nothing with his weapon.

Why had Grandpa trusted this driver of all people? How could he have thought that this man would keep his word? The whole village knew that he was an idiot. A swindler. Someone who was said to beat even his parents when he was drunk. Da Lin could not stand him. Whenever he had seen him coming down the street, he had crossed to the other side.

It was pitch black outside. He could not even see the faint light of a farm building. At this rate they would soon be standing out here with their luggage with no idea what to do next. The thought did not frighten him. Ever since he had seen the policeman lying bleeding in the courtyard, he had felt nothing any longer. Or at least not much. As though all the things that were taking place now were happening to someone else. He was merely watching. From a safe distance.

After the policemen had left, he had stuffed a few things into a bag, following Grandpa's instructions. Then he had sat in the courtyard and waited.

When the car came, he got in. Grandpa said nothing. He did not even wave. He turned and hobbled back into the courtyard before they drove off.

Da Lin understood then that he would never see his grandfather again. There was no "see you soon" to be said any longer. Not for them.

The police would come looking for him and since he would not be there, they would arrest his grandpa. He would resist, just as Papa had resisted, and they would beat him, like they beat Papa.

He would never see the farm again. The dog. The chickens.

He would never see the billiard table again. The table tennis table. Of all the things his father had made for him, the catapult was the only thing he still had.

He was not even sure if he wanted to see his mother again.

Paul had promised his grandpa to deliver him to her in person. He had seen Grandpa write her address and mobile phone number down on a piece of paper.

But what did that mean after all? Maybe she had moved house long ago, to Shanghai, or back to Shenzhen. Maybe she had a new husband and a new child. Why else had she not come home for Chinese New Year?

What would happen to him if his mother no longer wanted him?

He could not go with them to Hong Kong. And there were no other family members. They would probably leave him on a street corner in Beijing. Or in a restaurant. Wait here for us, we'll be back, they would say. He would sit there and wait. And wait.

He did not feel anything even at this thought

Or at least not much.

———

Paul and the driver were still arguing.

Da Lin dug a stone out of his pocket and put it in the sling. He was about to raise the catapult, but the driver was too well protected by his headrest. The weapon was useless inside the car.

Da Lin saw the tip of a metal rod sticking out of the seat in front of him. He pressed his knee against it until it hurt. He pressed harder. He felt the cold metal pierce his flesh, just a little a first, then deeper as he pressed harder.

The pain felt good.

Blood ran down his leg.

It was pleasantly warm.

III

It took a while for Luo's tears to dry. There was no one left to hold them back for. Along with the grief he felt over the parting from Da Lin, he felt a burning pain in his leg that rose to his hips and only subsided gradually.

Luo sneezed and looked round. The courtyard already looked as deserted as it would be in a few hours. Through the open gate, the wind blew in one cloud of dust after another. The table tennis table and the billiard table were already covered in a gray layer. The house door, which was open, creaked. The dog lay at his feet dozing.

His thoughts turned to the policeman. Judging by the location of the wound and the blood loss, his chances of survival were slim. Perhaps he had already bled to death on his way to the hospital. Even though the man had often treated him badly and tormented him in interrogations, Luo was surprised to realize that he felt something like pity. Not so much for the man but for his family. A child would lose a father. A woman her husband. Parents their son.

They have turned us into a people of murderers, he thought. Even a twelve-year-old. They have sown so much rage and hatred, so much bitterness and despair, they have done us so much injustice that we don't know how to help ourselves except through violence.

They.

Who were they? Luo had not found a satisfactory answer to this question yet. The Party. The communists, whom he had previously been one of. The people in power and their henchmen. But they were everywhere – in every village and in every family. They. We. The longer he thought about it, the more they and we merged into one.

He had wished for Da Lin to have a better life. But he had

given up on this hope after Zhong Hua's death. Now he could do nothing more for his grandson. Ever since the accident with his leg he had thought often about taking him to Beijing. He had postponed it from one month to the next because he could not bear to be parted from him.

Da Lin.

How dear his grandson was to him. Now he had had no choice but to entrust him to a family he barely knew.

Luo heard the cars coming from a distance. There were at least three of them, probably more. Their speed increased as they approached.

If the police let him talk he could claim that he had made the shot with the catapult. They would be happy to have someone admitting to the crime.

It was always about guilt and punishment, not about justice.

The cars braked sharply. Doors were opened and slammed closed. He wanted to face them standing, so he got up.

They ran towards the gate. There were more of them than he had expected. For a moment he felt frightened. The policemen would want him to feel their anger. If so, from what he knew of them, they would beat him up thoroughly before they asked any questions.

He shut his eyes and thought about his son, and his fear went away. The first policemen stormed into the yard and came directly towards him. He felt that Zhong Hua was beside him.

He had not felt him so close since his death.

They stood by the side of the field with their luggage. Paul was on the verge of losing hope. Ever since the car had disappeared around a corner, an almost complete silence had surrounded them. He reached for Christine's hand and held it tight. In the darkness they were only able to find the edge of the road with some difficulty.

He did not even know which way they should be walking. Back towards where they had come from or in the direction the car had taken, in the hope that there was a village behind the next hill? And what then? Even if they found a village after a few kilometers, who would help them there? So late at night. How could they explain who they were, where they came from, and where they wanted to go?

They stepped onto the road and started walking the same way the car had gone, in silence. Da Lin held onto Christine's other hand and Paul carried David.

Over an hour later, they heard a car approaching behind them. In the distance they saw two headlights, which disappeared behind a rise of land before appearing again. When they came into view, the brakes were applied and two men stared at them in astonishment through the windscreen. Paul signaled at them to stop and for a moment it looked like they were hesitating, but then they drove on.

The second car, half an hour later, did not even slow down.

Neither did the third.

The fourth car stopped fifty meters away from them. Paul ran towards it as quickly as he could, but when he had nearly reached it, it started moving again and disappeared into the darkness.

Paul could see that Da Lin and Christine were getting tired. It was long past midnight. They sat down by the roadside to rest. When he saw another car approaching in the distance, he stepped a little way into the road and waved for help.

The car slowed down but did not stop.

When the next car came, Paul stepped into the middle of the road and waved both arms. The driver stepped on the accelerator and drove straight at him. If Paul had not jumped aside at the last moment, he would have been run over.

Did they take him for a highway robber and fear an ambush?

One hour later a vehicle stopped.

It was a small pick-up truck. Three Buddhist monks and a young man were squeezed into the driver's cab. They rolled the window down.

"Where do you want to go?"

Paul could only shrug helplessly.

"Should we take you to our monastery?"

"Yes, please."

"Get in."

They climbed onto the back of the pick-up truck and kept Da Lin and David between them. The monks gave them a thumbs-up through the rear window. Paul nodded at them, exhausted and grateful.

The oncoming wind was cold. They crept behind the driver's cab and huddled together. Despite the biting cold and the rumble of the truck, Da Lin, David, and Christine all fell asleep within minutes.

Paul fell into a trance-like state somewhere between sleep and semi-wakefulness. At some point he realized that they had come to a stop. He heard voices. Christine and the children were still sleeping. Someone spread a blanket over them. Paul was too exhausted to find out where they were.

———

The vibration of the phone in his trouser pocket woke him shortly after sunrise. A text message from Zhang.

where are you?
Paul replied immediately: *on the way to hongyang*
is luo with you?
no
where is he?
??

Shortly after that the phone rang. Paul was startled. They had agreed only to phone each other in a desperate emergency. Or was it not Zhang at all? Who else had his number?

"Hello?" Paul spoke quietly so as not to wake the others.

"It's me," Zhang said. "Where are you?"

"I don't know exactly," Paul said, sitting up. "I think we're in a monastery. We were driven here by some monks in the night."

"Do you know where Luo is?"

"No. I think he must be at his farm."

"He's not there. When did you leave?"

"Yesterday afternoon."

Zhang took a deep breath. "I've just arrived. It's bad. Chairs and shelves have been thrown around the house and the table and chest of drawers have been smashed to pieces. There's a dead dog in the yard. And blood everywhere."

Paul was too horrified to speak.

"Hello?"

"I'm still here."

"Did you get my message with the address in Hongyang?"

"Yes."

"Get in touch as soon as you know where you are. I'll try to meet you in Hongyang."

Paul would have liked to talk to him for a while longer. The familiarity of his voice did him good. But Zhang ended the call without another word.

Christine, Da Lin, and David were still asleep. Paul could

not stay lying down any longer. His back ached from lying on the hard surface. He climbed off the back of the truck. A fire had been lit somewhere. The smell of wood smoke spread over the courtyard. A gentle breeze sounded the wind chimes on the roof. The monastery consisted of only two buildings and one temple, with an encircling wall. In the temple he found three statues of Buddha with colorful fairy lights wound round them. There were biscuits and plastic flowers laid before them as sacrifices.

He sat down on a wooden stump in the rising sun. Reddish-brown monks' robes were hung out to dry on the washing line next to him. A young monk walked up to him. It was one of the three monks who had taken them on board the truck last night. Paul got up and bowed.

"Thank you so very, very much. You have helped us a great deal."

The monk just smiled. "You must be hungry."

"A little."

"Come with me."

He led Paul into a small dining room, took a bowl from a shelf, filled it with rice and stir-fried vegetables, and put it on the table.

"Tea?"

"Yes, please."

Soon they were sitting facing each other, in silence.

The monk examined him closely. He could hardly take his eyes off Paul. It was as though his guest was an exotic creature to be studied in detail.

"This tastes good," Paul said with his mouth full. "Thank you very much."

The monk grinned. Then he started laughing. It was a laughter without malice; he was not trying to hide anything or pretend anything; it was neither aggressive nor embarrassed.

Eventually Paul could not help but join in.

The monastery's abbot entered and the novice fell silent and stood up immediately. He bowed respectfully and, after hesitating briefly, left the room.

"Welcome," said the abbot in a gruff voice. He sat down opposite Paul and sized him up thoroughly. He was about the same age as him and had deep lines on his face, strong hands, and a big belly. Paul got the impression that he had spent most of his life working on the land.

"Thank you very much. We are grateful for your hospitality," Paul said, hoping that the monk would not ask too many questions.

"Where do you want to go?"

"To Hongyang."

"That is far away."

Paul nodded. "Is there perhaps a taxi in the village that we could take?"

The abbot poured himself some tea. "I don't think so. But we could take you to the bus. It goes to Xian. There will surely be a connection to Hongyang from there."

"I . . . I'm not so keen on taking the bus," Paul said evasively.

"I thought so."

A tense silence followed. The abbot cleared his throat. "I was told that you were standing by the side of a road in the middle of nowhere."

Paul could not think of any good reason to give for this, so he merely nodded and said nothing.

The abbot drank his tea and waited for an explanation. When none was forthcoming, his face darkened. "Are you tourists?"

"Yes, we're from Hong Kong."

"From Hong Kong?" the abbot repeated, sounding curious. "That's far away."

It didn't make any sense. Everything that Paul said would make the monk more and more suspicious. "And we have to get to Hongyang urgently. How long does it take to get there by car from here?"

"I think it will be eight to ten hours. What do you want to do in Hongyang?"

Paul ignored the question. He hesitated before saying what was on his mind. "Could the driver maybe . . . ?"

The abbot shook his head. "I'm sorry. That's too far. We need him here. I would like to help you, but I'm afraid I can't."

Paul could not stop himself. "But how shall we get to Hongyang, then?"

"By train or by bus," the monk said coldly.

Paul's strength left him. It was as if all the air was slowly draining out of him. His head and shoulders grew heavy and his back slumped.

The abbot watched him calmly. "How urgently do you need to get there?"

"Very."

"How much money do you have with you?"

"About 2,000 yuan's worth, in yuan and Hong Kong dollars."

"That's all?"

"Yes."

"Hmmm. No jewelry?"

That hadn't crossed his mind. He thought for a moment. "Two gold wedding rings. They were expensive. My wife is wearing a necklace but it's not valuable."

The monk shook his head, disappointed. "I don't think I can find anyone in the village. Give me everything you have and I'll ask around."

"Thank you. Thank you very much."

The relief was short-lived.

He wanted payment upfront.

Their eyes met, and suddenly Paul did not know if he could trust this man. The money and the jewelry were all they had.

What were they to do if the monk could not find anyone to help them but did not return the money? Or simply disappeared with it immediately? Took it for himself and reported them to the police?

"Well? Don't you want to go and get the money and the rings?"

Paul did not know what it was. The man's voice, in which he suddenly thought he could hear greed? His body, which seemed more tense than before? His eyes, which were avoiding his? Or was he just imagining it all? The doubts wormed deeper into him. Suspicion had a voracious appetite. He hated himself for having such thoughts. The man in front of him was the abbot of a small monastery! A person who probably spent his life meditating and helping the poor instead of pursuing the Chinese dream of accumulating great wealth somewhere in a city. And who was making a generous offer to help.

Out of compassion.

Or out of greed?

"Perhaps it would be better for us to take the bus," Paul heard himself say.

"Are you sure?"

Was his doubt a well-meant warning or a threat?

Paul was completely thrown. He could no longer tell what was what. "Yes."

"No problem. We'll take you to the bus station. There are only two buses a day. One in the morning and one in the evening. You should still be able to get the one at nine. Then you'll be in Xian in the early evening."

Had he made a mistake, turning down the offer? From the man's voice, he could detect no disappointment over losing a good deal, more relief at getting these strangers off his hands again so quickly.

Paul's phone vibrated. "Excuse me."

He dug around in his pocket for it.

they are on my trail

Paul was about to put the phone away when a second message arrived.

do not get in touch. take the battery out of the phone. pastor lee is expecting you

"That was a friend," Paul said hesitantly. "He's asking us to get to Hongyang as quickly as we can. It's an urgent family matter for my wife."

V

She would not give up her wedding ring. Not under any circumstances. She did not care what Paul and this dreadful monk said. She would rather have the two gold crowns torn from her mouth.

Yes, they could have the necklace but it was cheap costume jewelry. The abbot cast a brief glance at it and shook his head dismissively.

He was more interested in another chain, made of silver with an amulet from her mother. He assessed it like a jeweler and took it.

No, she didn't have anything else, apart from her jade talisman of course. It was always in her bag, even though, looking back, she had to admit that it had not remotely fulfilled its function in any convincing way. It had not saved her from marriage to her first husband, nor helped her to gain material success. And on the cold and rainy day in February that she had first met Paul on Lamma, it had been lying on top of the chest of drawers in her bedroom.

It was a small shimmering green dragon, supposedly dating from the Ming dynasty. It had been a present from her father when she was born. She had been told that he had received it from his father in turn. It was the only memento she still had from her father. As a child in Hong Kong, she had protected it like a treasure. Before going to sleep, she had often put it under her pillow in the hope that it would bring her closer to her father and brother. On some nights it had worked miracles: they had appeared to her in her dreams and spoken to her; when she woke, she thought both of them were really standing by her bed.

Christine had always thought that the amulet had more symbolic than material value, but if she read the monk's expression correctly, she had been wrong on that count. Very wrong.

Yes, she was prepared to exchange it for being driven to Hongyang, but that was all she would give up. She would keep the cash and the rings.

The abbot looked carefully at the jade dragon again, from every angle. He held it against the light and studied the patterns in the stone. He stroked it almost tenderly.

He would definitely be able to find someone in the area to drive them there in exchange for two thousand yuan and the dragon.

"One thousand. Not one yuan more." She hoped Paul would keep out of this. He was no good at haggling.

"One thousand five hundred."

"Done."

The monk's satisfied smile told her that she should have driven a harder bargain. He reached his hand out for the jade dragon.

Christine shook her head. "Only when we arrive in Hongyang."

He let his arm drop and looked disappointed. "I'm afraid I can't help you then."

"Why not? I give you my word."

"Because I won't find anyone who will trust you."

"But you expect me to trust a stranger?"

"No, of course not." There was a thin and cold smile on his face. "But you don't have any choice."

"We'll give you the cash now," Paul said. "We'll keep the dragon until the driver has taken us to Hongyang."

The monk cast him a look of contempt, then turned as if to leave. Christine could see Paul grinding his teeth with rage. He sat up to say something, but did not manage to get a single word out.

"We have to get to Hongyang by the quickest way possible," she called after the monk. "We have two children with us ... We need your help."

Without reacting, the monk went to a shrine in the middle of the courtyard, pulled a handful of joss sticks out of an old canister, lit them with a candle and bowed several times in front of the shiny gold statue of a fat and happy laughing Buddha.

Christine walked over to him. "We need some security."

"Security?" The abbot paused for a moment. "You're clearly not from China. Security is a rare commodity here. I would even say that it does not exist."

He gave her a bitter smile and bowed once more. Christine understood that there was no point trying to convince him or to bargain with him anymore. They were in his hands. They had to accept his conditions.

He put the smoking joss sticks in a bowl filled with sand, bowed one last time, and walked towards the exit.

Paul was standing behind her now. "It's too great a risk. We'll find another way," he said quietly.

Christine turned around angrily. "There's no other way," she snapped at him. "Have you forgotten what Zhang wrote in his message? We have to get away from here."

She walked after the monk and gave him the jade dragon without saying a word.

———

Barely half an hour later, they were called to a vehicle. It was the same small pick-up truck and the same young driver who had taken them on board the previous night. He greeted them with a friendly but tired smile. He looked exhausted and his eyes were glassy, as though he had a fever and had barely slept in the short night. The four of them squeezed onto the passenger seat next to him. Da Lin sat on Paul's lap and Christine held David tight on hers. It was hot and crowded. She was sweating and could neither move nor hold on to anything. With every bump in the road, her head bounced against the metal wall behind them. After half an hour she got pins and needles in her right foot. After an hour she could not feel her legs any longer.

The driver said nothing. He coughed and yawned in turn and he drew breath with a rattling sound. Christine was afraid he would fall asleep any minute.

"Thank you again for taking us last night."

She wasn't sure if he understood her. Instead of replying, he yawned.

"Are you a friend of the abbot's?" she asked, just to say something.

"No, I sometimes make journeys for the monastery."

"Have you ever been to Hongyang?"

"No."

"Will we make it in one day?"

He shrugged. "How should I know?"

She stopped short for a moment. "Don't you know the way?"

"No."

Had they fallen into the hands of a cheat again, who would kick them out and leave them on a deserted country lane after a hundred kilometers? She gazed at the young man's profile. He looked friendly, almost innocent, but what did that mean anyway? She had lost all sense of whom she could trust or not. All she knew was that she did not want to be threatened with a knife and thrown out of a vehicle again. She and Paul would only be forced out of the truck by violent means and this slightly built man would not be capable of that.

"The abbot said we should head toward Xian then take the highway to Beijing, and there will be signs at some point to show us the way."

"It would be better for us to avoid the highway," Paul said.

"I don't know another way," the driver said.

"Do you have a map with you?"

"No."

At some point David grew hungry and needed the toilet. They stopped at a service area, right in front of a large restaurant with many cars, coaches, and a few trucks parked in front of it. There were also two police cars.

"Drive on," Paul said immediately.

"But I need the toilet," David protested. "Otherwise I'll pee myself."

"We'll stop by the roadside after this."

"And I'm hungry."

"Why don't you want to stop here?" the driver wondered.

"I'll go with him," Christine said. Before Paul could object, she opened the door, got out, and took David in her arms. She wanted to avoid the driver asking more questions and becoming suspicious.

The restaurant had a large dining hall with windows on one side. Behind the counter, a dozen cooks stood with their woks hissing and steaming over open fires with tongues of flame shooting out. It smelled of garlic and hot oil. Waitresses shouted orders at the cooks and dogs roamed the tables, pouncing on any discarded food that fell on the floor.

Christine saw a small WC sign at the other end of the hall. She was halfway across the room when she noticed the police officers. Three men and one woman were walking slowly through the rows of tables watching the guests. Clearly looking for something. Or someone.

She stopped and wondered what to do. One of the policemen was walking directly towards them. Christine was afraid that if she turned on her heel then and left the restaurant, she would attract undue attention.

David tugged at her arm. "Mama, I need to go," he said impatiently. "I really need to go."

She did not want her son to wet himself. She wanted to set an example for him and be strong, stronger than her fear. Christine gathered her courage and walked towards the policeman as calmly as she could. With every step her heart beat louder. He looked at her carefully.

"What a cute little boy," he said with a friendly smile. "What's your name?"

"Bao," David said. "And I need a pee urgently."

The policeman laughed out loud and stepped to one side. "Then hurry up."

Christine could have screamed with relief in the toilet. Had the Chens given up the search for them? Maybe they were no longer in any danger at all, and didn't know it. She thought about Zhang's text messages. He could be wrong.

When she returned to the dining hall, the police officers were standing together in a corner, discussing something. Two of them were looking around the room and another was making notes. She held David tight in her arms and walked as quickly as she could without running towards the exit. Suddenly she heard one of the police officers shout something. Christine increased her pace.

Loud cries for her to stop.

She ran out into the car park and stared at the spot where the pick-up truck had been.

It was gone.

She looked around and ran, without thinking, across the car park towards the coaches. One of the doors was open and the driver was slumped across the steering wheel, asleep. Christine boarded the coach.

"This isn't our car," David whispered.

"I know."

"Why . . ."

"Shhh . . ." she said.

They crept down to the seats at the back of the coach and looked through the tinted windows at the policemen, who had followed them after a few moments. They looked through the parked cars fleetingly and spoke to people who were just arriving. A young couple pointed hesitantly at first then with eager nods at the motorway. The police officers hurried to their car and drove off in the direction indicated by the passersby.

Christine's whole body was shivering.

"Where is Papa?" David wanted to know.

"I don't know. Come on, let's look for him."

They found the pick-up truck not far away, hidden between two trucks laden with pigs grunting and squeaking pitifully. Christine was furious.

"Are you crazy?" she screamed. "How could you drive off without us?"

"We didn't drive off. We parked here instead because people were staring at us so much by the entrance." Paul's calm reply made her even angrier.

"It's your fault the police almost caught us." She did not know what to do with her rage. She was on the verge of really lashing out at him.

"I said right at the beginning that we shouldn't stop here."

"You left us in the lurch."

"We did not," he snapped back at her. "What are you saying? I merely asked the driver . . ."

"You merely asked the driver," she interrupted. "Just like you merely left David for a moment in the hotel!"

That silenced Paul.

Their son held his hands over his ears. "Don't fight," he said quietly. "Please don't fight."

The driver had watched the argument with amazement and confusion. If he wasn't suspicious before then he certainly is now, Christine thought. It would be an easy matter for him to bring them to the next police station.

It was Paul's fault. Everything was Paul's fault.

The Ghost Town

I

They did not say a word to each other for hours. The confined space in the driver's cab of the pick-up truck was scarcely bearable. Paul had the feeling that Christine even found the contact with his body unpleasant. He slid as close to the door as he could, but their shoulders were still touching. He thought about sitting on the loading area at the back, but it started raining, so he discarded that idea.

Da Lin grew heavier and heavier as time passed. Paul's back and legs hurt, but there was no way to distribute his weight differently.

David had fallen asleep in his mother's arms. Christine sat motionless, staring straight ahead all the time. She did not reply to the two or three questions he asked her. He tried to imagine what she was thinking, but had to admit to himself that he had no idea what was going on inside her. Her rage at him grew with every passing day. He had never seen an outburst from her like the one in the car park. She was at the end of her tether, and her fear and her doubts were directed increasingly at him. He knew himself well enough to recognize what his reaction would be: retreat.

He could not respond any other way.

We are prisoners, for a lifetime.

———

When they arrived in Hongyang the skies had cleared and the low-lying sun was already casting long shadows. The city was in the middle of a wide plain and was much larger than Paul had thought. In the evening sky, rows of high-rise buildings towered in the distance, like the towers of a fortress.

Paul hoped that the anonymity of a city would give them safety and that Christine would feel calmer. They turned off the ring road into a road with three lanes. The traffic thinned and soon they were the only vehicle around for some distance.

The first buildings they drove past were the shells of new buildings that stood cold and naked like ruins on half-finished streets. Behind those was a cluster of four-story buildings. They had been finished, but were clearly not inhabited yet. Paul looked up and down the buildings but could not see any lights in the apartments, any curtains in the windows, or plants, chairs, and washing lines on the balconies.

Christine looked out of the window in disbelief. "Are we in the right place?"

A sign by the side of the road, 'Hongyang New Town', was the answer to her question.

Paul took the phone from his pocket and read the address out loud. "Beijing Lu, Block 4, building no. 3."

"Do you know the way?" the driver asked.

"No. We'll have to ask."

There was nobody on the street they could ask for directions. They looked for a shop or restaurant, but every place they saw was closed, with its shutters down, or boarded up. Their driver followed the signs to the town center. They did not come across a single other car, and waited several times at empty crossings. The traffic lights and the street lights were working.

The town center stretched over a few streets, and seemed just as deserted as the other areas. A gray office building with mirrored glass stood among the other buildings, but it was unlit. The windows had not been cleaned, and the panes of glass were covered in a thick layer of sand and dirt. On one side of the building the first letter of a neon advertising sign had been put up. Next to it, loose cables dangled from the wall.

An unfinished footbridge arched across the road.

There were piles of construction rubble at certain traffic junctions. A pedestrian precinct had not been completed: there were two wheelbarrows and spades by a pile of sand and stones.

It looked as though the inhabitants had fled the town over-night. But why?

Eventually they came to a building site where several workers were sitting by a flickering fire and drinking beer. The driver got out and asked for directions to Beijing Lu. The workers laughed and told him the way, pointing as they did so.

———

Shortly after that, the driver let them out in front of one of the high-rise buildings in which no lights seemed to be on. Christine asked him to wait, but he had barely put their bags down on the pavement before he said a hurried goodbye and drove off.

On the large panel of doorbells at the entrance to the building, there were only a few names and initials. Most of the slots were empty. Paul found a handwritten name tag by one buzzer: P. K. Lee.

A short man wearing large glasses opened the door, only by a crack at first. He looked suspiciously at Paul, Christine, and the two children before he let them into the flat. They stood in the hallway facing each other in silence for a long moment. There was a crucifix on the wall. Around it, someone had wound a string of multicolored fairy lights that flickered on and off constantly. Paul could see Da Lin recoiling from the crucifix, disturbed.

"Who are you?" the pastor asked them in a deep, forbidding voice.

"My name is Paul Leibovitz. This is my wife and these are our children," Paul said. "I . . . I thought you knew about us."

"I was told that someone who needed help would be arriving. But I was expecting only one person." He wrinkled his brow as he looked at each of them in turn. "I suppose you need somewhere to sleep."

Paul nodded.

"My flat is too small. I can't possibly put you all up here. I'm sorry." He did not sound as though he would be giving much thought to where else they could stay.

How much? The thought darted into Paul's mind. The more difficult the situation, the more money he would demand. "We only have a thousand yuan . . ."

"Five hundred," Christine interrupted.

"You think I want money from you?" The pastor snorted in outrage.

Before Paul could say anything in reply, Lee turned on his heel, disappeared into a room and slammed the door closed behind him.

They heard him making a phone call and ending it after a brief exchange. Then a second short call. And a third.

After a few minutes he returned holding a piece of paper with a name and address on it. "This woman is in my church. You can stay the night with her. It's ten minutes' walk to her flat from here."

It was a long march. Paul carried the luggage and Christine followed him with the two children. Every step was torture. He felt naked and defenseless on the wide pavements and empty streets. There was not a single tree or bush in sight. There were no cars parked on the road, not even a rubbish bin or a bench they could have hidden themselves behind if a policeman had come along. He had hoped for the anonymity of a big city but in deserted Hongyang they were more conspicuous as pedestrians than they had been in the village they had left.

II

Qian Gao Gao also lived in a dark high-rise building with no names by the doorbells. Pastor Lee had only written flat 28A on the piece of paper.

A quick buzz and the door was opened for them.

They stepped into a two-story foyer with red carpet and white marble walls. A chandelier hung from the ceiling. Below it was an empty reception desk covered with a thick layer of dust.

Only one of the four lifts was working.

On the twenty-eighth floor there were neither numbers nor names on the flat doors. Paul walked down the corridor and tried to listen for sounds from any one of them.

Suddenly a door at the end of the corridor opened and a woman stepped out. "Are you my visitors?" she said. "Why are you creeping around like that?"

Qian Gao Gao was a stout woman, not much shorter than Paul. She was wearing yellow pajamas or loungewear with pictures of Winnie-the-Pooh on it, along with a red silk dressing gown embroidered with the Chinese character for 'double happiness'. Her feet were in black and white panda slippers with ears sticking out on top.

"I didn't mean to give you a shock," she said apologetically when she saw their fearful faces. "Come in."

From the door the musky smell of men's cologne wafted towards them. They walked down a long hallway piled with boxes big and small. Some of them were still unopened but crepe paper, Styrofoam balls, and wood shavings spilled out of the others.

The hallway led to a living room. Paul looked around searching for the man who could be wearing the cologne.

"You must be hungry?"

When she got no reply, she leaned down to David, who had

been staring at her slippers in fascination all this time. "You must surely be hungry?"

"Yes," David said quietly.

"I thought so. I am too," she said, and laughed.

"Do you like dumplings?"

He made a sound that she took to mean agreement.

"Wonderful." She walked over to the open-plan kitchen consisting of counters, a central island, and three refrigerators side by side. She opened one of the fridges and took out several packets of frozen dumplings.

"Can I help?" Christine asked.

"You can set the table. The food won't take long." She put chopsticks, bowls, and small plates on the counter. Then she added mugs, a thermos flask and a jug of warm water. Paul noticed her bright red nail polish and her plump hands, with several gold rings set with diamonds and rubies on her fingers. Either her complexion was pale or her make-up was almost white, making the deep red of her lips stand out all the more.

Christine and Da Lin laid the things on the oval dining table, which had a crucifix and an oil painting of the Virgin Mary with her child hanging above it.

David pulled his father over to a giraffe figure that was more than two heads taller than him.

"Is it real?"

"No. It's made of cloth. But it's quite big, isn't it?"

David nodded in awe.

"Giraffes are my favorite animals," Qian Gao Gao called from the kitchen area.

"Not mine," David whispered.

Soon after, two bowls of steaming dumplings and a bottle of vinegar were on the table. Paul was about to start eating when Gao Gao folded her hands, closed her eyes, lowered her head and started to pray:

Every good thing
Everything we have
comes, O God, from You
Thanks be to You for all this
Come, Jesus Christ, be our guest
and bless what you have given us.

She paused for a moment, opened her eyes, looked round at them and smiled. "Bon appetit."

"I'm going to eat very quickly now," David announced. "Then I'm going to go to bed very quickly. And tomorrow morning I'll get up quickly and eat very quickly."

"Why don't you take your time?" Christine wondered.

"Because I'm now doing everything very quickly. Then we'll be at home more quickly."

A smile flitted across Da Lin's face.

"Did you make the dumplings yourself, Mrs. Qian?" Paul asked. "They're delicious."

"Call me Gao Gao," she replied with her mouth full. "I don't make anything myself. I hate cooking."

"Where do you buy your food then, Mrs. Qian, I mean, Gao Gao? All the shops we saw were closed."

"I only buy things online, and frozen, if possible. Everything is delivered to me. I have croissants and pain au chocolat for breakfast if you like."

"Pain au chocolat?" Paul repeated.

"Yes, supposedly baked fresh in Paris, frozen immediately, and flown to China. I don't believe it, but they really taste as though they were from a boulangerie."

"That sounds good."

"I'd like to ask something," Christine asked cautiously.

"I'm listening . . ."

"What's going on with this town?"

"You mean the empty streets?"

"Yes."

"Isn't it wonderful? No traffic. No jams. The air is good."

"Doesn't anyone live here?"

"No. Hongyang New Town is a ghost town." Turning to the children, she added, "You mustn't be frightened. It's not haunted."

"There aren't any ghosts in a ghost town?" David asked, for reassurance.

"No."

"What's a ghost town then?" He was clearly confused.

"A town in which there are many, many homes, but only very few people."

"But why are the homes empty?"

Gao Gao smiled. "You're a clever boy. But I'm not a clever woman, so I can't answer your question."

"How many people live here?" Christine asked.

"The town has been planned and built for nearly a million people. How many people really live here? Maybe fifty thousand. Probably fewer."

Gao Gao's gaze wandered to Da Lin. "You there, are you always so quiet?"

Paul could see Christine shifting uncomfortably from side to side on her seat. They had not discussed either with Da Lin or between themselves how they would introduce him. At Pastor Lee's he had simply declared that Da Lin was his son without much thought. What should they say if he contradicted them on that now?

Da Lin's intense gaze lay on Gao Gao for a moment, but in the end he merely nodded. Paul hoped she would not feel annoyed by his silence.

"He is the quieter of the two," Christine said.

David and Da Lin yawned almost in unison.

"The children are tired. I'll show you where you can sleep."

Gao Gao got up to lead them to two rooms. The doors opened only halfway, and with difficulty. Both rooms were piled to the ceiling with boxes and packages. The cartons even blocked part of the windows. Paul pushed some of the piles aside to find a double bed in each room.

Christine said that she wanted to sleep with David in one of the rooms. Paul could share the other one with Da Lin. It was a sensible arrangement, but Paul still felt stung by how firmly Christine made the decision without discussing it with him beforehand.

Da Lin fell asleep in minutes. Paul gave his son a goodnight kiss. Christine had disappeared into the bathroom.

He wanted to go to her, but the door was locked. He knocked hesitantly.

"Christine?"

"Yes?"

"Open the door."

"Why?"

What kind of question was that? It hurt him to have to answer it. "Because I want to see you."

He heard her moving around in the bathroom.

"Christine?"

"Yes."

"I want to talk to you."

"Not now, Paul. I'm too tired. Tomorrow."

He knocked one more time.

It sounded as though she had turned the shower on.

III

Christine closed her eyes and ignored Paul when he knocked again. She was tired. She was exhausted. She did not feel like talking. Not tonight and not tomorrow either. There was nothing to say or, at least, nothing that she could put into words at the moment. Later, when they were safe. Perhaps.

Warm water ran down her face, over her shoulders, her breasts and her stomach. She turned the temperature up, until her skin was burning and her shoulders were turning red. The bathroom filled with steam.

This was the first time she had taken a shower since she had left Hong Kong more than a week ago.

There were half a dozen bottles of shower gel on the ledge, and just as many bottles of shampoo and conditioner. She picked up a bottle and sniffed it. Then a second one. Lavender. She used something like this in Hong Kong. The familiarity, if only of the smell, did her good.

She washed her hair thoroughly and spread shower gel over her body a second and a third time. As though the events of the past few days were a layer of dirt that she could wash herself free of if she only used enough soap.

Christine had a flicker of feeling safe for the first time since they had fled Shi. She couldn't say why, but she felt protected by this woman with her big laugh, in this untidy, chaotic flat full of boxes and cartons. As long as they were with her, no one would find them. Paul had said that Beijing was no more than a day's journey away from here. Or a night's journey. Gao Gao surely must have a car. With her help it might be possible to get to the US embassy.

She thought about Josh and her mother. About their house and their beautiful garden on Lamma. They would be back there soon. Enjoying the mild autumn days. The peace. The security.

Playing with David in a sandpit. Watching butterflies. The time in China would seem like a bad dream and very far away indeed. She would get up first in the morning, as usual, have a shower and get ready. She would kiss both of them goodbye while they were still asleep, and take the ferry to Central. And in the early evening she would return and Paul and David would be standing at the pier waiting for her.

Everything would be the same as it had been before.

Christine reached for a towel and wiped the mist from the mirror. She got a shock when she saw herself. She had grown even paler and must have lost several pounds while on the run. Her face looked thinner and the faint lines around her mouth and eyes were much deeper. Her pelvic bones stuck out like a starving person's. Her legs, which had always been thin, were now even thinner and less shapely. As if she was standing on two sticks. Her breasts had lost all pertness. They looked fragile and vulnerable. How weak she was. How quickly her body could waste away. Christine crossed her arms over her chest as though she wanted to hold herself or protect herself from something. The thought of Paul seeing her in this state was unpleasant, almost repellent.

The longer she looked in the mirror, the more unbearable she found the sight. She took a bath towel and wrapped herself in it.

The fear returned, but it was no longer the same. In addition to the specific fear that her child would be taken from her came a general panic. She could not say exactly what it related to. The feeling that something had gone off track and was lost forever, never to be retrieved. The deep-rooted belief that things would turn out all right in the end was gone. They had robbed her of that feeling once before, when her father died and she had escaped from China. Back then she had been overcome by a deep mistrust and fear of people. She had freed herself of that feeling only through great effort and an agonizing struggle. It had taken many years before she finally felt the ground beneath her feet again. Paul had been a huge help with that. And now? She had retreated into the bathroom alone and been happy the door could be locked. She did not want to see him. She did not want to be touched by him. Christine felt the distance between them growing, and it only made everything worse. She needed him. She longed for him. For his sense of humor. His strength. His warmth.

She did not feel any of these things now. He felt more and more like a stranger to her with each passing day. Even in his appearance. He had a full gray beard now. He had lost weight and his face had grown thin. He looked years older.

Her feelings did not obey her any longer. Her life was betraying her.

She was losing control over herself.

Or had she ever had it? Had that belief just been an illusion?

After hesitating a little, Paul went back to the living room, where the strong smell of men's cologne still hung in the air. He did not want to go and lie down awake and alone next to the sleeping Da Lin just yet.

Gao Gao sat rapt in front of the biggest television he had ever seen. She paid no notice to her guest. On a shopping channel, a man was rhapsodizing about the advantages of a brand new generation of rice cookers.

Paul went to the window and looked out into the darkness. He could see the outlines of buildings opposite, but there were lights on behind only a few windows.

He was lonely and helpless. And furious.

He had not deliberately got their child kidnapped. He was not suffering any less from this situation than Christine was. Her behavior was only making the situation worse. For all of them. She was still turning her back on him, and he did not know how he could reach her. That made him feel afraid. In the high-rise building opposite, a half-naked man appeared at the window of one of the few lighted apartments and stared across curiously. Paul took a step back and turned around.

Gao Gao was still fiddling with the remote control. On the couch next to her were a tablet and half a dozen credit cards that she was clearly using in turn for her purchases.

Paul went to the other end of the room, where there was a white Steinway grand piano. Among the many plush toys on it, he found the photo of a young woman with an older man by her side. They were standing on the Tsim Sha Tsui harbor promenade in Hong Kong. The woman was slim and beautiful. She was wearing a figure-hugging black dress and a pearl necklace. Her hair was pinned up and she had a Prada handbag in one hand. Her companion also looked impressive. He had a

Louis Vuitton shopping bag hanging from his shoulder. She had her arm in his and both of them were smiling at the camera, proudly and confidently.

He picked the photo up and looked at it for a long time.

"My father and I."

Paul started. He had not heard her coming up behind him.

"It's a lovely photo."

She took it from his hand and put it back on the grand piano. "Do you go to Hong Kong often?"

"I used to."

"Now no longer?"

"No."

"Why not?"

She looked at him for a moment. "You're a curious person."

"I don't mean to be impolite," he said apologetically. "I only ask because we live on Lamma."

"The island without cars and with lots of seafood restaurants?"

Paul had to laugh. "Yes."

"Is it boring there?"

"It depends on what you're looking for. We don't find it so. When was the photo taken?"

"That was three years ago."

He thought he had misheard her. The woman in the photo looked ten years younger and was at least four stones lighter.

A sad smile flitted across Gao Gao's face, as though she could tell what he was thinking.

"Does your father live in Hong Kong?"

"No. He's dead."

Paul swallowed. "I'm sorry."

They stood opposite each other in silence. He stroked a plush toy rabbit in embarrassment and felt a desperate need for a drink. "Do you have any whiskey, by any chance?"

"Yes. Would you like one? I also have French red wine. Or champagne?"

"Will you also have something?"

She hesitated for only a moment. "A glass of champagne. Why not?"

She fetched the champagne from the fridge and put glasses and a bottle of whiskey on the table. "Ice?"

"No, thank you."

He opened the bottle, poured her a glass, and put the champagne back in the fridge. When he returned, she had poured him a generous measure of whiskey. They sat down, and Gao Gao turned the TV off.

Paul took his glass. "Thank you very much."

They clinked glasses and both of them took a big sip.

"What's the smell?"

She took a couple of deep breaths through her nose. "What do you mean?"

"A strong men's perfume."

"I don't smell anything," she said shortly.

V

Gao Gao seldom drank alcohol, and she felt the effect of the champagne from the first sip. A comforting warmth spread through her body. Just like before.

Her thoughts turned to her father.

He had brought her up with the knowledge that there was one person to whom she meant more than everything else in the world. That had been both a blessing and a curse.

Her mother had given her life and paid for it with her own.

Her father had been father and mother to her. He had never married again and had been discreet with his lovers. She had never seen even one of them.

For that she was grateful to him.

She took a second sip of champagne. Oh, this outrageous, seductive lightness of being. If only it could last forever.

Images passed through her mind's eye. Old black and white photos showing a little Gao Gao with the housekeeper and the nanny.

They had lived in a detached house in a compound for senior party cadres and military personnel. Walls had separated them from the world outside. Policemen had kept watch over the entrance. And the exit. There had not been many children there and the days had been long and dull, despite all the household staff.

Her father had worked a great deal, but had made an effort to be at home on time every evening. After having dinner together, he read to her, and put her to bed. As soon as she was asleep, so she was later told, he drove back to the office and chaired meetings or trained party cadres.

Even when he rose higher and higher in the party, he still kept to the evening routine with her.

She thought about the Sundays, which had been just for them, and which had become a fixed ritual, unchanged for years.

When she thought about it, if there was anything in her child-hood she missed, it was the tender intimacy of those Sundays.

They had risen early and walked to the market without having any breakfast before leaving. There, they had eaten pan-cakes or warm pork buns, and bought groceries. At home, they had spread everything out in the kitchen. Her father had explained the various kitchen utensils to her and showed her how to sharpen a knife, section a chicken, gut a fish, how to tell fresh vegetables apart, and when cooked winter melon and aubergine had reached the right consistency. They had made the dough for her favorite food, dumplings, and experimented almost every week with new fillings for them. The smell of lightly browned garlic. Of fried pork belly. A fine line between happiness and great grief.

"Would you like more champagne?"

Her glass was empty. So was his.

She nodded.

Paul got up to fetch the bottle.

Gao Gao slid back into the past. She saw herself laying the table for four, five, sometimes even six people, depending on who was coming. Gao Gao had made the decisions on how many guests came and who they were. They had greeted the guests at the door together and led them to the table. There, her father had started the conversation. While they ate, they had had lively conversations with his daughter's teachers, her favorite actresses, the neighbors, or the market stall woman who often gave her a sweet bun. Her father played all the roles with gusto, putting on different voices, and sometimes even changing seats, making Gao Gao laugh till she cried.

She remembered those meals as the funniest and most enjoyable dinners of her life, without any of those people ever having been in the house.

The feeling that she could rely on him no matter what happened.

'Xiǎo Chángjǐnglù', my little giraffe, had been his pet name for her, because she had not stopped growing. By sixteen she had grown taller than the tallest of her classmates.

When she got it into her head that she wanted to be a ballet dancer, he arranged for her to have dance lessons, even though aspiring to become a prima ballerina was not at all a suitable ambition for the daughter of an ambitious senior party cadre.

He was cold and distant to her first boyfriend. He was more well disposed to the second one. He took only a passing interest in all the later ones. As though he knew that it would never get serious with any of them.

Perhaps everything would have turned out differently if they had not set up a company to do business together. It had been his suggestion. China was going through a boom-time – everyone was taking what they could get, and as much as they could get. It was a gold rush, and anyone who hesitated or held back would suffer the consequences. Almost every senior party official in every province was granting privileges to their friends and families or was using front men to build personal corporate empires. Why should they be any different?

They made sure that her father stayed in the background. The mere mention of his name was enough, and if there were any problems, a phone call from him sufficed.

She got everything she wanted at the price she wanted. Land. Property. Building permits. Shares in companies. All her companies prospered. She made profits on everything she bought and everything she invested in. It was as though she had a license to print money.

Gao Gao had been unperturbed by this. "Let some people get rich first," Deng Xiaoping had said.

On their travels, Gao Gao and her father had of course booked separate rooms, yet they had often been taken for a couple. An older man and his young and beautiful lover. He had been uneasy about this at first, but later his pride in the compliments his daughter was receiving outweighed his discomfort. She was amused by it all.

Father and daughter. They had been very close.

But never closer than that.

———

"How long have you been living in this ghost town?"

His question brought her back to the present. The feeling of lightness dissipated. Dark clouds were approaching from the horizon instead. Gao Gao had another large mouthful of champagne. Perhaps that would delay their arrival a little.

"Are you really interested, or are you asking out of politeness?"

He replied with a cryptic smile.

"I'm not interested in small talk," she added.

"Neither am I," he said.

His glass was empty once more. "Do you always drink so quickly?"

"No."

She picked up the bottle and he nodded. She poured him another large whiskey.

"I seldom drink. But sometimes it helps."

"Only for a while," she said, and smiled.

"Anyway," he said, smiling back, "why do you buy so much stuff that you don't need?"

"Who decides what I need and what I don't?"

"Lots of it is simply lying around your flat in its packaging, still unopened.

She shrugged. "I enjoy it. I'm killing time."

"That's banned in some countries."

"What is? Shopping?"

"No. Killing time."

Was he being serious or was he pulling her leg? "Why?"

"Because it's so precious. We have so little of it."

She liked his sense of humor. "If you don't mind me asking, why do you all need somewhere to stay so urgently?"

He hesitated before replying, but held her gaze. His sad eyes reminded her of her father in the final months of his life.

"You don't have to tell me if you don't want to. You can stay as long as you like."

He lifted his glass in her direction and took a large gulp of whiskey before telling her his story. She believed every word. They wanted the child as a present. Why not? Everything had become a commodity, everything could be bought. Careers. Contracts. Permits. Friendships. Women. Why not a four-year-old child? Her father had told her about Chen before. They had often met at Party conferences. He said Chen was the most unscrupulous and power-obsessed of the Party cadres that he had ever met. He had sounded quite admiring of him. The children of the Party officials had grown used to getting what they wanted. She was one of them herself, so she knew that all too well. And who knows? If she had been a little luckier, or unluckier, she would still be one today.

She had seen the end coming. Not very long before it came, but all the clearer for it. Dozens of Party cadres in the neighboring provinces had been arrested in the course of Beijing's latest anti-corruption campaign. Was it time to sell some of her shares? Should she try harder to get an American or an Australian passport? Or try to get Singapore citizenship, even though, by comparison, it held less promise of protection in case of an emergency? Her father had always shunned the idea. It wouldn't look good for someone high up in the Party to be applying for dual citizenship elsewhere.

Suicide. That was the Party's official explanation. And it was the truth, for once.

Gao Gao had seen it coming and yet not known how she could have stopped it. It had been his life and he had had the right to end it the way he wanted to and when he wanted to.

Her father had stood up during a meeting of the most senior Party committee in the province and excused himself. He had something urgent to attend to and would be back in a few minutes. He had calmly walked up the stairs to the top floor, climbed onto the roof and jumped off it into the abyss. They said he had died on impact.

He had not left a farewell letter. Not that it had been necessary. What could he have said to her that she did not already know? This was his final and greatest gift to her, and he was paying for it with his life. The family members of Party officials who committed suicide were, with rare exceptions, spared further investigations into corruption.

A few weeks after his death she had visited the place where he had ended his life. She climbed the stairs one by one, overcame the protests of the building manager who unlocked the door for her, went to the very edge of the roof, stood with the tips of her toes over it, and looked down. Seven stories down. Seven, of all numbers. His lucky number; his unlucky number. Gao Gao had been born on the seventh of July and had made him a widower on the same day.

She saw the broken branches of the bushes in front of the building. Looking from here, the outline of his body could still be made out.

Should she jump? Did she want to jump? Seconds passed. Just a small step. Simply shift her weight forward and she would be together with him again. Gao Gao did not know what stopped her in the end. She had no husband and no children. The only person she would really miss had gone before her.

One week later, an article in the Party newspaper included a statement that the investigations would be extended to include the family of the Party Secretary. She got the message. The next day she sold her complete portfolio of stocks to the son of her father's successor. He had made her an offer that she could not refuse. It was under half the actual value but it came with a promise from his father that the authorities would refrain from any investigations into her affairs.

A few hours after the contracts had been signed, she had been cleaning out her office when she had broken down completely. Her old life had ended the way it had begun.

With the death of a parent.

———

Paul got up. He swayed a little on his feet, and held on to the armrest to steady himself. "I have to go to bed."

She nodded. "I still have to buy two rice cookers."

He disappeared into his bedroom and she turned the TV on again, spreading her credit cards out before her.

The bottle was empty. The champagne was no longer having any effect. The black clouds were advancing remorselessly and had almost reached her. The two rice cookers were quickly bought. She added a twelve-piece sushi master's knife set from Japan and eighteen red wine glasses. Express delivery.

She had used the wrong expression, she thought. It was not about killing time. It was about distracting herself. Some memories were too painful to bear without numbing herself.

A few weeks had passed between the end of her first life and the start of her second. She had spent the first two of those weeks in intensive care at People's Hospital Number 1. Her memories of that time were vague. A green curtain. Lots of tubes. Machines that had hummed at regular intervals or emitted frightening beeps. A nurse who had smelled of alcohol. Cramps. Pains in her lower body. Concerned faces by her bed.

When she read her medical records later, she learned that the doctors had practically given up on her. Her survival was a near miracle. She had been on the verge of multiple organ failure. Her body had been gradually switching off its functions, like someone going from room to room in a house turning off the lights. At the same time, her immune system had started to attack itself. The doctors could not explain the cause of this. They thought it might be an allergic reaction or a result of poisoning. Gao Gao knew better.

A young assistant doctor from Hubei province developed a particular interest in her puzzling case. He sat by her bed often, studied the results of her medical examinations and laboratory tests, and talked to her. She did not understand much of what he said, but his friendly, bright voice did her good.

At some point the nurses disconnected her from most of the machines and wheeled her into a private room. She did not know if it was a room to die in or to survive in.

It was a horrible room: small, with a barred window looking onto a courtyard that only got a little sunlight in the late afternoon. She did not have any visitors. Who would come? Her friends had turned their backs on her and after her grandmother had died her family had consisted only of her and her father, who was also her mother. Days passed in which she did not exchange a word with a single person apart from a few pleasantries with the nurses.

With the passing of time, she felt smaller and smaller and more and more helpless, as if she had been transformed back into the child sitting on a wall waiting for her father. But this time her silent fear had come true: he was not coming.

He had abandoned her.

For the first time since her childhood, she longed for her mother. She had no memory of her, of course not. No voice, no smell as a connection to her. How could someone miss a person they had never known? And yet. It was a deep, piercing pain that she thought had gone long ago.

She, too, had abandoned her.

She had stood on that roof and looked down. She could have died at the same spot but she had lacked the courage to make that one final step. What had actually stopped her from ending this desperate, lonely life? Gao Gao had cursed herself for her cowardice then, but now there were many days when she felt glad about it.

There was time enough for her to be dead.

VI

Da Lin did not feel like talking. The fat woman talked all day anyway. And when she was quiet Paul and Christine argued. Just like his parents used to. And the old couple in the house next door. Sometimes their voices had been so loud he had heard them in his house. Like the market traders arguing with their customers too. Why were grown-ups always fighting?

Christine had disappeared into her room. That was a shame. He would have liked to talk to her a little. Maybe she knew how his grandfather was. Or how long they had to stay here. Or if Paul had already called his mother and she was waiting for him. But Christine had a headache.

Paul too. He sat in an armchair and kept his eyes closed most of the time.

The fat woman had sat down in front of a TV. It was showing a movie about a bear who liked eating honey, and his friends. But the animals were not real animals, only drawings. David sat next to him, and whenever he felt frightened, he moved closer to him and took his hand. He did that often. Da Lin told him that the animals were drawings and that someone had just made up a story about them. But that didn't help. David was still frightened.

Time passed agonizingly slowly. There was nothing to do except watch TV. The woman wanted to play a card game with them but David did not understand the rules, so they decided to leave it.

He missed his grandfather. The dog. Even the chickens. It was horribly warm in the flat and you couldn't even open the window. And there was a funny smell.

Against one wall in the living room was a big glass box with water, plants, and two fish in it: one red and one white. He spent some time watching them swim from one side to another looking at him stupidly. But that became boring too.

Da Lin thought about the policeman. He simply couldn't get him out of his head. The way he lay motionless in the courtyard, with blooding flowing from his head. Like a rat. He had taken aim at him with his catapult and let go. But when the man fell to the ground, Da Lin had been surprised. How could such a small stone fell such a big man? But it was his own fault. If he had not broken Papa's cue and even laughed while doing it, nothing would have happened to him. It served him right. Was he still in hospital? Maybe he would never speak again. Like the old woman in the village. Something had burst in her head and since then she could not walk but had to be carried by her children. And when she spoke no one understood her. Da Lin thought about whether that made him feel sorry. A little; but then not really. It was strange. He had taken precise aim; he had wanted to hit the man, but he still felt that he hadn't intended to.

VII

He had not felt so lonely since Justin had died. When he had crept into bed with Christine and David that morning, she had got up and disappeared into the bathroom. She said he stank of whiskey. She avoided his gaze at breakfast. She had not returned his quick goodbye kiss. The more she withdrew from him, the less he could imagine them finding their way back to each other in Hong Kong. He knew that from his first marriage. Back then, during Justin's illness and before he died, there had also come a point when he and Meredith had grown so distant from each other that Paul had known they would never draw together again. It was over, no matter whether their son survived or not.

He was glad when Christine and Gao Gao left the apartment for a couple of hours.

Gao Gao had given him the phone number of a neighbor on the twenty-second floor before they left. If they got bored they could call him. Mr. Zhou was a bit crazy but quite harmless. He had something that the children were sure to be interested in.

Paul wanted to play a game with the boys first. Da Lin could not think of anything that he would enjoy. David wanted to play hide-and-seek. But when Da Lin found him quickly every time, he didn't want to play any more.

Paul suggested they play rodeo riders. He bent down on all fours. Da Lin climbed on his back. Paul bucked vigorously and Da Lin slid off and fell on his elbows. Now he didn't want to play anything any more. He crouched on the floor by the window and looked out. Paul propped his son on his back and crawled around the living room. David knew this game and held on tight to his father's hair. They galloped round until Paul's back hurt.

After half an hour, he called the neighbor.

———

Mr. Zhou was a short elderly man with gray hair that almost reached his shoulders. He was very pleased to have unexpected visitors. The three rooms of his flat were stacked with aquariums up to the ceiling. Some of them were as large as bathtubs while others were as small as shoe boxes; most of them were somewhere in between. There must have been hundreds of them. Swimming in them were fish of all shapes, sizes, and colors. The gurgle and pop of water and the sonorous hum of the many pumps filled the rooms. The air was warm and humid, and smelled of stagnant water. David and Da Lin stood still, not knowing where to look first.

"Would you like to feed the fishes?" Zhou asked.

The two boys nodded.

Zhou gave them small tins of fish food and showed them exactly what they had to do. He helped them with the first couple of aquariums, and when he saw that they were following his instructions precisely, he turned back to Paul.

"Would you like some tea?"

"Yes, please."

They went to the kitchen. A pile of water pumps, filters, motors, and replacement parts was piled up under the table. The fridge was crowned with a terrarium with two small tortoises in it and there was another one on the floor for salamanders and geckos. Zhou took two cups from a cupboard and poured the tea.

"Why do you have so many fish?" Paul asked, somewhat absently. He had never been very interested in aquariums.

"I actually wanted to sell them," Zhou said. "But I couldn't bear to part with them. Living creatures shouldn't be bought and sold." After a brief pause, he added, "You don't care much for aquariums, do you?"

"How do you know?"

"I can see it." Zhou smiled.

They drank their tea in silence.

"Do you live here on your own?"

"Yes. I get along better with fish than with people."

Paul gave him a questioning look.

"I can't read what's in people's hearts. They say something and do the opposite. I just don't understand it."

"Fish are quieter. That much is true." Paul had to smile at his own comment.

Zhou did not react, however. "You have two lovely children. Mine think I'm a loser," he said in a serious tone.

"Why?"

"Because I don't have anything other than a few hundred fish. The flat belongs to my son." He poured more tea for Paul and checked on the two boys briefly. They were entirely focused on feeding the fish. "But I live exactly the life that I want to. It's my decision. I'm a free person. My children don't understand that. They say I should work more. I ask them, why? They say, so that I will have more money and can enjoy life. I say, I enjoy my life. They don't understand me."

Paul nodded. He did not feel like having an intense conversation. He just wanted some distraction for himself and the children.

"Have you known Gao Gao for long?"

"Since she moved in here. And you?"

"No. She's a friend of a friend."

"Then be careful." When Paul did not react, he added, "Gao Gao cannot be trusted."

Paul ignored this too. He looked through the open door at a silver-gray fish in a large glass tank that was swimming behind a small fish. It was following the other fish as it criss-crossed through the water, past climbing plants and rocks. Suddenly, it made a jerky movement with its tail, shot forward, and the small fish disappeared into its mouth.

"Did you hear me?" Zhou asked, unperturbed. "She is very well connected."

Paul nodded. He wondered if he should ask Zhou what he meant. What kind of connections? Why should she want to harm them? To what end? He did not want to know more. They had no choice but to trust her, and if his intuition could be trusted, they had nothing to fear from this woman who was obsessed with shopping.

VIII

Come with me! It was more like an order than an invitation.

Christine was undecided. Leaving the flat meant putting herself in danger. Yet she also longed for distraction.

Gao Gao tried to dispel her doubts. They would be in her car driving from one underground parking garage to another and be back in two or three hours at most. She would not see anyone on the way.

And she knew everyone who attended the service in Pastor Lee's flat. All of them would have been willing to accommodate Christine and her family if they had had the space. She could vouch for every one of them. They belonged to an underground church, and they met in secret every Sunday. This showed how little they had to do with officialdom in China. Apart from that, they were Christians. It was part of their faith to help strangers in need. In the end we are all brothers and sisters. Fellow people. Creations of the same God. One big family.

It was an outing without risk. Christine would have other things to think about. It would do her good, just as Gao Gao herself always felt better for it.

Paul encouraged her to go. He wanted to stay in the flat and play games with the children.

————

The lift went straight down to the underground parking garage. For a building that was almost unoccupied, it was surprisingly full. Christine noticed several large Mercedes saloons, Audis, Porsches, and even a Bentley. "Why are there so many cars parked in the garage?" she asked. "I thought hardly anyone lived here."

"These are the third or fourth cars of the flat-owners," Gao

Gao said, grinning. "They're hiding them here. No one has to know how many cars a person has."

She led the way to a small van. When Christine opened the door, two boxes and a shopping bag fell out. Gao Gao had to clear the passenger seat before she could get in.

The light in the garage went out but came back on again immediately. They heard voices, and saw two men, one older and one younger, walking towards their vehicle. Gao Gao greeted them in a friendly manner as they walked past. They got into a silver-gray Mercedes sports car and sat in it.

Christine hurriedly closed her door.

"Don't worry," Gao Gao said. "That's the gay couple from the fourteenth floor. They sometimes sit in their new Mercedes for hours without driving it."

"Why do they do that?"

"No idea. Maybe they don't want to get it dirty."

Gao Gao was a brisk driver. The tires squealed at every turn in the parking garage and she drove up the ramp at full speed.

Christine gripped the handle above her door with both hands. "We're going to a church service at Pastor Lee's, aren't we?" she asked once more, to make sure.

"Yes."

"Did your parents believe in God?"

The thought amused Gao Gao. "No. Maybe my father did when he was young. His god was called Mao. Why do you ask?"

"I was just wondering why you go to church."

"That's a long story."

They stopped at a red light at an empty crossing.

"My father died three years ago. After that, I was very ill, and it wasn't clear if I would survive. A young doctor in the hospital told me about Jesus Christ properly for the first time. I listened to him only because I did not want him to go away. I was alone, and I liked his voice. At some point his strange stories began to interest me. A god who had created the world and who sent his son to earth as a sacrifice for the love of his people?"

They drove through the streets of the ghost town, which was as deserted on this Sunday morning as it had been when they arrived.

"The longer I listened to the doctor, the more I was drawn into his stories. He claimed that everything was connected. My mother's early death. My lonely childhood. The emptiness that I had often felt even as a teenager. The gold rush. The way I frittered money away on bags, shoes, and clothes. Everything was His will. He had been testing me, harshly and severely. He had led me into temptation and saved me in the end. Now he would free me."

Gao Gao stepped on the accelerator in order not to have to stop at the next red light. She almost ran over a meandering cat in the process.

"I didn't believe him," she said. "Who was He? Was there any proof He existed? If He did, why had He taken little Gao Gao's mother away from her? Where was He when my father leapt to his death? Why did He allow so much misery and sorrow in the world if He could give people full bellies and make them happy?"

"And did the doctor have an answer?" Christine asked in a skeptical tone.

"Always the same one: if you believed in Him, everything made sense, even if it sometimes remained hidden to humankind. If I was prepared to follow Him, he would give me a comfort I had not known before: a feeling of security. I would be raised up into a family, protected by a Father who would never leave me, no matter where I went or what I did. I just had to trust Him. Let myself go. Stop doubting. Believe. I couldn't resist this temptation."

Gao Gao turned into a parking garage. "And you?" she asked. "Are you religious?"

"No," Christine said. "I think I've never been to a church service. I went into St John's Cathedral in Hong Kong once. But only because it was raining so hard that I had to take shelter somewhere."

Gao Gao laughed. "Have you never been interested in it?"

"No. Gods and religions have never played any role in my life. Neither in my childhood nor in my marriage later, or in my everyday life with Paul. I don't give it any thought. I'm just superstitious."

"Do you go to see fortune tellers?"

"Yes of course. I believe in lucky and unlucky numbers. And in feng shui. There's a red ribbon hanging from David's bed that is meant to protect him. Next to the front door of my house I have set up a small altar, where I regularly make offerings of fresh fruit and joss sticks to appease the household spirits. I don't know if it helps, but I thought it couldn't hurt. My mother always says that there are five religions in China: Confucianism, Taoism, Buddhism, Christianity and Pragmatism. The last one is her favorite, and the most widespread one."

Gao Gao laughed again. "She's probably right."

———

The hallway in the pastor's flat smelled of roast meat. She heard a babble of voices through the open door. Young people, old people, and even families with small children had turned up.

Women and men were preparing lunch together in the kitchen. Gao Gao introduced her to a few people, who were immediately curious about her. Did she go to church in Hong Kong? No? A moment's unease. All the better that she found her way to God here with them, then. It was never too late. Once He had revealed himself to her, there was no going back; she would see.

It was only Pastor Lee who was no friendlier on seeing her again. He greeted her briefly, pressed a Bible into everyone's hands, and turned away.

Foldable chairs were tightly packed together in the living room. They sat down in the second row. Two young men, one with a guitar and the other with a violin, went to the front and started singing and playing. A mobile phone rang. Then another one. The young woman sitting next to Christine turned to her and hugged her. "God bless you."

Gao Gao had been right: the openness and warmth with which these people treated her did her good.

Years ago, Christine had asked Paul what he believed in. He had taken a long time to give her a satisfactory answer. When he held his newborn son in his arms for the first time, he said that he had found the answer. He believed in the power that was in this little heart. In every heart. In hope. In promises. In magic. He believed in the greatness, the tenderness, and the uniqueness that was within every living being. In the selfless love that it was possible to give. It was quite simply a straightforward belief in humankind: in love and in life, with all its tragedy and beauty.

His words had moved her then. She had written them down some time after he said them. His was a world view that trusted people, that believed in the good, and that did not include a god or a higher power. That spoke to her. We create peace ourselves. We create happiness ourselves. We create meaning ourselves.

Now she felt doubtful. Had there not been many bad things in her life? Her own brother had betrayed their father and driven him to his death. Destroyed her family. A whole country of people had been set loose on each other and had sunk into a bloody orgy of lies and betrayal, murder and bloodshed.

Had she not experienced too much sorrow and senseless pain to believe in goodness? Did she need to encounter a spoilt and crazed son of a senior Communist Party official who wanted to give her child to his girlfriend as a present to clearly see the evil in humankind? She had refused to see it for too long.

It had been simpler that way.

———

Pastor Lee stepped forward, stood behind a pulpit and spread his arms out. The congregation fell silent.

"Hallelujah," he said.

"Hallelujah," the believers chorused in reply.

"Hallelujah!" he said again, louder.

"Hallelujah!" echoed the enthusiastic response.

Everything seemed strange to her. Singing together. Praying together. The conviction with which the prayers were spoken. The passionate sermon. The pastor whispered, hissed, and screamed. Some words he spat out at them, others were delivered in a tone of awe, like precious things. He castigated the evils of the world in a long tirade. Sin found a home everywhere. In every one of us. Every beat of the human heart is evil from the start.

But there was salvation.

And the savior had a name. Let us praise him. Hallelujah.

Lord, forgive us for our sins, as we forgive those who have sinned against us.

Christine started to feel unwell. She felt very hot, and the air was stale. Her shoulders were tense. She slid from side to side on her seat and looked around her. The congregation was lapping every word up. Many of them had their eyes closed and heads bowed.

Lee told ever more bloody tales of fratricide and sacrifices from the beginning of mankind. She listened attentively, but felt that this was getting too much for her. The condemnation of sin. The demonization of humankind. The fury with which he spoke.

She would have liked to get up and go, but she didn't dare to. The pastor kept preaching.

And lead us not into temptation, but deliver us from evil. For yours is the kingdom, the power, and the glory for ever. Amen.

Christine could no longer stand it. She got up and made her way through the rows of chairs. The pastor cast her a disapproving look. It was just as warm and humid in the hallway and in the kitchen.

She sat on the stairs outside the flat. It was cool and quiet there. After a few minutes Gao Gao came to stand behind her. "What's wrong?"

"I'm sorry. I wasn't feeling well. I'm better now," she lied.

Gao Gao brought her a glass of water and sat down next to her on the stairs.

"Can I do anything to help?"

"I just suddenly found it . . ." Christine searched for the right word. "Too cramped. Too many people. I'm sorry if I offended anyone."

"No problem." The sound of the believers singing loudly came from the flat. "We're lucky there aren't any neighbors."

Christine thought about Paul and the children. About the US embassy and the security it represented. She just wanted to get away. "How far is it from here to Beijing?"

"About eight hours by car. Depends on the traffic."

Christine didn't dare to say what was in her head. Did she dare to ask such a thing?

"I know what you're thinking," Gao Gao said. "Your husband told me everything. I spent all night thinking about whether to drive you there."

She paused for a long time. "To be honest, it's too much of a risk for me. If Chen's son wants your child at any cost, he will do anything. You're safe with me in the flat. I don't know how he would ever find you here. But everything would change as soon as you were on your way to Beijing. I would prefer your friend to find another option. Can you understand that?"

Christine nodded. She had no right to expect more help. Would she do any different if she were in Gao Gao's position? Probably not. But she was still disappointed. Where did people draw the line in their willingness to help others? What sacrifices was a Christian prepared to make to help strangers in need? We are all brothers and sisters, she had said. Fellow human beings. Creations of the same God. One big family. Did that not count any longer?

What would Gao Gao do if they heard nothing more from Zhang because he had already been arrested? What would she do with them then? Kick them out of her flat? Tell the police about them, because the risk of keeping them under her roof had become too great? A wave of suspicion rose in Christine. It was a sickness that she had been infected with in China, she thought. A highly infectious virus that she now carried within her, and which took every opportunity to break out.

IX

Of course she could use the telephone. And yes, to Hong Kong too, of course. Wherever she wanted, as long as she needed.

Her mother did not answer the telephone. She was probably out with friends having dim sum or playing mahjong. Christine left a message and apologized for her long silence. Her mobile phone was out of order, she said, and she had made a last-minute decision to extend her trip and travel to Beijing and Shanghai as well. They were all well and would be back in the next few weeks.

Christine wondered if she should also call Josh in Australia. Since he had gone to Sydney three months ago to study architecture at university they had spoken on the phone regularly, often several times a week, if only for a few minutes each time. He mostly had questions on practical matters or needed her help. He must have tried to contact her and be getting worried.

Yes, fine to call Sydney, Gao Gao yelled from the kitchen. No problem.

His voice. It had been a good idea to phone him.

"Where are you, Mama?" He sounded worried.

"My mobile phone is broken. We're still in China." Her voice broke. When she had not spoken to him for some time, the feeling of missing him hit her even more strongly.

"How are you, darling?"

"Fine."

"How's your course?"

"Also fine."

"What are you doing right now?"

"Studying."

Josh was not a talkative person, and even less so on the telephone. He was like his father in that respect, Christine thought. They had spent a large part of their marriage in silence.

Exchanged a few words about the day over dinner and turned on the television after that.

Later on, the television had been on even during dinner.

"Can you transfer me some money?"

"Again? What for?"

"The course material is much more expensive than we thought."

"How much?"

"I don't know."

"Will five hundred Hong Kong dollars be enough?"

"Yes."

"I'll do it once we're back in Hong Kong."

"Thanks."

"Have you called Grandma?"

"No. Should I?"

"I'm sure she'd be glad to hear from you."

They fell silent. Christine was relieved that he wasn't asking any questions. She did not want to lie. Yet she felt annoyed that he didn't ask how they were. What they were doing. Whether his little brother missed him.

"When will you be back in Hong Kong?"

"Next week. We extended our trip."

He didn't say anything. As though it was the most normal thing in the world for them to stay in China for two weeks rather than two days. He probably had no interest in their trip at all.

She heard him breathing and wished he would say something. Christine suddenly felt afraid to end the conversation. His voice gave her the feeling of him being near, and a sense of familiarity. It was a link to her life before they had been forced to go on the run. When would she hear it again?

"Josh? Are you still there?"

"Yes."

"Is everything OK?"

"Yes."

"Then let's talk again soon. I'll call when we're back in Hong Kong."

"Bye then."

"Look after yourself."

" . . ."

"I love you."

A brief "You too" would have been enough. Two words. She didn't expect much.

He put down the phone instead.

Paul was right, she thought. He hated talking about serious things or asking questions with the phone pressed to his ear. He had to see the person he was speaking to in order to make sure that what he said was being reflected in their body language and facial expression, and to see if that was in agreement with the look in their eyes. He thought the telephone merely magnified a person's mood. It made the secure more secure, the anxious more anxious, and the lonely feel lonelier.

Christine was anxious and lonely right now. Speaking to Josh for even longer than she had done would not have changed anything about that.

X

One ring of the doorbell and two anxious looks.

"Are you expecting guests?" Paul asked suspiciously.

"No." Gao Gao went to the door. A deep male voice spoke through the intercom. Li Gang. Her only loyal visitor.

Since his wife's death a year ago, he often dropped by for a cup of tea on Sunday afternoons. Supposedly because Gao Gao had the best Oolong tea. But really because he was taking the opportunity to make advances to her that she rejected every time. Sometimes in a friendly manner, and sometimes in a brusque one.

He was twenty years older than her, almost her father's age. And a widower. That was unlucky, a fortune teller had once warned her. Apart from that, she had lost interest in sex. If she did feel the need for it from time to time, she satisfied herself. It was simple that way.

She opened the door and wondered if it would be safer to hide her guests from him. But if one of the children in the bedrooms made a noise, that could make him suspicious. It was better to say that she had a friend visiting from Hong Kong with her family. Gao Gao was about to tell Paul who was visiting and to warn him to be careful what he said, but Li Gang stepped out of the lift just then.

Christine and Da Lin had disappeared into their rooms. David was much too curious to follow. He hid behind his father's legs and stared at the stranger inquisitively.

Li Gang was both surprised and disappointed in the first instance when he saw Paul and David.

After hesitating briefly, he accepted the offer of a cup of tea. His daughter lived in Hong Kong and he was glad to hear that Paul lived there too. They talked at length about the city and about what had changed since it had been returned to China.

The conversation moved on to traditional Chinese wisdom, Chinese sayings, and the poetry of the Tang dynasty. Gao Gao had never met a Westerner who had even the sketchiest knowledge of this.

They defrosted a Black Forest gateau from a bakery in Qingdao that claimed to have followed an original German recipe. Christine and Da Lin emerged briefly to greet the guest, but quickly withdrew again.

Li Gang asked for a whiskey.

"You're a lucky man," he said to Paul. "A beautiful wife and two healthy children."

"I appreciate my good fortune."

"I hope so."

The two men clinked their glasses.

"Happiness is fragile."

Gao Gao looked at Paul. She wanted to let him know that this was an innocent remark by her guest. But fear darted into his face. He did not glance at her, but fixed his gaze on the man opposite him.

"What do you mean by that?"

Li Gang was taken aback by the question. "Exactly what I said! 'He who lives in happiness does not know what happiness means.' So the old Chinese saying goes." Don't you agree?"

Paul nodded, still feeling unsettled.

XI

They had told him not to leave the flat on his own. Gao Gao and Christine had impressed that on him several times yesterday. But he had been awake for ages. The clock showed that it was just after six. Everyone was still asleep and he was bored. What could possibly happen to him in this strange town? There weren't any people on the streets that he had to avoid. Apart from that, he would be back in half an hour at the most. No one would know about his little outing.

Da Lin picked up his catapult, opened the door quietly, and stepped into the hall. Not a sound could be heard. He liked the silence. It reminded him of Grandpa. He had often sat in the courtyard with him and listened for moments of perfect stillness. Grandpa had called that learning to hear the quiet. Most people couldn't do that.

He did not trust the lift. He had been unnerved by the speed with which it had shot them up to this height. He had felt an unpleasant pressure in his ears that had only gone after a mighty yawn.

A sign showed the way to the staircase. It was a narrow stairwell and the stairs seemed to go on downwards for such a distance that he thought he would never get to the end of them. There was a small pile of rubble next to the door to the stairwell. He picked up a lump of mortar, tossed it over the railing and listened for the sound of the impact. He waited in vain.

At the bottom of the stairs, Da Lin decided that he would take the lift on the way back, despite his reservations.

On the street, it was almost as quiet as it had been in the flat. There was the occasional birdsong from a couple of birds and he heard a car in the distance.

Da Lin leaned his head back and looked up at the block of flats. He had never seen such a tall building. When he closed his eyes a little as he looked at it, the tip of the building seemed to be boring straight into the low-lying gray cloud. He walked down the street and came to a fountain with no water in it. Next to it were six flagpoles with no flags on them. Da Lin picked up a small stone, placed it in his catapult and aimed at the top of one of them. A metallic sound told him that he had hit his mark. And a second and a third time.

At the other end of the square was a multi-storied building with a façade of glass windows. Parts of a neon advertisement sign were on the ground in front of it. It looked like the entrance to a large shopping mall. Da Lin was curious, so he crossed the square. The doors to the building were secured with heavy chains and locks. All except one of them. He needed all his strength to open it.

Inside, the stillness spooked him a little. There were lifts leading up and down. There were at least three floors. The golden railings gleamed and the floor had been mopped. The shop windows were clean. Everything was ready. Only the people were missing.

Suddenly he heard footsteps. Then two men's voices. They were far enough away for him to have time to find somewhere to hide. Da Lin looked around. There was not a flowerpot to be seen. He tugged at the door to a shop. Locked. He tried another.

The voices came nearer.

He pulled at a third door.

Then they saw him.

Perhaps everything would have been different if he had not run away but simply stayed where he was calmly. And told the men that he was a boy from the countryside visiting his aunt, had been looking around because he was bored, and now couldn't find his way back to her flat. With tears in his eyes. His grandfather had said that he was a good actor. Perhaps they would even have helped him.

But he turned and started running. Da Lin ran as though his life depended on it. They shouted at him to stop. He heard them start running after him, as though he had woken a hunter's instinct in them. He ran even faster and deeper into the labyrinth, and would most likely have escaped them if there had been an exit open at the other end of the mall. But the lift that led to the upper floors was blocked with wooden planks. The emergency exit door was locked. Da Lin was in a dead end. He heard the panting come closer to him. When they saw that he was trapped, they slowed down and stood still for a moment to catch their breath. They, too, were out of breath.

Da Lin turned around. They were only a few meters away from him. Tall, burly men in uniforms. He raised his catapult and they shrank back. It took a moment for them to realize that there was nothing in the sling. He tried to escape once more. He feinted first to the left then darted right and threw himself onto the floor, hoping to escape their clutches that way. In vain.

One of the two men caught him by the hair. Da Lin screamed in pain. The other man grabbed his back with two hands and lifted him up. Despairing, Da Lin flailed and kicked with all his might. One of his feet hit the man between his legs. The man groaned loudly and let him go. Da Lin struggled to get upright and ran off again. Now he knew the way to the exit.

They caught up with him twenty meters short of it. They threw themselves at him as though there was a reward for his arrest.

Da Lin fell. He threw his arms up around his head to protect it, thudded to the floor and heard something break.

The weight of the men on him. He could not breathe. He could not even scream.

The sweet taste of blood spilled into his mouth.

It was her fault. She had wanted them to take him along. Despite all his warnings, despite his express wish against it. Paul had predicted that Da Lin would be an additional risk to their safety. Christine had not believed him. She had thought him hard-hearted, and disliked him for thinking that way.

She had not had a choice after Da Lin's shot at the policeman, but she still felt responsible. That was why she did not want to wake Paul now and ask for help.

Da Lin had disappeared. She had searched the whole flat for him. What on earth had he been thinking? Since they had left his village they had not spoken to each other much. He had been quiet and withdrawn and she did not know what he was thinking. Was he homesick? Did he want to go back to his grandfather? Or was he afraid of seeing his mother again?

She thought about what to do. Simply wait until he returned of his own accord? Too dangerous. She had to go and search for him before the police picked him up. Maybe he was only taking the lift up and down. Or was playing in the foyer. She hoped to be back before Paul even noticed that she had gone at all. But she scribbled a note anyway and put it on the dining table.

He was not in the lift, or in the foyer.

She stood in front of the entrance to the building, feeling undecided. She had no idea where to look. She walked around the building. At the back of it she found a deserted pedestrian area. The empty shops had metal grilles drawn over them. The wind had blown a table umbrella and a couple of plastic chairs over, and they lay topsy-turvy outside the shops.

She went back to the road and stared blankly in the other direction.

A car was approaching in the distance. When she realized that it had a blue light on its roof, it was too late.

The police car drove straight towards her, suddenly slowed down, braked and stopped next to her. There were two policemen in front and on the back seat was Da Lin, who stared at her imploringly before he looked away. He had a cut on his upper lip and his cheek was swollen. His face was red. She could tell from his eyes that he had been crying.

The seconds ticked by. For a moment she wanted to faint. Simply collapse onto the ground. Hear no more. See no more. Let others take care of her. And him. And only wake up when everything was over.

The two policemen got out of the car. They took their time. They looked intensely suspicious of her. Christine automatically took a step backward.

"Security guards caught this brat in the shopping mall," one of the men said. "We couldn't get a word out of him. But when he saw you he suddenly blurted out that you were his mother. Are you?"

She could say no, was the first thought that shot into her head. No, I don't know this boy. He probably wouldn't even protest. There was no reason not to believe her. Which mother would deny her own son? The policemen would take him away and leave her in peace.

But a yes was an immeasurable risk. What had Da Lin done? What would she have to take responsibility for, as his mother? Would they hand Da Lin to her without any further ado or would she have to show some ID? She couldn't do that. Her documents were in the flat and she did not want to lead the police to Gao Gao, Paul, and David. Not under any circumstances. If she said yes, she could only hope that they would hand Da Lin over to her with a few words of warning, without wanting to know anything more about him.

What if they didn't? What if they started asking questions?

"Are you?" the policeman repeated impatiently.

She had to reply. The longer she said nothing, the more suspicious she seemed.

She had the choice. Yes or no?

Christine looked at the policeman, and at the other man. Her gaze went to Da Lin, who was cowering on the back seat and no longer dared to look at her. He must know that his fate lay in her hands.

"Yes." And gathering all the courage she had, she added, "Look at the state of him! What have you done to my child?"

"We'll tell you about it at the police station." The policeman opened the door and gripped her arm.

"Get in."

XIII

Paul was woken by loud cries from the next room. "Papa! Papa?"

Next to him, Da Lin's bed was empty. He hurried to his son. David was cowering under his blanket. "Where is Mama?"

"I don't know."

David sat up, looking worried. "Why don't you know?"

The wrong answer. "Because I've just got up. She's in the kitchen making breakfast."

David scrambled out of bed and ran into the living room.

A few seconds passed.

"She's not here."

———

Christine must have written her note in a great hurry. Her writing was normally neat and tidy, like a schoolgirl's. But Paul could hardly make it out this time.

Don't worry, she had written. She would be back in an hour at most. Below it was the time: 6:50 a.m.

It was now a quarter past nine.

David had kept his eyes fixed on Paul. "Where is she?" The worry in his voice.

I don't know, he wanted to say, but instead he said, "She's gone for a walk with Da Lin."

"That's mean. Why didn't she take us with her?"

"Because ... because she didn't want to wake us up."

"When is she coming back?"

"I don't ... soon."

"When is soon?"

"Sweetheart," he said, making an effort not to lose his patience, "soon can mean in ten minutes or in an hour."

David looked mutinous and said nothing, as though he understood that this unsatisfactory reply was the best he would get.

How could she have done this to them?

Paul went to wake Gao Gao up. He had barely told her that they didn't know where Christine and Da Lin were before she jumped out of bed, threw on a dressing gown, went straight to the television and turned it on. A few seconds later, a pin-sharp black and white image of the corridor outside the flat door appeared on the screen.

"I have a small CCTV camera above the door. It records the previous six hours." Gao Gao rewound the recording until they saw the door opening slowly and Da Lin stepping out. The time on the image was 6:25 a.m. Exactly half an hour later, Christine left the flat, walked to the lift, and disappeared.

The image froze on screen. David started to say something but then fell silent.

Gao Gao looked at her watch with concern. "I really don't know what it's possible to do in Hongyang for such a long time," she said, as if to herself.

"Is there a café or teahouse nearby?" Paula asked.

"No."

"A restaurant?"

"No."

Paul thought for a moment.

"A shopping mall?"

"Yes, but the shops are empty."

"Maybe they went to see Pastor Lee?"

"Not likely. But I'll phone him."

They were not there either.

Sitting on Paul's lap, David grew more and more quiet.

"Where is Mama?" he whispered.

Paul ignored his question. "Shall we play a game?"

"No."

"Shall I read you a book?"

"No. I want to know where Mama is."

"I told you already. She's gone for a walk."

"For such a long time?"

He could not bear to look at his son. David knew that his father was not telling the truth. Paul found it difficult to lie to him, and, even more so, to be caught doing it.

"Are you hungry?"

"No," he said sulkily. His chin wrinkled and his upper lip disappeared, as always happened when he was trying to stop himself from crying.

Paul stood up, carrying David in his arms, and started dancing. Gao Gao put on a recording by Teresa Teng, mimed to it and started dancing too. She looked like a drunken bear. Even David laughed when he saw her.

Suddenly the doorbell buzzed. They ran to the door and into the corridor. They waited impatiently for Christine and Da Lin in front of the lift.

The door opened slowly. Out stepped Zhang.

XIV

The two policemen kept their eyes on her every movement. The one in the passenger seat turned halfway in his seat to keep watch on her and the one driving kept his eyes on her in the rear view mirror while driving.

Christine was so frightened that she could barely move.

Da Lin had shrunk away from her. His T-shirt was torn at the neckline, as though someone had grabbed him there. She noticed a damp patch the size of a palm between his legs. Christine took Da Lin in her arms and immediately felt his body stiffening. She slid closer to him and pulled him to her. He hesitated briefly and stopped resisting. He sank into her lap, buried his face in his hands and started crying quietly. She looked out of the window at the empty streets and stroked his head.

At the police station, they had to remove their shoes. They took Da Lin's belt from him, as though there was a danger that one of them would hang themselves with it. A woman brought them to a windowless room and told them to wait.

There were four chairs in the room. Nothing else. The bare walls were painted white. There were several fluorescent strip lights on the ceiling. The door had no handle on the inside.

She crouched down in front of Da Lin and looked more carefully at his face. The swelling on his upper lip and around his left eye had grown worse. His chin was badly grazed. When he opened his mouth, she saw that two of his front teeth were missing. She cupped his face gently in her hands. She did not even have any water to wash his wounds.

"Poor boy. Does it hurt very badly?"

The hint of a nod.

"What did they do to you?"

Silence.

"Did they beat you?"

" . . . "

"Will you tell me what happened?"

No reply. When she tried to read his gaze he lowered his eyes.

"Are you thirsty? Should I ask for some water?"

It was pointless.

She sat down next to him and took his hand. She could feel him trembling.

He needed a doctor. She got up, went to the door and gathered her courage.

She knocked. Hesitantly at first, then harder. She kicked the door with her foot and shouted. After five or six kicks she heard noises in the corridor. A policeman opened the door.

"Stop that at once," he ordered.

She flinched and stepped back. "We need a doctor," she said in a flat voice.

"A doctor?" He looked contemptuous. "What for?"

She pointed at Da Lin's bruised face. "My son is not well. Someone has beaten him."

The policeman simply shrugged.

"We. Need. A doctor." She surprised herself with the sudden decisiveness of her voice. Her firm tone astonished the policeman too. "We don't have a doctor here," he said, suddenly becoming a little friendlier.

"Do you have painkillers at least? And a damp cloth?"

He disappeared and returned with a bottle of water, two pills, and a wet cloth.

Da Lin took the medicine and drained the bottle in one mighty gulp. Christine dabbed the cloth carefully at his chin to clean the wound. It was deeper than it had seemed at first. Christine stroked his hair away from his face, sat down and took him in her arms. He allowed her to do this.

She waited without knowing what she was waiting for.

Maybe they only wanted to establish their identities. Why were they here? Where did they live? When were they leaving? But she did not have convincing answers for even the simplest of questions. She was no good at telling stories and even worse at lying.

She grew more anxious with every passing minute. Any moment now, someone could come in and arrest her. Or Da Lin.

Christine thought about Paul and about his son who had died.

Waiting for the results of the medical tests had been almost unbearable, he had told her. The hours passed in the doctors' waiting rooms or in the hospital corridors, until a door finally opened and you were told to enter. Hoping for improvements. Helpless in the face of bad news. Everything turned on one simple sentence: "I'm sorry to have to tell you . . ." A few words were all that was needed to make life take a completely different direction. The blood cell counts were worse. Or they were fine again.

She had always thought she could imagine what Paul had felt then. As a mother, she knew what it was like to worry about a child. Now she knew how wrong she had been. She could not possibly have imagined how he had felt. Her whole body was in revolt. How Paul must have suffered for months.

Hours passed.

At some point Da Lin lay down on the floor and fell asleep. She sat down next to him and put his head on her lap. He held her hand as he slept. A child's hand, she thought, pulling him closer to her. How thin he was. She could feel every single one of his ribs. She lifted his upper body onto her lap so that he would not catch cold from the cold stone floor.

Soon she lost all feeling in her legs.

————

Christine heard footsteps. A policeman entered and, in a brusque voice, ordered her to follow him.

On her own.

She asked for a blanket for Da Lin. After hesitating for a moment, he brought her one and Christine tucked it gently under the sleeping boy.

They walked down a long, badly lit corridor, past several empty rooms. The police station seemed to be as under-staffed as the town was under populated. The policeman led her into a room, pointed her to a chair and sat down behind a desk. There was a form and a pen in front of him. And a catapult.

"What is your name?"

"Wu."

"Wu what?"

"Christine Wu."

"Don't you have a Chinese name?"

"No," she lied.

A gesture of disapproval. "And the boy is your son?"

"Yes."

He looked at her for a long moment. "Not much likeness," he said, smirking. "Not on the outside, at least."

She shrugged. What did he expect her to say in reply?

"How old is he?"

"Twelve."

"What's his name?"

"Da . . . Da . . ." Christine started stammering. Should she give his real name? If they were searching for him, she would be giving them a lead. "Damien. Damien Wu."

"Damien? What kind of name is that?"

"British."

"Does he live with you?"

"Yes."

The sardonic look on his face showed that he did not believe a word she was saying.

"Where do you live?"

"In Hong Kong."

He looked up, surprised. "What are you doing in Hongyang, then?"

"We're tourists."

"Tourists? They don't come to our town often. What exactly are you here to see?"

He was enjoying her uncertainty.

"Nothing. We're here visiting a friend."

"I see. A friend."

"Why do you want to know all this?"

He ignored her question. "Where were you before this?"

"In Xian," she lied. "We went to see the terracotta warriors."

"And before that?"

"We were in Beijing. I wanted to show my son the Forbidden City and the Great Wall." She could hear how thin and false her voice sounded.

The policeman didn't even bother to write anything down. He leaned back in his chair and crossed his arms behind his head. "Beijing, Xian, Hongyang. You're travelling through the country in a zigzag. Have you been to Shi?"

He knows, she thought. Of course he knows.

"Where is that?"

"In Sichuan province. You should know that." He picked up the catapult, examined it carefully, tugged at the elastic band and laid it back on the desk.

"It's well made. Does it belong to your son?"

She did not reply.

"Does it belong to your son?" he repeated, in a loud and threatening tone.

Before she could reply, the door opened and Da Lin entered. A second policeman followed him.

His giant frame almost filled the doorway. He was wearing a uniform with several stars on the lapel, and looked about the same age as Paul.

She had seen him before. It took her a few seconds to realize where.

XV

The strong smell of someone who had not washed for several days wafted out of the lift towards them. Zhang had exchanged his monk's robes for rags. The jacket was torn at the sleeves and the gray trousers were dirty. He had bound a strip of fabric around himself as a belt. His shoes did not have laces in them. He was unshaven and he had lost weight.

"Who is that?" David whispered.

———

Gao Gao found an unopened box of men's clothing for him.

"Do you wear men's clothes as well?" Paul asked.

"No. But I couldn't resist buying them. They were on special offer. Seventy percent off."

"The aftershave too?"

"Which aftershave?"

"The one the whole flat smells of."

"No," she said in a somber voice. "That's my father's eau de toilette."

While Zhang took a shower, Gao Gao prepared rice, vegetables, and red-stewed belly pork from the freezer.

David did not leave his father's side. "When is Mama coming back?"

"In half an hour."

"For sure?"

"Yes. Do you want to draw a picture in the meantime?"

"No."

When Zhang came out of the bathroom, they both could not help laughing at the sight of him. The red turtleneck jumper was two sizes too big, as were the green jacket and the blue trousers. He looked like a clown.

Zhang sat down and ate quickly. Every now and then he spat

a small bone onto his plate, and he took a second and a third helping. Paul did not feel hungry. David sat on his lap and they looked on as Zhang and Gao Gao ate.

"Where's Christine?" Zhang asked with his mouth full.

Paul hesitated before replying. "We . . . we're not sure."

Zhang put his chopsticks down. "What do you mean you're not sure?"

"She's gone for a walk," David said in a firm voice.

"And the boy?"

"He's gone for a walk with Mama."

"For a walk?"

Paul could see that his friend required a further explanation. "They're sure to be back soon." He hoped that his son would not hear the helplessness in his voice.

Zhang looked at Paul and David in turn and back at Paul again. It took Paul a while to understand what Zhang was trying to tell him. He took David over to the television and put on the Winnie-the-Pooh film that they had watched together the day before. He promised to come back to sit with him in a moment, and then went back to the dining table.

"I have bad news," Zhang said in a low voice. "The policeman is dead."

"Are you sure? Or is that just a rumor?" Gao Gao asked.

"Quite sure. He bled to death on his way to the hospital. A former colleague of mine in Shenzhen looked into it thoroughly for me."

"What's happened to Luo?" Paul asked.

Zhang dropped his gaze. "He was the first one to pay the price," he said, in an even lower voice.

Zhang did not know how he had died. Or he wanted to spare them the details.

Out of the corner of his eye, Paul saw Winnie-the-Pooh licking a pot of honey clean.

"Papa, when are you coming?"

"In a moment."

"The boy is wanted for murder. They've started a massive search for him." Zhang paused and drank some tea. "And for you."

"How do the police know who we are?"

"They don't know your names yet. But they have descriptions of you. Fairly detailed ones. A neighbor must have seen you."

Paul took a deep breath in and out, but still felt that he could not get any air. "Why us?"

"As accessories to murder. You were there when the boy took a shot at the policeman. Now you're helping him escape."

Paul closed his eyes and buried his head in his hands. Zhang did not have to tell him what that meant. Now they not only had the henchmen of the crazy son of a senior Party cadre after them. They were also subjects of an official police search. A policeman had died. To pin his murder on them was a simple matter. Would the US embassy be able to help in this situation? China did not allow any foreigners who were being investigated for murder to travel. Not without demanding a price. And in China murder came with a death penalty.

Paul felt faint. Zhang's hand on his arm. He opened his eyes and looked into Gao Gao's concerned face.

"What's wrong, Papa?" David was standing next to him.

It took Paul all his strength to lift the child onto his lap. "Everything's fine, sweetheart. Everything's fine."

XVI

The police officer was clearly a few grades senior to the one who was interrogating her. The younger man automatically sat up and sat ramrod straight at the desk, as though awaiting instructions.

At second glance, Christine remembered where she had seen the man before.

"Thank you," he said to his colleague. "You may go now. I'll take over."

The younger man stood up immediately. "Yes, Detective Superintendent." He left the room without saying anything further and closed the door.

Da Lin remained standing a few meters away from her, clearly frightened. She opened her arms wide but he didn't dare to move. He gave the detective superintendent a questioning look. When the man nodded, he ran to Christine.

Despite his height and the uniform, the man did not seem threatening. He had an unusually calm air. He gave a deep sigh.

"The boy is wanted," he finally said. "And so are you."

I'm sorry to have to tell you . . .

"What for?"

"Murder," he said in a serious voice.

Christine held on tight to Da Lin.

"There . . . there's been a mistake," she stammered.

He shook his head, picked the catapult up from the desk and looked at it for a long moment. "I'm afraid not. I'm going to have to put you under arrest."

She felt the urge to retch. Not here, though, she thought, not here. She asked for the toilet.

"Not now," he said flatly, looking at his watch.

She took a deep breath, hoping to calm her stomach that way. The urge grew stronger. She swallowed a few times and clamped her jaw tight.

The policeman passed her a wastepaper bin in the nick of time.

The sour smell of fresh vomit filled the room. She retched until she was only bringing up greenish-white bile. Da Lin turned away in revulsion.

The man stood in silence opposite her. For several minutes. He seemed completely unmoved, merely looking at his watch every now and then.

Stomach acid burned in her throat.

Suddenly he opened the door. "Follow me. Both of you."

He led them deeper into the building. They went down into the basement and walked down a long corridor. At the end, they climbed up some stairs to a door that he opened by keying in a code.

Out in the yard was a black van with tinted windows.

"Get in," the policeman said.

Christine hesitated. What did the detective superintendent intend to do with them? Would they be taken to a jail to be interrogated? Why not in an official police car? Were they to be secretly transferred to Shi? She did not want to leave this ghost town. At least they were near Paul and David here. Everything in her resisted this. If she got into the van she would never see them both again.

"Get in now," he ordered in a stern voice. "Come on."

She opened the automatic sliding door to the van. Behind the steering wheel she saw Gao Gao.

XVII

How soft her hands were.

Da Lin had not really wanted her to stroke him. He didn't like the feeling of someone else's skin on his. He never allowed anyone to touch him. The only exception had been his father. He had often held his hand as he went to sleep, clinging on to it as tightly as possible. Less often, he had also held his hand when going on walks together. His father had patted him on the head now and then and Da Lin had felt happy whenever that happened. Apart from that, he did not like to be touched. Not by Grandpa. Nor by Mama. And definitely not by other children or other people.

It was different with Christine. Her hand glided through his hair as she stroked him tenderly. Nothing in him resisted. Her gentle, regular movements soothed him. Her warm body, that he could curl up to, and her smell, all helped calm his fears. His mouth and chin did not feel so painful when she held him tight. She whispered something in his ear. Da Lin did not understand a word, but her voice told him that he was not alone.

He hoped she would never leave. He wanted someone who would stay with him. Da Lin reached out for her hand and held it tight. He would never let it go again.

Why had she saved him? She could have said no. She could have claimed not to know him. The policemen would have driven on with him and they would never have seen each other again. Everything would have been easier for her that way.

He did not know whether she could really protect him, but with her by his side, he felt there was someone looking after him.

He would have liked to show her how grateful he was, but how? By giving her a present? All that he owned were the clothes on his back. The policemen had taken away the catapult his father had given him. And even if he still had that, what would

Christine have done with it? He still had the second billiard cue at home. But would she be glad to have a cue?

A present! A small one would be enough. But there was nothing he could give to her or share with her.

The inside of his mouth still hurt terribly.

He hated crying. Tears were a sign of weakness. He felt small and helpless when he cried. The last time he had cried was after the death of his father. But only for a short while.

Now he sobbed without restraint. Christine held him even tighter. He realized for the first time how it did him good not to have to hold his tears back.

Da Lin grew tired and his eyelids started drooping. He lay down on the floor to sleep.

How cold it was.

He thought about his father. And about Grandpa.

Half asleep, he felt her sitting down on the ground next to him. Tugging him onto her lap.

Her lap was soft and warm.

She covered him with a blanket. He wanted to fall asleep like this and never wake again.

Beijing

I

They had to get out of the city. By the quickest route. The family was now in even greater danger. Gao Gao had understood that, and not hesitated for a moment.

Li Gang had phoned and given her brief instructions. Where she had to be and when. How to get to the rear entrance of the police station. What she had to do there and what they had to say if someone asked what she was doing there.

He had hung up as she was about to thank him.

Typical Li Gang, she had thought. He was the only link she had to her previous life. They had met many years ago when he had been one of her father's bodyguards. She had seen him at official events and dinners and every now and then he had accompanied her father home and been on duty there too. She had liked his unassuming air. The laid-back manner and the inner calm that he projected. He was the only one she had seen reading books. Tang dynasty poems! Once she had even seen him read a volume of political essays. She had forgotten the title, but she remembered that it had been banned shortly after. When she encountered him again and he told her that her father had made him the chief of police in Hongyang, she thought it was a joke. He did not fit her image of policemen. The role fit even less well with what she had thought of him.

"You don't know my story," he had said to her, with no indication that he was going to tell her anything.

She had thought often about his statement since. You don't know my story. How apt this was in many cases. We seldom know a person's story. How little we know about the backgrounds to their actions. The real motives behind their deeds. Yet we always have an opinion. We judge. We evaluate.

She was no exception, even though she had made efforts ever since to be more careful.

His help would come with a price. Gao Gao was under no illusions there. Everything had a price. Li Gang was no Samaritan, and he also owed her nothing. If he felt indebted to anyone it might have been to her father. Letting two criminal suspects go was a not inconsiderable risk for him. He would have thought things through carefully. As the chief of police he clearly did not fear betrayal by one of his subordinates. And he must have a plausible explanation ready if it was needed.

What would he want from her? He was not especially interested in money. She would probably have to submit to his advances the next time. Widower or no widower. The thought of it did not fill her with gladness but it also did not repulse her. It was a long time since she had slept with a man. Maybe it would even be fun.

————

The main road was incredibly empty and they made good progress. Zhang was in the passenger seat. He had not said a word since they had set off, and he replied to questions with only a nod or a shake of the head. Now he sat cross-legged next to her as though he was meditating. What an oddball.

But you don't know his story, she thought.

The others were huddled together in the two rows of rear seats. In the rear view mirror she saw Da Lin had fallen asleep on Christine's lap. Paul was reading a book to his son in a whisper.

They would arrive in Beijing late in the evening, and Gao Gao had no idea where they would stay the night.

Hotels were out of the question. She had neither friends nor acquaintances in Beijing. Not any longer. And even if she had known people, none of them would have been willing to take the risk of putting them all up for the night. Or perhaps she was wrong. She had forgotten Lin Dan. She had been at university with her in Beijing. Lin had also made a fortune from property. From what Gao Gao knew, she lived alone in a large flat near Tiananmen Square and owned a string of flats spread out over the whole city. Gao Gao passed her phone to Zhang and asked him to ring Lin Dan.

Lin Dan was not pleased to hear from her. That was clear from the tone of her voice, no matter how much she claimed the opposite was true. She did have room for a guest, she said, but only for one night and only for one person. A group of six people? Not with the best will in the world. She would like to help, but under these circumstances ...

Gao Gao remembered another contact. Yu Xiang was also a friend from university. When she called, he was in Singapore. He would be back in ten days' time at the soonest. He'd be pleased to see her next time.

One more hour to go till they were in Beijing.

Her last hope was Hong Mei, the daughter of a woman from her church. She visited her mother regularly and also came to their church services, even though she was a Buddhist. Gao Gao always liked talking to her. She was a madwoman. She spent her life saving dogs and cats. She fought for animal rights though even human rights were on shaky ground in China. But she was fearless. She had lain down in front of lorries to block them from delivering cats to Guangdong province for human consumption. She had simply trusted that the driver would not drive over her. Placed his humanity under duress and appealed to it. Total foolishness, Gao Gao thought, if you really considered everything. There was a fine line between courage and stupidity. Last year, Hong Mei had travelled to the famous dog meat festival in Yulin and gone on hunger strike in protest, at the People's Square. The dog meat eaters had not taken kindly to that at all and she was badly beaten up. The police had intervened to take her to safety in the end.

Hong Mei recognized Gao Gao's voice immediately. Of course she could stay overnight with her at short notice. Yes, even with her visitors. It would be quite cramped but for one or two nights it would be no problem. As long as no one was allergic to cat- or dog-hair. She shared her home with twelve pets.

II

The city looked dark, almost sinister through the tinted windows. There were hardly any people on the streets and most of those who were walking around had strips of gauze tied over their mouths and noses. Paul could not see much through the windscreen either. By his estimation, the visibility was only a hundred or two hundred meters at most before street lights, traffic lights, buildings, trees, and cars disappeared in a dense gray-brown haze. At first Paul thought it was mist or smoke fumes, but Gao Gao told him that the whole of Beijing was enveloped in a thick cloud of smog. That was normal at this time of year.

A young woman's voice was giving her directions on her mobile phone. As far as Paul could make out they were driving north on the first ring road then past Houhai lake and turning off Gulou Dongdajie into a narrow street.

Her house was in a *hutong* somewhere between Lamma Temple and the bell tower. He knew the area from visiting Beijing before. If he was not mistaken, the journey from here to the US Embassy would take between twenty minutes and an hour, depending on the traffic. They just had to drive eastward up to the second ring road. It wasn't far from there.

Gao Gao drove them quickly and confidently through the city, but had trouble maneuvering the wide van up the narrow alleys. Suddenly she braked hard. The diners at a street restaurant had to get up and move their foldable tables and chairs away in order for her to get through.

At some point they stopped in front of a gray wall. Someone opened a red gate for them from the inside and it took Gao Gao several attempts to get the mini-van through the narrow entry into the courtyard.

Paul saw immediately that they could not stay here long. The house consisted of two small cramped rooms and a kitchen.

There were cats everywhere. On the table. On the shelves. On the bed. On the couch. Three dogs were barking as if their lives depended on it. They were so small that even David was not frightened of them. The place stank of cat litter. When they were all standing in the kitchen, the room was full.

They heard a child cough in the house next door. Someone was snoring loudly somewhere. They could hardly have found a worse hiding place. Here the neighbors would know everything.

"I didn't know there would be so many of you," Hong Mei said somewhat helplessly, though not in an unfriendly tone. "But we'll manage somehow. Are you hungry or do you want something to drink?" Without waiting for a reply, she put mugs and a Thermos flask of tea on the table.

She pulled a drawer out from under a dresser and took out blankets and pillows. Gao Gao, Christine, and David could have the bed and Hong Mei would sleep on the sofa.

Zhang suggested that he, Paul, and Da Lin could sleep in the minivan.

Something in Paul resisted this. He did not want to spend the night without David and Christine. He suddenly had a childlike fear of separation.

"Should I sleep in the mini-van?" Gao Gao asked.

"No, no," Paul said.

Each of them took a pillow and a couple of blankets and got into the minivan. Paul made a bed for Da Lin on the second row of rear seats. He would sleep in the middle row and Zhang settled himself into the front passenger seat, leaning it back as far as it would go.

It was chilly in the van. It was going to be a cold night. Da Lin had fallen asleep after only a few minutes. Paul laid his own blanket on the boy as well.

Zhang sat in front and looked back at them both. "What are we going to do with him?"

"We'll take him to his mother tomorrow." Paul knew that this was not the reply to Zhang's question. "Or do you have another suggestion?"

Deep in thought, Zhang chewed at the nail of his little finger. "And what if the police are waiting for us at her place?"

Paul had not thought of that. Da Lin's mother was the only lead for the police and her address would be the first place they would look for him.

"What do you know about her?"

Paul thought for a moment. "Not a lot. She's called Yin Yin and from what I understand from Luo, she wanted to go to one of the coastal cities to earn money. She ended up in Beijing and works in a factory here."

"Officially? Is she registered in the city?"

"No idea. Probably not. It would be very unusual for someone in her situation."

"If she hasn't registered then the authorities don't know where she is. There are a hundred million migrant workers. She could just as well be in Shanghai or Shenzhen. Do you have the name of the factory and her address?"

"Only her address. And a mobile phone number."

"That's good to know in an emergency. We'll have to see if the police are waiting for us at her place tomorrow. Maybe I should go first and you should stay with Da Lin in the van to begin with. I'll attract the least attention."

Paul nodded. "And what if...?" He did not finish his sentence. There were too many "what-ifs" going through his head.

What if the police do know where Yin Yin lives?

What if she's moved away in search of work?

What if she doesn't want her son?

There were no answers to any of these questions, and he could not expect Zhang to have them either.

"Tell me, how did you get to Hongyang?"

"It was difficult. My nephew gave me a lot of money. That helped. Buses. Taxis. Pick-up trucks. And still I had to make a few detours."

"What will you do when we're gone? Will you go back to Shi?"

"I can't do that. There are too many people there who know who helped you." He stroked his thin beard thoughtfully. "I know an abbot in Tibet. He's the leader of a small, semi-official monastery. It's very remote. That will be a good place for me to disappear to for a while."

"Didn't you say that you'd had enough of religion in your life?"

Zhang strained his face into the faintest of smiles. "That's right. Maybe I'm not strong enough for a life without religion."

"I doubt that. I don't know anyone who is stronger than you are."

Zhang did not respond. Paul started feeling the cold.

"Would you like my blanket? I'm warmly dressed."

"Are you sure?"

"Yes."

Paul wrapped himself in the blanket thankfully. "What don't you go back to Shenzhen?"

"What would I do there?"

The harsh, almost abrasive tone in which Zhang spoke made Paul think that his friend had already thought about this and rejected the idea. He was not sure if he should say what he was thinking. "Maybe see your son?" he asked carefully.

Zhang's eyes narrowed and his lips thinned until they almost disappeared. Paul feared an angry reaction but instead Zhang wrestled with himself for a long time before he replied. "I don't know . . ." he said at last, and repeated himself. "I don't know . . ."

Three words in which there was so much longing and sadness that Paul did not know how to respond.

He looked out of the window. A door opened and a neighbor staggered into the courtyard. He was clearly drunk and did not notice them.

Zhang spoke into the silence. "Getting to the embassy doesn't mean you'll be safe."

"What do you mean? Surely they won't hand us over to the Chinese police?"

Zhang tipped his head from side to side. "The policeman is dead. You're wanted for murder. Or as accessories to murder. The authorities won't let you leave the country before that is cleared up. There are no witnesses apart from the boy. There could be difficult negotiations."

"Do we have an alternative?"

"No. At least in the embassy you won't need to fear Chen and his henchmen."

Before Paul fell asleep he thought about Christine. He felt such longing for her that it was almost a physical pain.

When Justin was ill, he and Meredith had turned away from each other without realizing it. When they did become aware of it, it was too late. It was a little different with Christine. He was full of anger and sadness. He did not understand her. Sometimes he wanted to shake her and scream at her. He withdrew but he was not turning away.

How he yearned to lie down next to her now. To simply put his arm around her and feel her warmth. Her smell. But he was afraid that she didn't want him to be close to her at all.

During their journey in the van he had tried several times to stroke her head from behind. She had shrunk back every time.

Touching her would have made him feel so much better.

III

There was only room for one person on the narrow bed but they had squashed onto it anyway. Gao Gao lay next to the wall and fell asleep in minutes, snoring. David lay half on his mother and thrashed around in his sleep. Christine felt too hot. Her whole body itched but it was so cramped on the bed that she could not scratch herself. One of the cats jumped onto a shelf above them in one big leap. She was afraid that it would land on them any moment. A pounding pain crept from her tensed shoulders into her head.

One of the dogs howled in his sleep.

She could not stand being cramped any more. She slid out of the bed and lay down on the floor. It was hard and cold.

She crept into the kitchen to see if there were any chairs that she could place side by side. She found only three stools that were too small to sleep on.

A clock above the door showed that it was 2:13 a.m.

She found a pile of old towels that smelled of cats. She took them from the shelf, thinking that she could create a makeshift sleeping place for herself in a corner.

"Can I help?"

She turned. Hong Mei was standing behind her.

"I didn't mean to give you a shock," she said.

"It's very cramped in bed. I can't sleep."

"Ah, I thought so. You're welcome to sleep on the couch."

"What about you?"

"I'm not tired."

Christine was hesitant about accepting the offer. It was the middle of the night. Why was the young woman not tired? What else could she do at this hour?

"I don't need much sleep," Hong Mei added, as if to reassure her.

"Do you have any pills for a headache?"

"No, I'm sorry. I never get headaches."

"Any painkillers at all?"

She shook her head.

"Shall I make you some tea? That might help?"

"I'm afraid not."

"Shall I massage your shoulders?"

Christine was unnerved by Hong Mei's helpfulness. What did this woman want from her? "No, thank you. I'll be fine."

There was a grayish-white cat with big eyes on the couch. It jumped up and arched its back as Christine approached. Hong Mei picked it up and carried it into the kitchen.

The couch was too short but it was fine if she drew her legs up to her chest. She heard Hong Mei making tea and sitting at the table. David murmured in his sleep but Christine could not make out what he was saying. After that it was quiet again.

She was wide-awake and felt thirsty. She got up and went into the kitchen. Hong Mei was slumped over the table with her head on her arms, asleep. Next to her were a ring binder and a pile of newspaper cuttings.

Two cats slunk silently around her and watched her every movement with suspicion.

Christine drank a glass of water and lay down on the couch again. She drew her legs up and pulled the blanket up till it covered half her head. When her eyes finally closed it was already getting light.

———

Hong Mei had bought warm steamed buns and vegetarian dumplings for breakfast. She made tea and unearthed biscuits from a drawer. But no one apart from her and the children had any appetite. Paul and Zhang shared a bun and Gao Gao ate a dumpling and bit into a second one but put it down again, staring blankly into the distance. Christine did not touch anything. No one spoke.

Paul was standing next to her. She felt his hand on her shoulder but pulled away with the excuse that she was helping David with his meal.

She had not done it deliberately. It had been her body's automatic response, not something she had thought about. That made it even worse. She did not want to lose Paul. She did not want to raise a child on her own for the second time. To have a second failed marriage. To go to bed alone once again, to wake up alone. To spend lonely evenings in front of the television. To have no one to satisfy her body's desires. All the things her mother would say. Everything would be much worse than it had been the first time. She loved Paul more than she had her first husband and David was closer to his father than Josh had ever been. And there wouldn't be a third chance for her.

She wanted to talk to Paul. But how was she to explain what she herself did not understand?

The fear was too enormous. She had crawled into the deepest corner of her soul and left no room for any other feelings. Her strength was ebbing. Under the pressure, she was beginning to crumble, to dissolve, to become another person. The Christine she had known before this journey had disappeared into a thick mist that grew ever more dense.

They turned into a narrow street. Da Lin pressed his face to the window in order to see better. He saw a shop selling fruit and vegetables. A tea shop. Stray dogs. A restaurant had put tables out on the street under some trees. A few diners were already sitting there drinking beer and eating. A man squatted by the curb mending his bicycle tire.

He could not see any policemen or police cars.

They passed a run-down building with a large neon sign on it. They must have got it wrong. This was not a factory, not as far as he could see. Not even a small one. This was a hairdressing salon. That was emblazoned on the sign. There were several women sitting in front of the salon, all wearing very short skirts and extremely tight T-shirts.

"Is this the right address?" Gao Gao asked, sounding doubtful.

"Yes," Paul said.

"Are you sure?"

He nodded.

They drove on, turned right three times and finally stopped in front of the salon.

"I'll ask for Yin Yin," Zhang said.

"I'll come with you," Da Lin said from the rear.

"I don't know if that's a good idea," Paul said.

"Yes, it is," Da Lin said, and before anyone could say anything he had opened the door and jumped out onto the street.

Paul quickly got out of the van. As they walked towards the salon, Da Lin reached out to hold his hand. Both their hands were icy cold.

"I think we're in the wrong place," Paul said. He stood still.

Da Lin did not reply but tugged him forward.

The women looked them up and down briefly, not seeming unfriendly, but indifferent.

"We're looking for Yin Yin," Paul said.

"Who are you?"

"Friends."

"She doesn't have any friends," one of the women said. The others tittered.

"She is my mother," Da Lin said, in a quiet but determined voice.

The women fell silent immediately. They looked away and did not speak.

"Where can we find her?" Paul asked.

When the women did not answer, he repeated his question politely. When there was still no reply, Paul opened the door to the salon and they went in. It was warm inside and reeked of perfume. Three women were lounging on the sofa staring intently at a large screen. A narrow stairway led to a kind of gallery and there was a curtain in the doorway.

"We're looking for Yin Yin," Paul said again.

"She's with a customer," one of the women said, without taking her eyes off the television.

They heard low groans and the squeaking of bedsprings from a room at the back.

Da Lin gripped Paul's hand and looked up at him. "What do they mean she's with a customer? Where is my mother?"

"She's not here. She'll be back soon," Paul said, hurriedly pulling him outside.

They waited in the car. Da Lin could tell from the grown-ups' faces that something was not right. They reacted to what Paul told them with an embarrassed silence. Christine had hugged him. How could his mother have a customer when she was not even there? Or was there another salon where she was working?

They saw a man leave the salon. Soon after that his mother came out and looked up and down the street.

"There she is," Da Lin called. "There she is."

His mother looked very different from the way he remembered her. Like the other women, she was wearing a short black skirt and a T-shirt that was much too tight. She had painted her lips bright red. Da Lin thought she looked awful. Suddenly he was no longer sure if he wanted to see her at all.

"Should I go with him?" Christine asked.

Luckily, Paul said, "No, I'll go." Da Lin did not like the thought of Christine face to face with his mother.

They got out of the van and went towards his mother. He automatically reached out for Paul's hand again.

V

"What are you doing here?"

Paul took a deep breath. This was what he had feared.

Her voice was deep and her tone was cold. He wished he could have gathered Da Lin up in his arms and turned away on the spot. But there was no way to spare him the next few minutes.

He could feel Da Lin's hand growing even colder.

She looked Paul up and down. The face that was looking at him was not a beautiful one. Small suspicious eyes with dark rings beneath them, heavily made-up out of necessity. Narrow, hard lips made to look wider with gaudy red lipstick. She looked tired and haggard. He suspected that she was on drugs.

"Who are you?"

"Could we speak in private somewhere?" Paul asked in as calm a manner as he could manage.

She looked around her. "Where?"

"In the salon, perhaps?"

"There's no space there."

"In a restaurant?"

Yin Yin thought for a moment. Then she turned on her heel and opened the salon door. "Come in."

She reluctantly led them up the stairs and into a small room with two beds and two chairs. The ceiling was so low that Paul could not stand up straight. A bare red light bulb hung from the middle. He sat down with Da Lin on one of the beds. Yin Yin perched on the other one. The air in the room was heavy and warm.

"Why aren't you with Grandpa?"

Da Lin had been staring at his mother all this time and shrinking into himself. Now he looked down and did not answer her.

"I'm talking to you."

"His grandfather can no longer care for him," Paul said.

"I can't either." She hesitated briefly. "What's happened to Luo?"

Paul did not want to tell her anything, not about the death of the policeman, nor about Luo's. Not yet, at least. From what he saw of her, he feared that she would not want to keep her son with her if she knew that the police were looking for him.

"His health is not good. He can ..."

"Is he dead?"

Paul didn't know what he should say. It was Da Lin who helped him.

"Yes," he whispered. "Grandpa is dead."

Yin Yin sighed heavily. "And who are you?"

"We're friends."

"Whose friends?" she asked. Her tone of voice made it clear that she thought the statement completely absurd.

"Your father-in-law's."

A suspicious look. "I don't believe a word you're saying. He never knew what a friend was."

From somewhere below they heard quiet groaning that grew louder and louder with each second.

Paul was finding the situation more and more unpleasant. He started sweating.

They could feel the violent movements even up here. A brief cry. Silence.

"Shall I take you back to the van?" he asked.

Da Lin shook his head.

They sat in silence. Yin Yin looked Paul straight in the eye, refusing to let him look away, as though she was waiting for him to suggest a solution.

"You can't stay here with me," she finally said in a firm voice. "I have no room for you."

Paul was so startled that he thought he had not understood

what she had said. Maybe it was her Mandarin, which she spoke with a heavy Sichuan accent. "What do you mean?"

"It's quite simple. Da Lin can't stay with me."

Maybe it would have been different if he had heard a note of regret in her voice. A hint of sadness. A feeling of guilt. A pang of conscience.

But maybe, he thought later, that was too much to expect. Perhaps her brusque, harsh tone and cold manner was her way of hiding what was going on inside her. With hindsight, he regretted the way he reacted.

In the moment, though, Paul felt nothing but rising anger and indignation.

"What do you mean he can't stay here with you?" He had to make a great effort to keep his voice down. "Where should he go? Do you want to leave him on the street? Da Lin is your son. You have a goddamn duty to care for him. Who else should do it? His father is dead! His grandfather is dead! You can't sit there and say he can't stay with you. He has to. He has to. You're his mother! Apart from you he has no one left."

Yin Yin looked at him expressionlessly and said nothing.

Paul had worked himself up into such a fury that he did not realize that Da Lin had started crying.

VI

What was going through the mind of a mother who had not seen her son for nearly two years and did not even embrace him? Who said that she had no room for him even though she knew that there was no one else who could take him in? Christine could hardly believe what Paul told her. How could a person be so cold and hard-hearted?

Her indignation did not last long. She thought about her dead brother. He had not been able to escape to Hong Kong as a child and had spent his life in China. They had not heard from each other for more than forty years. After they met again, Christine had wondered every so often what would have happened to her if she had stayed in China. It was a matter of luck, not merit, that she had been able to grow up in Hong Kong. What kind of person would the China Years have turned her into? Certainly not into a mother who rejected her twelve-year-old son. So she thought. So she hoped. Was it foolhardy to even think she had the answer to such a question?

Hard times created hard people.

Without looking at anyone, Da Lin crept past her onto the rearmost seat in the van, lay down, and curled himself up in a ball.

"What's wrong with him, Mama?" David wanted to know. "Does he have ow-ow?"

"Yes."

David clambered over the armrests into the back of the van and patted Da Lin. Da Lin did not resist.

"What are we going to do now?" Her question was directed at no one in particular. The reply was a helpless silence.

"We can't stay here anyway," Gao Gao finally said. She started the engine.

Christine was not able to formulate any clear thoughts. She felt nothing but a deep emptiness within her. What to do with

Da Lin? Was there a chance they could take him with them to Hong Kong? Or just to the US embassy in the first instance? Would they take care of him there? Probably not. Christine saw from Paul's exhausted expression that he could not think of a solution. Even Zhang, who she thought could see a way out of even the most difficult situations, sat slumped with defeat in the passenger seat.

David was the only one who knew what to do. He sat down next to Da Lin on the rear seat and kept on stroking him.

VII

Gao Gao turned north onto the first ring road. Her pale, almost translucent skin was flushed red in the face and the neck. She sat upright, gripped the steering wheel with both hands, and looked straight ahead with a strained expression.

"Where are we going?" Zhang wanted to know.

"I don't know."

She merged with the flow of traffic and Zhang got the feeling that she was simply joining in with the cars on the right-hand lane rather than actively determining the speed she was driving or the direction she was going in.

"Do you have any suggestions?" she asked, without looking at him.

He did not. Zhang turned around. He saw Christine and Paul sitting next to each other like a couple of strangers. She had leaned her head against the glass and was staring out of the window. He sat next to her with his head lowered.

He could not expect to get an answer out of them.

Zhang tried to focus. Going back to where they had spent the night was not an option. The longer they spent in Beijing, the greater the risk of being found. Paul and his family had to get to the US embassy as quickly as possible. Even if the authorities did not permit them to leave the country while they were wanted in connection with murder. That was a problem the diplomats would have to deal with.

He would find a solution for Da Lin later. He hoped.

The traffic began to slow down.

"Is there a hotel near the embassy?"

"No idea. Have a look." She passed him her phone.

Zhang found a Hilton Hotel less than ten minutes away. Paul, Christine, and David could take a taxi from there. That would be safer than if the three of them arrived in the van driven by Gao Gao. He entered the address into the phone for it to find the route. They were driving in the wrong direction.

Gao Gao braked hard, until they came to complete standstill.

"What's wrong?" Paul asked.

"Traffic jam," Gao Gao said.

Lots of blue lights were flashing three or four hundred meters away from them.

"An accident, probably."

Or a police roadblock, Zhang thought. Not very likely at this time of the day on the first ring road, but not out of the question.

Zhang could see that Gao Gao was getting concerned. She looked to the left and the right as if to see if she could turn round on the main road. "We're stuck," she said quietly, more to herself than anything.

The minutes passed and they did not move. The red spots on her throat grew larger and darker.

Suddenly they heard sirens behind them. A police car was making its way through the jam doggedly, followed by an ambulance.

"Where are we going?" Paul asked.

"To a hotel near the embassy. You'll take a taxi from there. We'll wait in the hotel with you for a little while."

Paul leaned all the way forward. "What about Da Lin?" he whispered.

Paul saw him first. A young man on a street corner. His hands buried in the pockets of a light jacket, waiting patiently on the spot as though he had turned up early for an appointment. Conspicuously inconspicuous.

He sized up every car that turned into Donglin Lu with watchful eyes.

It was the look of suspicion in his eyes that gave him away.

Christine kept her son hidden on her lap; he lay beneath a black blanket that stank of stale smoke. Her eyes were closed, as though she was asleep.

Paul knew she wasn't.

She had not believed that they would make it. Not when they had first fled, nor later on, as they had left Shi further behind them with each passing day. Not even this morning.

The traffic lights turned red and the taxi stopped. Christine opened her eyes briefly and he could see that she still did not believe it. One more street to go, he wanted to say. Look out of the window. Reassure yourself. Two hundred meters, maybe three hundred, no more than that. What was one more street after thousands of kilometers on the run?

The man on the street corner would not be able to stop them on his own.

Then he saw a second man.

And a third.

A black Audi with tinted windows, with its headlights off, drew up and parked not far from the security zone in front of the embassy. He noticed a group of young men lurking under one of the gingko trees, keeping watch.

"Don't stop. Drive on," he said to the taxi driver.

"The embassy is here."

"I know where the embassy is. Keep driving."

Christine. Alarmed. How fear could show so strongly on a face, Paul thought. That was something it had in common with love.

"But you wanted to go to the embassy."

"Carry on driving. Go!"

"Where to?"

Sometimes there were no answers to simple questions. Especially not to those questions.

"Where to?" the driver said again.

"Back to the Hilton Hotel."

The car made a sharp turn and the driver sped up in order not to have to wait at the next red light. The lights turned red just as they passed the junction. Paul turned round. He couldn't see a car following them.

They drove towards the ring road and stopped at the hotel a few minutes later. A porter opened the door for them, welcomed them warmly and asked them if they had any luggage.

"No luggage, thank you."

They hurried into the foyer. Paul looked round for Gao Gao or Zhang but could not see them.

"Are we in the right hotel?" Christine whispered.

"Of course. We were just here a few minutes ago. They said they would wait a little while." They stood in the foyer feeling lost.

"Can I help you?" the concierge asked.

"We're . . . we're looking for friends."

"Perhaps they're waiting in the café?"

They walked across the foyer and found Gao Gao, Zhang, and Da Lin in a corner at the very back of the café sitting in front of three slices of cake that were untouched. They were the only guests.

Paul told them what he had seen.

Zhang sank deeper and deeper into the cushions. "I was afraid that would happen," he said. "Did they see you in the taxi?"

"I don't think so."

Zhang buried his head in his hands. All eyes were turned on him.

"They're keeping watch on the telephones," he said. "There's only one way to reach the embassy now. Paul has to write a short letter explaining the desperate situation you're in, and ask for a diplomat to pick him up here from the hotel in a car. Vehicles with diplomatic license plates are not stopped when entering or leaving the embassy. Out of all of us, Gao Gao will attract the least attention. She must go to the consular section of the embassy on the pretext of applying for a visa and deliver the letter there."

He did not sound convinced by his plan.

"What if Gao Gao is stopped outside the embassy?" Christine asked in a doubtful voice. "The letter will say where we are. We'll lead them to us. They will only have to come and get us."

Zhang nodded.

"And what if they only read the letter in the embassy tomorrow morning? Or don't even accept it in the first place?" Paul added.

"I don't know. Does anyone have a better idea?"

They fell silent, deep in thought. After a while, Christine stood up and got some headed paper from the reception desk.

In a few sentences, Paul described the kidnapping of David, their subsequent flight, and the secret police outside the embassy. He did not mention the death of the policeman. Under his name, he added his American passport number and his date and place of birth so that his details could be checked.

Gao Gao picked up the letter. It was ten minutes' walk from the hotel to the embassy. She hoped to be back in two hours at the most.

IX

A waiter came to ask if they wanted anything else. They ordered some water, tea, an espresso for Paul, and an ice cream for David. Da Lin did not reply when they asked him if he wanted anything to drink. He had not spoken at all since the meeting with his mother. Apart from glancing at David a couple of times, he did not look at them at all. David did not leave his side.

Zhang grew more and more restless with every passing minute. He could barely sit still. He jiggled his left leg so hard that the water in the glasses sloshed around.

When Christine went to the toilet with the two boys he turned to Paul. "It would be better for me to leave with Da Lin now."

"Why?"

"The Americans won't protect the boy. And if the police come . . ." He let his words fade away without finishing his sentence.

"Where will you go?"

"We can stay one more night with Hong Mei."

"And then?"

"I'll travel to the monastery in Tibet and take him with me as a novice. He'll be safe from the police there for the time being. In a few years he can decide for himself if he wants to be a monk or to do something else. What do you think?"

"Hmm."

Zhang did not think Paul had been listening to him. He saw the tension in his friend's face, and wished he could do something for him. But they had come to the end of the road they had been travelling together. Now they could only wait and hope that Gao Gao would not be turned away and that a diplomat would take the letter seriously.

"What do you think?" he asked again.

Paul leaned back on the sofa and closed his eyes. "I don't want you to go," he said quietly.

Zhang took hold of his hand. He had never done that before in their friendship of over thirty years. Apart from his ex-wife and his son, no one else was closer to him than Paul was. Nevertheless, or perhaps because of this, he now had to look after the boy. Out of all of them he was in the greatest danger, and he had no one else.

"I don't want to either. But ..."

Paul interrupted him. "I know. How will I find you?"

"You won't. I'll contact you. But it will take some time. At least a few months. Probably more."

"Will we see each other again?"

"Probably."

X

There was *no room* for him.

And he didn't even need very much. He could sleep on a blanket on the floor. Even without a blanket if he had to. He would have left her in peace while she cut people's hair, and wouldn't have bothered her. He didn't eat much and didn't say much. So why couldn't he have stayed with his mother?

She had probably found a new husband long ago. And had another child. A new family, in which there was no room for him.

Da Lin thought about his father. That hurt.

Once the three of them had played billiards together. Mama, Papa, and him. Grandpa had looked on. It had been a warm summer's day, Da Lin suddenly remembered very clearly. Papa had wanted to show them a few tricks but it had been Mama who had won the games. One after another.

Da Lin saw the slight smile on his mother's face and the cigarette hanging from the corner of her mouth as she took the cue in her hands. He heard his father laugh. He did not mind losing.

He heard the clip-clop of horses' hooves in the distance.

He thought about Grandpa. If only he had stayed with him on the farm. Even if the police had arrested him and beaten him to death that would have been better than to be sent away by his own mother.

Or was that woman not his mother at all? She smelled totally different. She looked totally different. She definitely couldn't play billiards. His mother would never have worn such a short skirt. And that tight T-shirt. His mother would have been glad to see him and would have embraced him. She would have made room for him and shared her bed with him.

His mother was dead. He would never see her again. She was dead. She had been run over by a car and no one dared to tell him the truth. Who was that strange woman? Why had they taken him to her?

He did not want to go with this man, even though Paul said he was his best friend. He was old and sick. He would die soon. Anyone could see that. And then what?

He didn't want to go back to the ghost town either. And he couldn't go back to his village. Nor could he go to Hong Kong with them.

China was so big. There were so many people. Why was there no-one he could stay with?

Paul spoke to him in an insistent voice. Da Lin could not understand anything he was saying. He heard the sounds and tones as if through a wall, but could not make out a single word.

Christine wept. No one had ever cried for his sake before.

David held his hand and pressed it.

He wished he could vanish without a trace. Become invisible. Dissolve into nothing. Burn out like the sparks of a flame.

But he couldn't do that.

He still had something to do.

XI

Christine did not know how to say goodbye to Da Lin. She had tried to take his hand in the van, but he had pulled it away immediately. He only allowed David to touch him.

She did not want to leave him behind but she knew that she had no choice. Maybe there would be a chance to bring him over to Hong Kong later, she thought.

She tried to hug him but he shrank back.

She did not have the strength to stay silent. "We'll see each other again soon. I promise."

"Promises mustn't be broken," David said.

Zhang had already walked a few paces ahead and was calling for him. Da Lin lingered a moment longer with them. He did not have to say anything. The expression in his childish face was enough of a plea. Christine could stand it no longer so she looked down at the ground. Da Lin continued standing there. Zhang called his name once more. Slowly, he turned and followed him, without looking back even once.

Christine sat still for a while. Then she gestured to the waiter to come over and asked him for a knife. He gave her a puzzled look.

"A knife and fork," she added. "For the cake."

He brought her a dessert fork and a useless little knife with a blunt edge. She needed a sharp knife with a long blade. Whatever happened in the next few hours, she did not want to be unarmed. She wanted to be able to defend herself.

She asked for another knife with a sharp edge. She said she had to undo a seam.

The waiter returned with a kitchen knife. He was unsettled by her. She could see that in his eyes. When he had gone she wrapped the knife in a paper napkin and put it in her bag.

Christine looked at the clock. Gao Gao had left the hotel

more than an hour ago. Ever since saying goodbye to Zhang and Da Lin, Paul had been sitting motionless on the sofa. She found the sight of him alarming. He looked old. And exhausted. No more help could be expected from him.

David sat next to his father, drawing.

Christine could not stand waiting any longer. She got up and walked up and down in the café. She looked into the foyer, came back and walked back to it again. The women at the reception desk looked at her suspiciously. She ought to sit down so that her restlessness did not attract even more attention. But after a few seconds she got up again.

The concierge came up to her. "Can I help you with anything?"

"No, thank you."

Back in the café her eyes went to Paul. He was standing up looking for David.

Everything was horribly familiar to him. Waiting. Feeling faint. Feeling that he had lost all control over his own life. In the hospital he had met people who had reacted to this with rage and aggression. They shouted at the doctors and nurses and at each other. Others became very restless and manically overactive. They had constantly to be doing something because they could not deal with the loss of control.

Christine was one of those people. What did she need a long knife for? Why couldn't she just sit down by his side? She probably felt contemptuous of his passive behavior. But she was deluded. It was crazy to think that she could still change anything.

He did not have the power to fight any longer. They had been on the run from their persecutors for two weeks.

Now they had to give themselves up to fate. And endure it. With integrity and honor. He had retained those qualities after Justin's death and they would not be taken from him now.

The most important reason for him to be strong was his son. He must not see his father crumbling. He had to be an example to him.

David wanted to play tag.

"No, I'm too tired."

"Hide-and-seek, then." He told Paul to close his eyes and count to ten.

He put both hands over his eyes and peeked through a crack in his fingers. "One ... two ... three ..."

"No peeking," David cried and disappeared behind a thick curtain.

"Ten." Paul got up and pretended to look for him under a bench. And behind the cake counter.

Christine came back from the foyer. "Where's David?" Her voice was almost a shriek.

"We're playing hide-and-seek," Paul whispered. "He's behind . . ."

"Paul," she screamed. "How can you let him . . ." She was about to give him a tongue-lashing.

"But I'm here, Mama," David said in a disappointed voice, coming out from behind the curtain.

Paul crept under a table. He heard David counting.

Suddenly he found himself looking at a pair of smart black leather shoes right in front of him.

"Mr. Leibovitz?"

Paul came out from his hiding place.

"Samuel Adams, attaché at the US embassy. Are these your wife and son?"

Paul nodded.

XIII

Da Lin waited patiently until Zhang had nodded off. He went over to the couch to make sure that Paul's friend was fast asleep. Then he crept out of the house and closed the door.

On the street it took him a while to find someone he could ask for the way. There weren't many people walking about. Most of them had white cloths tied over their mouths and simply hurried on when he approached them. He had never seen so many people in such a hurry. An older woman stopped for him. He was lucky. The nearest police station was not far away.

Ten minutes later, he was standing in front of a new gray building. Wide steps that looked very dirty led up to the entrance. There were two sacks of cement on them. Workers were making a balustrade.

Da Lin hesitated. He had lain awake in the van last night and come up with a plan. He had gone through every detail. But now he was frightened. What would the policemen do with him? Beat him the way they had beaten Papa? Lock him up in jail? Was there a jail just for children? Or would he have to be with the grown-ups?

Paul and Zhang had thought he was asleep but he had heard every word they had said in the van. The policeman was dead. They were wanted for murder. It was unlikely that the embassy – or wherever they were heading for, Da Lin had not quite understood – would help them under these circumstances. Until the case was solved they would be stuck there. The worst-case scenario was that they might be handed over to the Chinese authorities.

All because of him. He was a burden that endangered all of them.

Da Lin did not want David to have to go to a children's home. He did not want Christine to go to jail. Or Paul.

There was a way to prevent all that.

Two policemen came out of the building. Da Lin turned his back to them. They did not take any notice of him.

His heart was pounding, just like it had yesterday when they were standing in front of the salon and asking for Mama.

His father had not been afraid of the police.

Neither had his grandpa. He had known what they would do to him and yet he had not run away.

Da Lin walked slowly up the steps.

It took all his strength to open the heavy door.

He stepped into a room where several policemen were on duty at their desks.

He felt sick. His stomach lurched.

A policeman looked at him suspiciously. "What do you want?"

Da Lin was afraid he would not be able to get the words out. That he would never again be able to leave the world of silence. Since Papa had died he had been in that world so often. But now he wanted to speak.

Just three sentences.

Three sentences that he had given careful thought to.

Even if they were the last ones he would ever speak in this life.

He thought about Christine. What she had done for him. He heard her voice and knew that he was not alone.

We'll see each other again soon. I promise. She had said that when they parted.

Promises mustn't be broken, David had said in a determined voice, taking Da Lin's hand. He could still feel the little fingers between his.

"What do you want?" The policeman got up and walked over to him. How tall he was. He had big hands and short, thick thumbs. Like little sausages.

Da Lin wanted to say something. He took a deep breath. Opened his mouth.

Nothing.

His lips were refusing to form the sounds. His tongue lay like a lifeless piece of flesh in his mouth. He was afraid that words had failed him forever.

"Open your mouth, brat, or get lost." The man and his deep threatening voice were making everything worse.

Da Lin summoned all his remaining strength and tried to concentrate.

Just three sentences.

He had practiced them that morning when he was on his own. He had managed to say them quietly but clearly. He took another deep breath.

"M-m-m-my n-n-ame is D-D-D- Da Lin."

"I can't understand a word you're saying. Speak up!" The sausage fingers grabbed him by the collar and lifted him effortlessly.

The next sentence was the difficult one. He had to speak more slowly in order not to stammer. Word for word. Da Lin worked himself up to it.

"I. Killed. A. Policeman."

The sausage fingers let him go. "What did you do?"

"I. Didn't. Mean. To."

Hong Kong

I

Christine lay in her bed and gazed at the play of the bamboo shadows on the ceiling. Next to her, Paul was tossing and turning. He was breathing unevenly but he did not wake up. She got up and went into David's room to check that everything was all right.

For the third time that night.

He was sleeping peacefully in his bed.

It was warm. She opened a window and cooler morning air streamed in. The clock with the penguins on it showed that it was nearly six o'clock. The first birds were starting to sing.

Christine sat on the floor and watched her sleeping son. He had cast off his blanket, cushioned his head on his small hands and drawn his knees up to his chest.

She could not get enough of looking at him. His black curls and his soft limbs, that seemed even more delicate to her than before. He was a small child. Even at birth he had been small. Paul did not like to hear that.

She wished she could spend all night by his bed looking at him. And all day. Stroking him, cuddling him, burying her nose in his hair, and inhaling the smell of him. He made it quite clear to her that she was too clingy and it sometimes got on his nerves. He would slip out of her grasp then, and keep his distance, or go away and play in his room. But she couldn't help herself.

The weeks in China had left their mark. Sometimes he woke in the night and cried out for them. He had never done that before. It was harder for him to concentrate now. Before, he had liked doing jigsaws and had shown unusual patience searching for the right piece. Now he swept everything off the table when he could not immediately find the pieces. She felt he was more moody and irritable, though Paul disagreed.

She thought about the mug of hot chocolate that he had dropped yesterday. His favorite mug! David had been inconsolable. They had gathered up all the pieces and Paul had managed to painstakingly glue all the porcelain shards back together. The cracks were still clearly visible but there was not a piece missing and, amazingly, it did not leak.

But David had continued howling bitterly while holding the mug in his hand. "It's not the same," he sobbed.

She felt the same way. The whole family had been put back together from shards but it was no longer the same.

It would just take some time, Paul said.

She doubted that. The mug would not be the same anymore, no matter how long David continued using it.

She heard the alarm go in her bedroom. Before the day began properly, Christine slipped back into bed and curled up to Paul's back. She put one hand on his chest and felt his heart beating. He was awake; he turned around. They lay nose-to-nose and knee-to-knee. She stroked his face.

He had shaved off his beard and his face had filled out again. From the outside he did not look very different from the Paul that she remembered. His smell, too, was more familiar to her once more.

"Good morning," she whispered.

"Good morning."

Just like before, yet nothing was like it had been before. Since they had returned to Hong Kong they had not kissed properly once. Fleeting kisses of greeting, yes, but greater intimacy was out of the question. They crept around each other. Were considerate of each other's moods and needs. Made efforts.

To what end?

Were they trying not to damage the other person any further? To get closer and achieve a tentative rapprochement? Or simply to achieve some peace, security and normality?

Some days she looked in the mirror to reassure herself that she was still Christine Wu. She had put on a little weight and her body was beginning to regain the shape she was familiar with. Yet she often found that she still looked strange to herself.

When she walked into the kitchen there was already a bowl of congee and a small pot of green tea on the table. Paul had made a habit of getting up at the same time as she did. While she had a shower he made some breakfast for her. She told him every morning that he didn't need to do this. He could sleep in, because David often slept till eight or nine. But he insisted on doing it.

Paul sat at the kitchen counter with an espresso, writing an email. He would have his breakfast with David later.

Christine sat down next to him. "Have you heard anything from Beijing?"

"No."

"From Zhang?"

"No, not from him either."

Since they had returned six weeks ago they had tried to find out what had happened to Da Lin after his arrest. For the first few days, Paul had tried to contact Yin Yin, but her mobile phone number had been disconnected. He tracked down the number of the salon, but when he called and asked for her they hung up on him. They had asked the US embassy to find out from the Chinese authorities where Da Lin was. But all they were told was that the boy was in police custody.

Christine had written to Gao Gao several times. She had made enquiries, but also made no headway.

More than anything, she hoped that Zhang, through his contacts, might manage to find out something about what had happened to Da Lin. But they had not heard anything from him since his hurried email from Beijing. Paul's attempts to reach his friend had gone unanswered.

Not a day passed in which she did not think of Da Lin and how much they owed him. David had named one of his toy pandas Da Lin, but had not talked about him now for some time.

"Should we make enquiries at the embassy?"

Paul shut his laptop. "We could. But I don't think that would make sense."

"Why not?"

"Da Lin is not American and we are not his relatives. Why should the Chinese authorities reply to yet another enquiry?"

"Is there nothing else we can do?"

He furrowed his brow in thought. "I'm afraid not. Not at the moment. We have to wait until Zhang gets in touch or until we can speak to Yin Yin."

"I find that very difficult."

"I know. I do too."

She ate her congee, deep in thought, and sipped her tea. Paul watched her.

To be able to sit in silence with each other again without having the feeling that they were not talking about something was a first step, though Christine was not sure which direction it went in.

In her first marriage, when she found out about her husband's affair, she knew immediately that it was over. Right away and without a trace of doubt. She could not forgive him the years of betrayal, not under any circumstances. The trust between them had been irreparably damaged. It was the end. Over.

With Paul it was different. He had not betrayed her, not lied to her. Perhaps she herself had been deceived in him but if that were the case, it was her own fault, not his. They did not have to be reconciled; there was nothing to forgive.

They had been overwhelmed. Who would not have been? They had experienced an extreme situation they had not sought out, one in which there had been nowhere left to hide. They had been forced far beyond their limits, had looked into the abyss and, shocked, had flinched away from what they had each seen in the other.

And in themselves.

Neither of them had blamed the other. Yet deep wounds remained. Could they be healed? And if so, what was needed apart from time?

II

Since their return Paul had been seized by a barely containable urge to keep moving. Every morning after breakfast he left the house with David. They walked to Pak Kok, to the northern tip of the island, and counted the container ships that were anchored only a few hundred meters away.

Each time his son was impressed anew by how the huge ships kept afloat despite their size and how he sank in the water even though he was small and light.

They walked to Hung Shing Ye beach or on to the isolated bay of Lo So Shing. When David could walk no further and started whining, Paul hoisted him onto his shoulders. On the way back they often had a meal in one of the seafood restaurants.

Today he planned to do something different. He wanted to go for a short walk by himself first and then pick Christine up from the ferry. He had asked her to take the afternoon off because he wanted to go for a walk with her and spend some time just with her. She was often too tired in the evenings and the weekends were for David.

Paul said goodbye to his son and his mother-in-law, put another water bottle in his bag, tied his boot laces tighter and set off. He went down the steps to the valley and walked past the small fields in which old men and women were weeding, breaking up clumps of soil, or digging for beetroot. They greeted him with a nod; he was a familiar face to them. Paul returned the greeting.

———

Christine was one of the last to disembark. Her dress flapped in the warm autumn breeze. She was no longer the same, but no less lovely.

They hugged, not in an exaggerated way, but affectionately.

They strolled through the town and bought some warm waffle-balls to take with them. Christine did not want to take the dirt track on the ridge over the hills because she did not like the many stray dogs there. So they took the main path instead, on which they encountered only one or two people walking towards them.

It was here that they had met for the first time on a cold, rainy Sunday afternoon. He had been on one of his daily walks and she had been looking for Sok Kwu Wan village and the ferry back to Hong Kong. Paul had sought shelter in a viewing pavilion on the top of a hill and had been looking at the leaden-gray, choppy waters. He had jumped when she had spoken to him from behind. The rain had fallen on her back and she had stepped a little closer to him.

He had liked her immediately, though it had taken him a long time to admit it to himself.

Now they were standing on the same spot. A calm, deep blue sea stretched out before them, glinting with the light of the sun.

Was she reliving the same scenes or were her thoughts still in the office? Or in Shi, in Beijing, or with Da Lin?

He took her hand. She looked into the distance and was silent.

"Christine," he said. "Where are you?"

"Here," she said pensively, without looking at him.

Paul did not know whether to believe her.

"And you?" she asked. "Are you thinking about that cold, rainy day in February?"

"Yes."

"That was a long time ago."

"Do you think so?" The way she had said that did not sound good. Defeated and withdrawn. Far away. A story without any meaning in the present.

"Nearly seven years."

"And?"

"And nothing."

He wanted to talk to her. He had been wanting to talk to her for days. He wanted to hear how she was. Did she feel safe in Hong Kong now or was she frightened? Did she think about Da Lin often? What did the friendly way in which they kept their distance from each other mean? He could not read her silence. Paul searched for the right words to begin this conversation, but could not find them.

Two seagulls circled above them before they dropped down to the water in an elegant swoop.

"Paul," she said in a serious voice, "can you imagine living somewhere else?"

He gave her a sidelong glance. He had not expected this question. "Why do you ask?"

"Just because."

"Just because? I don't believe that. Are you frightened, living in Hong Kong?"

"No, not frightened." A lone hiker passed them. "But I don't feel comfortable in the city any longer."

Paul thought about this. In the thirty years and more that he had lived here, Hong Kong had become his home, the only home that he had ever known.

"I don't know," he said evasively. "I've never thought about it. Where would we go?"

Christine continued looking at the sea. "No idea. Australia? Maybe Sydney?"

"Hmm." He heaved a great sigh. "Hong Kong is my home. I don't want to be driven from it by anything."

"I don't want to drive you away from it," she retorted.

"I don't mean you," he said.

"Who, then?"

"Whoever or whatever is responsible for making you feel uncomfortable." He paused and added, "You're not alone."

"I know."

They fell into a pensive silence.

"Come on," she said and tugged him on to continue their walk. "It was really just a thought."

They followed the path and turned right shortly before Sok Kwu Wan to Lo So Shing. There was a snake on the warm rocks a few meters away from then. Christine stopped short, startled. Paul stamped his feet hard, but the snake did not move. Only when he threw a stick at it was it shocked into movement, disappearing into the undergrowth.

There was no one else in the bay. Even the lifeguards' hut, where there were normally a couple of men repairing buoys or nets to keep the sharks out even in the off-season, was empty.

The sun cast long shadows but it was still pleasantly warm. They walked down a few steps to the beach and sat down under a palm tree. Christine lay down on the sand and closed her eyes.

Paul watched the gentle lap of the waves and considered taking a swim.

"Will you come into the water?"

Christine sat up, looked at the sea in silence and shook her head.

"Kiss me," she suddenly said.

Paul gave her a kiss.

"Not like that. Properly. Like before."

He hesitated for a moment. Like before. If only it were that simple.

She kneeled down in front of him. Took his face in her sandy hands.

"Close your eyes," she said quietly.

The tips of their noses touched. Their lips. Very gently at first. Tentatively, shyly, as though it was their first time. Then the passion returned.

Aroused, she whispered, "I want to make love to you."

"When?"

"Now."

"Here?"

She nodded.

Paul looked around. There was no cover to be seen anywhere and the undergrowth was full of insects and snakes. But the bay was isolated and not overlooked in any way. It was very unlikely that another hiker would stumble upon Lo So Shing at this time of day. But the uncomfortable thought of being surprised by someone outweighed any desire.

She kissed him even more passionately.

"Come on," she whispered, pulling him to her.

Little by little, he succumbed.

He felt more and more uplifted with every passing minute of their passion. He had seldom felt so protected in his life. Everything fell away from him in their movements. His fear and his doubt. His sadness and his gloom.

III

The day did not start well. Christine missed the ferry at 7:50 and the next one was twenty minutes later. To be at work on time she would now have to rush through the city. She hated arriving anywhere bathed in sweat.

On the ferry she noticed three men she had never seen before. Of course she did not know who every passenger on the morning ferries was, but after four years she knew almost all of them by sight. She noticed totally unfamiliar faces. Especially as the men were dressed in a way that made them stand out. Their ill-fitting suits did not blend in with the other commuters on their way to offices in Central, Admiralty, Wan Chai, or Kowloon. It was almost always visitors from China who wore ridiculous jackets and trousers like those. The city was full of them now, but they seldom made their way to Lamma; only at weekends, if at all.

Christine was one of the first to get off the ferry. She was in a hurry and took two steps at a time as she climbed the staircase from the pier. On the pedestrian bridge to the International Financial Centre she noticed that the three men were following her.

She thought about turning back. She had done that once in the last few weeks, when she had given way to a panic attack. She had taken the next ferry back to Lamma. It had not helped. She had not felt better there either. Only in the evening had she begun to feel calmer, and she had not been able to explain to Paul why she had become so anxious. It was a vague, undefined fear, which only made it worse. She was not actually worried about her personal safety or about Paul's or David's. She did not think that anyone would go as far as to kidnap her son from Hong Kong. But three strange men on the ferry were enough to unsettle her.

Her sense of security had been shaken to the core. Her daily life had acquired a completely different feeling of fragility.

But she did not want to allow fear to control her again. The best way to cope with his fear, Paul had said, was to confront it, not to run away from it.

Christine entered the IFC Mall and the scent of freshly baked bread wafted over to her from a supermarket. She slowed down and came to a halt after a few meters.

She couldn't do it.

A woman stepped on her heels and continued walking without saying a word to her. In order not to be carried along by the swell of commuters, she made her way through them to the wall and waited there. The three men from the ferry walked past without looking at her.

She leaned against the wall and slid down it slowly until she was sitting on the ground. Two security guards came up to her immediately and told her to keep moving. No one was allowed to sit on the floor here. She walked past the Prada boutique. In front of the Tiffany store there was already a line of tourists from the People's Republic. Christine recognized them by their ill-fitting clothing. And their worn-out shoes.

Her phone rang. Her boss. She cancelled the call.

As the moments passed her fear subsided. What remained was the unsettling knowledge that she had been on the verge of a panic attack. Fear glowed in her like the embers of a fire, and a mere gust of wind was all that was needed to fan it into flames.

She sat down in a coffee shop and thought about Da Lin.

It was only because of him that they had been able to leave much faster than they had expected. They had been at the US embassy for three days. The police had interrogated them there, in the presence of diplomats. The ambassador had advised them not to mention that David had been kidnapped in Shi. From the doubt in his voice when he had asked them about the kidnap and responded to their replies, they could tell that he was not sure what to make of that part of the story himself.

Then came the news that the twelve-year-old boy who had murdered the policeman had given himself up. His statement was plausible and completely cleared Paul and Christine of responsibility. There were no further charges against them and they were free to leave the country.

The ambassador's representative had accompanied them to the airport that very day to make sure that there were no unanticipated problems at immigration control. Christine had shown her passport with her heart pounding, and been fearful to the very last moment. Even when the doors of the Dragon Air Airbus had closed, and the plane had been taxiing to the runway. Only when the plane had gathered speed and lifted off a few seconds later had she burst into tears of relief.

Since then she had thought about Da Lin every day.

She drafted another letter to the US ambassador in her head. If only they could find out how the boy was and where he was. If she had an address for him she could write to him regularly and send him things. Perhaps she should turn to the Chinese authorities in Hong Kong? But on what grounds? They were not even related to him.

Christine wondered if they would put a twelve-year-old boy on trial. Murder carried the death penalty in China. But for a child too?

The feeling that it was their fault allowed her no peace. They had set in motion the train of disastrous events. If only they had not turned to Luo for help ... If only Da Lin had not borrowed the bicycle from the neighbor for David ... If only they had not gained his confidence, he would not have thought of hiding them from the police ...

If only. If only. Her conjectures drove Paul mad. Life is not a series of 'if onlys', he said. He was right, of course. Yet she could not let go of these thoughts. They twisted and turned in her mind in an endless loop.

She saw Da Lin before her. His thin body. The grave look in his big eyes, which had already seen far too much. His tentative smile, that was so hesitant but had a warmth to it that she had rarely seen in anyone else before.

She saw him walking into the police station on his own. She could hardly bear the thought of it.

She had promised to return when she said goodbye to him. Now she knew that she would not be able to keep that promise.

Her phone rang again. Paul. She would have liked to speak to him, but didn't trust herself to right then. She didn't want to worry him.

Christine's gaze wandered through the shopping mall, searching in vain for distraction.

She felt alienated from her own city. The more she thought about it, the more uncertain she felt. If Hong Kong was no longer her home, where was home? She did not want not to have a home.

Her mother would never move to the US or to Australia with them. Could she leave her on her own?

No.

Or could she?

Her boss rang again. She should pick up the call and make her excuses. She did not have the energy to lie. So she switched the phone off altogether.

Christine got up and set off without knowing where she was going. She stepped out into Exchange Square and took the pedestrian bridge toward Lan Kwai Fong. Once there, she zigzagged through the narrow, overcrowded streets in search of a place to sit down and think in peace. The coffee shops were too noisy and full of people. On Wyndham Street she saw a sign pointing the way to the Catholic Cathedral of the Immaculate

Conception. It was only two streets away on Caine Road, walled in by high-rise buildings.

How quiet it was in the church. She could not hear anything from the city apart from distant, muffled noises.

A man stepped into the church after her, crossed himself and went towards the altar. Christine followed him.

Several visitors were kneeling in the front rows. Two women stood up and scurried past her quickly.

The stillness was unusual and it felt good. Christine sat down on one of the wooden pews in the middle and looked around her. The walls and pillars were whitewashed and there were scarcely any ornaments or pictures. The crucifix hung from the ceiling.

The tension fell away from her gradually. She felt safer behind these thick walls. As though the church was a place that had nothing to do with the world outside.

She thought about Gao Gao and the church service in the ghost town. She did not have the dedication that the believers there had, praying to their redeemer.

What did she seek in the cathedral? Succor? Deliverance? A savior? No. She did not want to be saved, and she did not want to be set free. She wanted to feel protected, and she could do with help and support, but she would not find those things here. Other people might, but not she.

The church was a place of peace. Of safety. Of reflection. And that was worth a great deal.

Christine sat in the pew for a long time. People came and went. Someone practiced a piece on the organ. When she got up, she felt better.

She had to speak to Paul. Urgently.

It was one of those late autumn days on which Hong Kong was most beautiful. The sky was clear and blue over the city and a strong wind had blown the dust in the air out to sea the day before. The temperature was 25°C and the humidity was less than fifty percent.

Paul and David were waiting for the ferry. David had a posy of flowers in one hand and a ball in the other. He ran up to Christine on the pier and proudly gave her the flowers. They strolled up and down the main street and had freshly pressed orange juice in Green Cottage like they always did. They played soccer at the sports ground; Christine stood in goal and did not defend any of David's shots. He shouted with joy at every goal. That was another thing they liked to do regularly.

At home, Christine put David to bed while Paul cooked, lit candles in the garden, and hung a couple of lanterns in the frangipani tree. He prepared two simple dishes, some of her favorites – fresh mango with mozzarella and red peppers with basil – and spaghetti all'arrabbiata as the main course. And he opened a bottle of her favorite Tuscan wine.

He made every effort. As though nothing had changed.

Christine served the starters onto two plates. "Do you think we were born sinners?"

He stopped short. "Is that a serious question?"

"Yes."

"Sinners? No, I don't think so. What makes you say that?"

"Pastor Lee in Hongyang said that in one of his sermons. He said it was in the Bible."

"I think it is. But it's a terrible way to view the world, don't you think?"

"A realistic way, perhaps."

Paul leaned his head back and looked up at the night sky, in which a few stars were twinkling. They could watch him thinking. "No," he countered. "I'm convinced that every human being has the potential to do the most wonderful and selfless things. But also the most horrible things. It depends on the circumstances. Bad circumstances create bad people."

Christine had expected a reply like this. She thought otherwise. "But who creates bad circumstances? Bad people."

He smiled. "Which came first? The chicken or the egg?"

She started eating, not knowing quite how to turn the conversation in another direction. "Have you heard anything from Beijing?"

"No. I'd tell you immediately if I did."

"I wonder where Da Lin . . ."

"Christine," he interrupted her in a slightly weary tone.

"Why do you immediately get annoyed whenever we talk about Da Lin?"

"I'm not annoyed," he said. "But it doesn't help at all to constantly be speculating about what's happened to him. We can't do anything for him at the moment."

"Don't you feel guilty?"

The question surprised him. She could see that from the searching look in his eyes and the way he tipped his head to one side. "No," he said, finally.

"Why not?" she asked in surprise.

"What happened was not our fault. We were victims, just like Da Lin is a victim. I could only feel guilty if we had had the chance to do anything differently. I don't think we did. What did we do wrong?"

"What do you mean? If we had not come to stay with him at the farm . . ."

"Christine, I'm sorry to be interrupting you again. We were on the run. We had no choice."

She poked around at the mango on her plate in silence. It

was delicious but she had lost her appetite. "Have you heard anything from Zhang?"

"No, not from him either."

"Do you think about him often?"

He put his fork down, had a sip of wine, and sat back in his chair. "Yes. I miss him. I only noticed how much I missed him when I saw him again. I miss the closeness between us."

"Do you worry about him?"

"Yes. He wasn't well when we saw him in Shi. He was lonely. After everything that has happened since, he won't be doing any better."

"Will you phone Mei or his son to ask if they have heard anything from him?"

He shook his head. "I think he'll get in touch with me first."

They ate their pasta in silence.

"Paul," she said finally, "I've thought things over again."

"I know what you've been thinking about."

"And?"

"You want to leave Hong Kong."

"Yes."

He sat up straight, pushed his hair away from his face and looked at her thoughtfully, without saying anything.

"I'm frightened. Are you?"

"No," he said.

Something in his tone of voice made her prick up her ears. "Not at all?"

Paul thought for a long moment. "Now and then, perhaps." He paused again. "But I won't let myself live in fear. I want to decide where I live or not. If we . . ."

"Me too," she interrupted. "I thought it would get better with time, but it isn't. We've been back for over two months, and seeing an unfamiliar face on the ferry is enough to get me into a panic. I have the feeling it will get worse."

"Hmmm." He sipped his wine. "Have you thought about getting some professional help?"

"What kind of professional help?" she asked, unsettled.

"There are therapists who specialize in dealing with fear."

"Are you crazy?" Christine threw her napkin onto the table angrily. "I don't need a therapist. I'm not imagining things. Someone tried to kidnap our child. If we had been less lucky we would now be stuck in a Chinese jail, with no chance of release. Have you forgotten that?"

"No. But . . ."

"But what?"

"We're safe here."

"What makes you think that?" she retorted.

"Because Hong Kong is not yet part of China."

"No?"

"Not completely. There are agreements and contracts that guarantee Hong Kong's autonomy. 'One country, two systems.'"

"Are you serious?"

He was silent.

"You think I'm paranoid, don't you?"

"No," he said weakly, sounding unconvincing. That only made her angrier.

"People who get into a panic for no reason need help. There are good reasons for my fears. I'm not imagining things."

"Why do you think you would feel safer in Sydney?"

"What kind of question is that? Because it's further away, and not part of China."

"Hong Kong is my home," he said, almost sullenly.

"Mine too! As though . . ."

"Shit," he suddenly said, standing up. He walked up and down the terrace restlessly. "I don't want to leave."

V

Zhang got his phone out from beneath his monk's habit with some difficulty. He had been expecting this text message for too long to wait till he was back in the monastery to read it. His hands were red and frozen from the cold and they hurt. It took some effort for his stiff fingers to press the keypad. The phone vibrated again. Even in this remote Tibetan high plateau, the world could reach him.

The sender was a former colleague from Shenzhen who had been working in Beijing for years. They had often gone on patrol together as young police officers and had got along well. He had immediately agreed to make enquiries about where Da Lin was when Zhang had asked him to. His messages had not been encouraging and had grown gloomier and gloomier. The boy was in police custody. He did not speak. He did not eat. Zhang had sent his former colleague Da Lin's mother's address but she could not be found; neither could any other family members. After that there had been no contact. He had not heard anything from Beijing for over three weeks.

Zhang read the message a second time and let his hand fall. Da Lin had died the night before. Alone in hospital. No one had been with him, not even a nurse. According to the police, he had starved himself to death.

Zhang wondered how to let Paul and Christine know. In this remote place there was no internet access and he did not know their phone numbers off by heart. They had been saved in his old phone, which he had been forced to discard while on the run. Apart from that, they could not do anything anyway. Da Lin was dead.

Zhang picked up the phone, took a deep breath in and out, and tossed it in a wide arc down the escarpment. He saw it fly through the air for a couple of seconds before he lost sight of it. He did not want to be contactable any longer. Not by anyone.

Could he have saved him? For the first few days after Da Lin's arrest he had tortured himself with this question day and night. If only he had not fallen asleep on that fateful afternoon ... If only they had immediately set off for Tibet ...

After much thought, Zhang had concluded that it would have made no difference. Da Lin had known exactly what he was doing. The boy had decided to help Paul, Christine, and David. Would Zhang have had any right to stop him? More than ever, he now believed in karma. It was the only explanation for Da Lin's brief, tragic life. The punishment for misdeeds in his previous life. In his next life he would be rewarded for his sacrifice. Wherever he was now, he was better off than he would be in this world. It was a comforting thought, though he knew Paul would argue vehemently against it.

The icy wind grew stronger. Zhang sought shelter behind a stupa. His gaze wandered over the snow-covered valley.

Although he had been born and bred in Sichuan, he had only been to Tibet once before. It had been in the summer, on a kind of delayed honeymoon with Mei. The landscape had moved him at first, then impressed him, and finally made him feel fearful. He still dreamt about it years later. The bleak mountains and valleys. The craggy rocks, the wide-open spaces, their bareness. He found nothing about the landscape inviting. He had felt unpleasantly overwhelmed by it, lost and lonely even with Mei by his side. The longer they travelled through the landscape, they more he found it repellent and even hostile to human beings.

At the end of the trip he had been glad to be back in subtropical Shenzhen with its colors, its warmth, its humidity, and its bursting vegetation.

Now it was different. Snow made the landscape brighter, if no more inviting than before. It was still bleak and inaccessible, but it didn't matter to him now. He felt that the isolation spread out before him, the lack of people, and the monotony of the days reflected his inner life. For years he had tried to detach himself from the world through meditation. To let go. To not get worked up over corruption among his colleagues, or the demands of his wife, or the alienation from his son. He had only succeeded in making the first steps. Now he felt the detachment that he had sought for so long. There was no-one and nothing he felt an attachment to any longer. He doubted if that was really a state of being to strive towards.

In the past few weeks something had happened to him, but he was not clear what had caused it.

Was it the last time he had spoken to his son on the phone? Unlikely. Even though the wordlessness between them had hurt him. Especially the way his son had ended the silence without a word of farewell, but by simply pressing a button.

Was it the knowledge of the farmer tortured to death? Probably not that either. He had seen many murder cases as a police detective.

Was it seeing Paul again and saying goodbye to him for the last time?

Or was it simply the end point of a journey that had started many years, perhaps many decades ago?

There was no point in looking for an answer. It would not change anything.

It had started snowing. His feet were so cold he could barely feel them. Zhang turned to walk back to the monastery. Each step through the deep snow was difficult for him. He pulled his robes over his head and round his face. The cold and the gusts of mountain air made progress more difficult than he expected.

The monks had warned him that it was not a good time to go for a walk. But he had not been able to receive any text messages in the monastery. His mobile phone only had reception a few hundred meters away.

The snow grew heavier. It was hardly possible to see the outline of the monastery.

Zhang came to a stable. He was completely out of breath. There were probably still a hundred meters to go before the gates. He was not sure if he would make it. He could stay here and wait till the cold crept from his hands and feet into his arms and legs, until it had his whole body in its grip, made him tired, and sent him to sleep.

He leaned against the wall of the stable. He could shout for help but the monks were meditating. They would not hear him from behind the thick walls of the monastery. He dug out a hollow in the snow with his hands and crouched in it. In the silence he heard the rustle of the snowflakes falling. They covered his shoulders and his head and after a few minutes he was completely covered in snow. He had no more feeling in his hands or in his feet.

He heard the voices of two novices. They were not too far away. They were struggling through the snowstorm calling his name repeatedly. He only had to answer their call.

They came towards the small white mound by the stable wall and walked a few meters past him without seeing him.

The men were slowly walking further and further away.

"Hello," he called out, a few seconds later, as loudly as he could. "Here I am."

VI

Paul put the breakfast dishes into the dishwasher, sat at the kitchen counter, opened his laptop and looked up the latest stock exchange figures from the US, feeling anxious. He had bought highly speculative stocks in the last few days and weeks, betting on the market falling. It was a very risky business. He had trusted his intuition more than the opinions of almost every financial market analyst. One look at the closing figures from the New York stock exchange told him that he had been right. If he sold now, his profit would be more than his entire income in the previous year. And that had already been a very good amount. But should he wait until the market fell further? If his intuition and the figures were not wrong, it would fall by ten or maybe twenty per cent. Should he hold?

Paul stared at the figures from New York. One year's income! In one click. It was incredible. He used to find people who bought speculative shares rather suspect, but now he was feeding his family with the proceeds. Hold or sell?

He heard David upstairs. He was awake and calling for him.

Paul entered half a dozen "sell" trades. He wanted to enjoy the day with David and not think about the market all the time, checking the figures on his phone and worrying about whether he should have held on to the stocks after all. He waited for the confirmation, shut down the laptop, and went up to David's room. David was sitting in bed playing with his toy pandas.

Paul raised the blinds. Birds were singing outside and the hibiscus bushes were blooming in rich reds and yellows in front of the window. A mild, sweet scent was coming into the room from the frangipani tree. "Shall we go swimming after breakfast?"

David nodded enthusiastically.

Paul took the mail from the postman absently. He was too busy packing towels and swimming gear for himself and David to look at it closely. A letter from a bank, two bills, and a large envelope from the People's Republic of China. Paul could see that from the postage stamp. It was addressed to Paul Leibovitz and Christine Wu. There was no sender on the back. He put the small pile on the kitchen counter and carried on looking for swimming armbands.

They were the only people swimming at the beach.

He thought about Christine.

———

The envelope with no sender was addressed to them both. They opened it together in the evening. There was no letter inside, only two photos, without any writing. Christine turned them round.

She screamed, loud and long, and dropped the photos. Paul was just able to stop her from falling to the ground. He hugged her and led her to the couch.

From his room, David called, "Mama? Mama?"

"Everything's fine, sweetheart," Paul said. "Mama just hurt herself a little. It's nothing serious."

"Will she have to go to the hospital?"

"No, no, honey."

Christine buried her face in his shoulder. "Have you looked at the photos?" she whispered.

"No."

Paul tried to get up to look at them. She held him back. "Don't go."

He held her tight but began to feel anxious. He could not imagine what kind of photos would have made her react so strongly.

"Is it about Da Lin?"

She shook her head.

"Zhang?"

"I don't think so. But maybe."

Paul could not wait any longer. He got up and she let him go reluctantly.

He walked over to the kitchen counter and looked at the photos.

It took him a few seconds to realize what his eyes were seeing.

VII

A scratching noise woke Paul that night. It sounded as though someone was trying to open the front door. Christine was fast asleep.

He got up quietly, pushed two slats of the venetian blind apart and looked out of the window. He could not see anyone on the terrace or at the entrance. Was someone in the house? He listened. Stepped quietly into the corridor. The sound was coming from the living room. He walked to the top of the stairs and thought about whether there was anything on this floor he could use to defend himself. A knife? A candlestick? From the bathroom he took the bamboo frame that they used to dry hand towels and went down a few steps. The scratching stopped briefly then started again.

"Hello?" He listened. "Hello? Is someone there?"

Paul crept into the living room. Through the large glass door to the terrace he saw a stray cat on the decking in front of David's sandbox, scratching at it as if it was sharpening its claws. When Paul went up to the glass it disappeared into the bushes in a few swift movements.

He collapsed onto the sofa, feeling exhausted. Until this evening he had thought that it was only a matter of time before they regained a feeling of security. The power of the everyday and routines would help them.

He had been wrong. And if he was being honest, he had to admit that he had also been feeling deeply unsettled. Most days he managed to suppress these feelings but they came to him in the night all the more strongly. He had dark dreams or lay awake for hours waiting for any suspicious noises.

Paul went into the kitchen and took out the two photos that he had slid between the cookbooks in the evening. The sight was almost intolerable. Two horribly distorted corpses. A man and a woman. One small, the other well built. The woman was lying on her side and was so disfigured that he could not identify her. He had no doubts about the man. The large dark mole on the forehead. That was the couple that had brought David back to him.

Christine was right. They were no longer safe in Hong Kong. He could not rule out the possibility that they might try to kidnap David from Hong Kong.

They had to leave. But where should they go? He could trade his stocks almost anywhere. All he needed for that was a fast internet connection. But he did not have friends or family anywhere else in the world. Nothing apart from the language drew him to America. Going to be with Josh in Sydney was an option, at least in the short term. Paul doubted that they would get the necessary visas and permits to migrate there at their age. Taiwan? It would not be far away enough from China for Christine to feel safe. He could apply for a German passport but nothing drew him to the country where he had been born. He had not been there since he had moved from Germany to New York with his parents in the 1960s.

It didn't matter where they went, Christine had said to him. The main thing was to get away. Far away.

London? He had been there often with Meredith, and he had grown to like the city more and more with each visit. He had toyed with the thought of moving there several times. But he had never made the move because he did not want to leave Hong Kong.

But Hong Kong had changed. It was no longer the place that had become his home. The former British crown colony had turned into a Chinese city, not overnight, but gradually. Over one million visitors crossed the border every month and more and more Mandarin was heard on the streets. Chinese corruption money was driving property prices up. The press was becoming less and less critical of the People's Republic. Deng Xiaoping's promise of "One country, two systems" had turned into "One country, one and a half systems", and it was only a matter of time before it would be "One country, one system". They would export not only China's laws to Hong Kong, Paul thought, but also China's lawlessness. When Hong Kong had been returned to China in 1997, it was meant to stay autonomous for fifty years. But Beijing would not wait so long.

London. The more he thought about it, the more he liked the thought of living in a part of Europe. He was familiar with the continent from his travels and had always felt comfortable there, especially in Italy and France. And why should they not learn Italian?

What drew him to Europe was what was most important to him now. Safety. The freedom to live without fear. The freedom not to be frightened of the police. Or the law. Protection from the kind of people who want to make a present of a child. A continent where the laws apply to everyone and no political party or party functionary is above the law. Where no one disappears without a trace into jails or labor camps for weeks, months, or years.

"We are a traumatized people," Zhang had told him many years ago. Paul had disputed that back then, and thought for a long time that his friend was exaggerating.

He checked that all the windows were closed and that the front door and the terrace door were properly locked before going upstairs and creeping back into bed. Christine woke up.

"Europe," he whispered. "We're moving to Europe. What do you think about that?"

"When?"

"Whenever you want."

VIII

The decision to leave Hong Kong filled Christine with an unexpected sense of euphoria. Her anger at Paul turned into a physical desire that she had not felt since David had been born. The fear and gloom of the last few weeks and months were dispelled. In their place came a feeling of lightness that helped her to say goodbye. The last day in the office. The last ferry ride to Hang Hau to a final dinner with girlfriends. At no time did she have any doubts about the decision. Quite the opposite. The closer their departure date was, the happier she grew.

The biggest problem was discussing it with her mother. She would not want to come with them and Christine was tortured by a bad conscience for leaving her alone in Hong Kong. A good Chinese daughter would never do something like that. Or only in an extreme situation. Was their situation extreme enough?

How would she react to the news? Paul and Christine considered talking to her about it together, but in the end they decided that it would be best for mother and daughter to speak on their own.

Wu Jie was already waiting in front of the house when Christine came to get her. They went to Man Fung, a seafood restaurant in Yung Shue Wan harbor. Christine had actually wanted to take her mother to a more expensive restaurant in Wan Chai or Tsim Tsa Tsui, but her mother thought that was an unnecessary waste of money, and refused.

They were taken to a waterside table, and they ordered thousand-year eggs, smoked tofu, steamed perch, and pak choi. There was a light breeze from the sea but the air was warm and mild.

Wu Jie buttoned her jacket up anyway. She often felt the cold. Probably because of her age, Christine thought. "Are you cold? Shall we sit somewhere else?"

Her mother shook her head.

The waiter brought the eggs, mustard, and ginger, a small dish of peanuts and two Cokes. They sipped their drinks and looked at each other in silence. Her mother had never been one for many words. She was not one to ask questions. Nor to talk much if it was up to her. If she said anything she spoke in short sentences and chose her words with care. Her voice often sounded more brusque than she intended it to.

After they had come back to Hong Kong, Christine had only described what had happened to them in China in broad brushstrokes. She had not wanted to worry her mother too much. Wu Jie had listened quietly to everything and not said a word about it. They had not talked about it since then.

Christine ate a couple of peanuts. "How was today with David?"

"Fine."

"What did you do?"

"We played. And painted." Wu Jie helped herself to half an egg, put a piece of ginger on it, dipped it in mustard and bit into it. "The eggs in Sampan are better."

"We'll go there next time," Christine said, suppressing a sigh. "How's your knee?"

"Better."

"Have you been to the doctor?"

"What for?"

There were things that she should just not talk about with her mother.

The waiter placed the fish and vegetables on the table. The sauce slopped over the edge of the plate and soaked into the tablecloth. Christine dabbed at both spills.

"Mama," she said. "There's something I have to talk to you about."

Her mother picked up her chopsticks and tried some fish, then some vegetables.

"Paul and I have decided that it might be best if we moved to London with David."

Her mother continued eating calmly. Without looking up, she spat a long fish bone onto her plate.

"Just for a year to begin with," Christine added quickly.

Wu Jie helped herself to some tofu.

Christine jabbed at the food nervously with her chopsticks. She knew how uncommunicative her mother was, but she still could not read this silence.

The move to Lamma had done her mother good. She was happier here than she had been in Hang Hau. She walked around more and had soon found friends to play mahjong with. She looked much younger than her seventy-six years. Above all, it was her young grandson who had brought her to life. She would miss him most. And he would miss her.

"What will you live from?" she finally asked, with her mouth full.

"Paul's trading of stocks and shares is going well. Very well, in fact. He can do that in London too."

Her mother nodded. Christine tried to read her expression and was shocked by how her mother's face seemed to her like a stranger's at that moment. The small eyes that were always a little too moist, the somewhat fixed gaze, the thin, almost non-existent lips. Nothing betrayed what was going on inside her. She sat there in front of her, bent right over with her shoulders slumped.

"When?"

"In four weeks."

Her eyes flickered briefly. She picked up a piece of fish and it slid out of her chopsticks. The second time too.

Christine felt the impulse to reach for her hand but she decided against it. "I'm sorry," she said quietly.

Wu Jie looked at the water for a long time. She sipped her

drink, started to say something, then fell silent. "Don't be," she finally said in a firm voice.

"Would you like to come . . .?"

"No. I'll be fine on my own."

Christine wondered if she was making a mistake. Could she really leave her mother behind in Hong Kong?

Wu Jie helped herself to some more pak choi and rice. "London is a good idea," she said decidedly. "Not only for one year."

What was her mother thinking? Hadn't she often voiced her discomfort with the fact that David spoke better English than Chinese, that Paul read German fairy tales to him and not Chinese ones, that he seemed to be better at eating with knife and fork than with chopsticks?

"A tree will die if you move it. A person will be revitalized when he moves. So goes the old Chinese saying. Don't worry about me. It's better for David not to grow up in China." After a brief pause, she added, "It was better for you too."

"What?"

"Not to grow up in China. But he is luckier than you."

She grew more confused by what her mother was saying. "I don't know what you mean."

"We had to swim to get away. You almost drowned. Now you can simply get on a plane." She separated the rest of the fish from the bone and took another piece. "It will keep going on, don't forget that. There will always be victims . . ."

"What do you mean by that?"

"Exactly what I said." Wu Jie put her chopsticks down and cleared her throat. "I hope he still knows who I am when we see each other again."

IX

He had never been with David on the Peak before. Christine had taken David there often. They had taken the cable car up the steep mountain and returned very happy about the outing every time. On their last day, Paul wanted to make a trip to Hong Kong's highest mountain with him. Christine had to sort out some things for her mother, so did not have the time to come with them.

To Paul, there was no place better to say farewell to the city. And no place more difficult.

Paul had taken his first son to the Peak often. Even as a two-year-old, Justin had been amazed by the views of the city, the harbor, and the South China Sea on their many walks around the summit. Paul walked on the mountain every year on the anniversary of Justin's death.

They took a taxi from the ferry to the Peak Tram terminus in Central. From there, a footpath led up to the summit. It was an ascent of almost five hundred meters, a distance that he had easily covered before, sometimes even with Justin on his back. That had been ten years ago.

They walked up the steps parallel to the tram tracks. After that, the steps grew more and more steep. Paul was sweating and out of breath. David asked when they would get to the top.

"Soon," Paul said, breathing heavily.

They turned into Chatham Path, which led away from the road into thick undergrowth. David couldn't walk on any longer; he wanted to be carried. Paul heaved him onto his shoulders. From here onward, there was no longer a road to the Peak from which they could get a bus or a taxi if they needed to. They stopped every few meters for a short rest. But after a few minutes Paul was so winded that they turned back to May Road and got a taxi.

They bought ice cream in the Peak Galleria and strolled toward Lugard Road, a pedestrian path that had once gone right round the summit. Paul slowed down. Something in him was resisting this. He heard Justin's voice. Shortly before he died, he had asked him if they would climb the Peak together one more time.

"But of course," Paul had said.

His son had lifted his head weakly, smiled at him and asked, "Really?"

Did he want to know the truth? Did he want to hear: "No, Justin. No, I don't think so. You're too weak for that and I can't carry you up five hundred meters. There's no hope now. We'll never stand on the Peak together again." Of course he did not want to hear that. No-one in his right mind would have managed to say that to an eight-year-old child.

"But of course," Paul had said a second time. Justin had smiled faintly and sunk back into his pillow. A little white lie. The right answer. Who could doubt that? Yet Paul could not forgive himself for it to this day. He had effectively left Justin on his own by feeding a silly, utterly ludicrous hope instead of telling the truth, sharing it, and thereby making it more bearable.

David looked wonderingly at his silent father.

"What's wrong?"

"Nothing."

"Then let's go, Papa."

"Wait. I don't know . . ." Paul said, hesitating.

"Please, dear Papa, I want to show you something." He walked ahead without turning back and had already turned the corner before Paul started moving to catch up with him.

A couple of turns later came the view of the city and the harbor. Paul was struck anew by it every time.

Two lizards scurried across the path in front of them.

"Does the Easter Bunny go to London as well?" David suddenly asked.

Paul stopped and squatted down in order to look David in the eye. "Of course the Easter Bunny goes to London."

"How will he know where we live?"

"We can write to him and tell him."

"I can't write yet."

"You can draw him a picture of London and of our house."

David nodded, satisfied. "How long will we stay in London?"

"For one year. Then we'll see how things are."

"Why isn't Grandma coming with us?"

"Someone has to look after our house. Grandma will do that with one of her friends from Hang Hau."

"Will they look after my toys too?"

"Yes, they'll look after your toys too."

David walked beside him for a while, deep in thought.

"Papa, when will I be five?"

Paul stroked the hair away from his son's face. "That won't be for a while yet."

David thought hard about this. "And when will I be six?"

"One year after that. And then you'll be seven, eight, nine, and eventually you'll be as old as I am."

"How old are you?"

"Very old."

"As old as Grandma?"

"Even older than that."

"Thaaaat old?" His son gave him a piercing look. "And when will I be four again?"

"Hmmm." Paul suppressed a laugh. He could see how seriously his son meant it. "Never, I'm afraid."

"Why not? Doesn't it start from the beginning again?"

Paul was silent. David waited for a reply.

"Papa?"

"No, it doesn't start from the beginning again."

"Why not?" David looked more amazed than disappointed. "A movie starts from the beginning again."

"You're right there." Paul picked David up in his arms and held him close.

"Have I ever told you that I had a son before?"

"Was he also called David?"

"No. He was called Justin."

"Where is he now?"

"He's dead."

"Why?"

"He was sick."

David nodded in a matter-of-fact way. He calmly finished his ice cream and licked every one of his fingers clean.

"I used to come up here with him often."

David looked around him. "Shall we play something?"

His father put him down on the ground. "What shall we play? Planes? Horses?"

"Let's play tag," David said, and ran off.

Paul looked at him. Only yesterday he had been lying in his palms. A naked, blood-smeared body with pale skin, shimmering almost blue in places, and with crumpled little hands. A miracle weighing 3,333 grams and measuring 49 centimeters long, fragile and vulnerable. Now it was running away from him and he had to hurry not to lose sight of it.

"Come and catch me," his son called.

Paul hurried after him. A couple of big steps later, he had caught up with him and held him tight. David wriggled and screamed with delight.

"Again!"

He let him go and David ran on again.

Paul caught up with him and let him go. Over and over again.

And each time Paul felt a little freer. The burden that had lain on him like a thick, heavy crust for the last few weeks, perhaps months or years, without him being aware of it, crumbled and fell away. The laughter of his child. The life in his hands. The joy of playing tag, the exuberance, the carefree feeling drove it away.

Paul caught up with David and grabbed him in his arms. He lifted his child up again, tossed him in the air, caught him and pressed him close. He would never let him go again.

"Not so tight, Papa. It hurts."

Paul was startled, and put him down again. "I'm sorry, sweetheart. I didn't mean to hurt you."

David darted his father a look of annoyance.

Then he laughed. "Catch me if you can!"

And off he went.

ACKNOWLEDGMENTS

I've been travelling to China for over twenty years. First as a journalist, then as a writer. In this time, many, many people have helped me. They have told me their stories and let me into their lives. They have shared their fears, grief, dreams, and hopes with me. I dedicate this book to them too. It's impossible to name them all here and some of them have asked not to be mentioned for reasons of personal safety. I'd like to thank Zhang Dan as a representative for them all. She accompanied me on my travels as a translator, researcher, and a good friend, and explained her country, her culture, and the recent history of China to me with endless patience. Without her fearless help, the novels of my China trilogy would not have been possible.

Naturally I owe my editor, Hanna Diederichs, many thanks. She has worked with me on all three volumes with great care, rigor, and passion.

Over the years, my son, Jonathan, has grown into an extraordinarily attentive and critical reader of my manuscripts, who has helped me a good deal with his questions and suggestions. My friend Stephan Abarbanell was always there at the right time with the right words. From my mother, I learned early on the power and the magic of good stories.

My very special thanks go to my wife, Anna. She is my first reader. Her critical comments and ideas, her patience, her praise and encouragement, and her support in times of deepest doubt are a fundamental help in the creation of my books.